MW00899224

Hidden by the Gargoyle

DEVIL SPRINGS
BOOK THREE

C.C. WOOD

Copyright © 2024 by Crystal W. Wilson

All rights reserved.

No part of this book may be reproduced in any form or by any electronic or mechanical means, including information storage and retrieval systems, without written permission from the author, except for the use of brief quotations in a book review.

Any similarities to real persons, living or dead, are coincidental.

PROLOGUE

My heart was pounding in my chest as I packed clothes and toiletries in a bag.

Dax Tremaine was on his way here. For me.

My hands shook and I nearly dropped the bras I was pulling out of my dresser.

For years, I'd wondered how it would feel to be waiting for Dax to pick me up. Only, in my daydreams, he was picking me up for a date. Not because I needed protection from a threat that I didn't truly understand.

I'd long since gotten used to Aunt Minnie's premonitions. She saw things that I couldn't and refused to talk about them.

Like the time she forced me to stay home from a party that I'd really wanted to attend in high school. She was more insistent than I'd ever seen her. We had a huge knockdown-drag-out fight about it. I'd been so angry with her.

Then, the next morning, we heard about a single car accident in the same area as the party was being held. On the road I would have taken to come home. A witch had gotten power-drunk from practicing black magic and crashed into a tree. She hadn't survived.

I knew then that my aunt had seen my death in that crash. That was why she'd kept me home. Since that day, I almost never argued with her when she had premonitions and asked me to follow her instructions. I trusted her with my life because she'd probably saved it on more than one occasion.

Now, I was about to go home with the gargoyle I'd had a crush on since I was old enough to understand sexual attraction. The gargoyle I'd secretly been in love with for nearly a decade.

All because my aunt had a vision about the blood god sleeping beneath the mountains near our town, Devil Springs. A god that I would somehow awaken with my magic.

Magic that I never thought I would possess, since I didn't manifest my powers during puberty.

Then, there was the problem of Leona Mansfield, a lion shifter and local businesswoman. For some reason she had a vested interest in this god and his powers, and she would do whatever was necessary to gain access to them, including finding a warlock who would help her for the right price. Edgar Sommerton had never been my aunt's favorite person. Now, she loathed him because he had agreed to help Leona free the blood god. Somehow, they believed that they could control him and, thus, his magic.

It wasn't until they kidnapped Sela Ward, the human mate of the wolf pack's alpha, that Minerva realized what they were trying to do. Only Sela wasn't human. She was a witch. A powerful one who had suppressed her powers her entire adult life.

Their plan had failed, but Minerva and I knew them both well enough to understand that they weren't giving up. They were going to find another way to achieve their goal.

Now that Minerva had a premonition of my destiny to wake the blood god, it was only a matter of time before they discovered that I was the key to getting what they wanted.

They had already kidnapped one woman. We both knew they wouldn't hesitate to do the same to me if they got what they wanted in the end. Which meant I needed to put myself beyond their reach.

Hence, the gargoyle who was coming to pick me up. They were guardians by tradition and nature, which made him the perfect candidate to keep me safe.

"Ally, Dax is here," my aunt said from the door to my room.

I stuffed a few more things in the bag and zipped it.

"I'm ready," I told her. The lie sounded almost believable coming from my lips.

Aunt Minnie walked over, cupping my face with her hands. It was strange, really. She was only eleven years older than me, but she had taken on the role of my surrogate mother with ease after my parents died.

"Call me every day," she said.

"I will."

"And listen to Dax. He's been a guardian his entire existence. If he tells you to do something, please do it without question. I want you to be safe."

"I will," I answered, barely refraining from rolling my eyes.

She smiled at me, leaning in to kiss my cheek.

"I love you."

I hugged her. "I love you, too."

She released me, her golden eyes gleaming. In that moment, she looked so much like my mother that my heart ached.

"Time to go."

I followed her downstairs, carrying my heavy bag in one hand and my backpack, which held my laptop and purse, slung over my shoulder.

Dax Tremaine stood at the base of the stairs, his huge arms crossed over his chest. His pale skin gleamed in the sunlight streaming in through the windows. His dark brown hair was cut short and close to his scalp on the sides but longer on top. Deep blue eyes that were nearly purple locked on me as I came down.

My knees went weak as I reached the last step and I stumbled. I dropped the bag and landed against a hard chest with an oomph. Two hard hands closed around my biceps, keeping me steady even as my backpack slid down my arm to bang against the back of my legs.

"You okay?" Dax asked, looking down at me with concerned eyes.

My heart raced and a blush rushed to my cheeks because I knew he could probably hear the pounding of my runaway pulse.

"I'm fine," I said, straightening and stepping away. "Thank you."

His gaze tracked me as I slung the weight of the backpack over my shoulder and went to pick up my bag.

His hand closed over the strap at the same time mine did.

"I've got it," he said, his voice gravelly like the stone he could turn into at will.

My face heated even more. "It's okay—"

He didn't let me finish. His other hand hooked the top loop of my backpack, taking it off my shoulder, and he hefted the duffel bag that held my clothes as though it weighed nothing.

"I've got it," he repeated.

Without another word, he carried them out the door and to the SUV parked in front of Aunt Minnie's house.

I glanced at her, feeling hopelessly awkward. She smiled at me, her expression reassuring.

"It will be okay," she said. "Just trust me."

"I do," I told her, blowing out a breath.

It was me I didn't trust. I was nervous enough around Dax the few times I saw him a month. Being around him all the time was going to be much, much worse.

Then again, maybe I would be able to get over this ridiculous crush if I was near him for an extended length of time. Maybe some of his gross habits or personality flaws would come to the fore and I would get over the wild longing that filled me whenever I saw him.

Dax came back to the door and nodded at Minerva. "I'll text when we arrive at the resort." His impassive eyes came to me. "Let's go."

I gave Aunt Minnie one more hug, taking comfort from her

lavender and sunshine scent. Then, I followed him out the door into the unknown.

CHAPTER
ONE

The ride was quiet. But that wasn't unusual when I was with a certain gruff gargoyle.

Since I'd turned seventeen, I hadn't been much of a talker around Dax. I was always so worried I would say something embarrassing.

As I stared out the window, I remembered the times before I became a teenager and realized that I liked Dax as more than a friend. I'd never been a chatter box, but Dax had always managed to bring me out of my shell just a bit.

When I'd come to Devil Springs at the age of eleven, I'd been in the throes of the deepest grief I'd ever experienced. Both my parents had died in a car wreck. Apparently, all the safety and protection charms in the world couldn't protect witches from a head-on collision with a drunk driver.

I remembered walking through the days in the fog of sadness and silence, missing my parents so fiercely that I felt as though I was dying.

Minerva had done everything she could to ease my transition but, after six months, I wasn't getting better.

Until Dax had come over to fix her gutters.

I'd never met a gargoyle before, so the novelty had pierced the cloud of pain hovering over me. Barely.

It was his calm, quiet presence that had eased me. He seemed so strong and big, as though nothing could hurt him. Especially when he'd partially shifted to allow his wings to come out.

He'd asked me to hand him tools as he worked on the gutters. Sometimes, he worked in silence, but occasionally, he would ask me a question. Nothing intrusive or deeply personal. He asked about my favorite book. My favorite color. A couple of times, he told me stories about my aunt, Minerva. Things that she never would have told me herself, yet they made me smile.

After he was done fixing the gutters, he'd come back to replace a few of the shutters on the house that had been damaged by a hailstorm and he didn't have to ask for my help. I would drift outside when he arrived and stay until he left.

Between his quiet strength and Minerva's gentle and loving efforts, I'd finally emerged from beneath the fog of grief and begun living again.

I'd always felt like I could talk to him about anything, until I reached the age of seventeen and my eyes had suddenly opened to the opposite sex.

My platonic love for him had morphed into something I didn't fully understand. I felt hot and flushed around him. Tongue-tied. It took me a while to realize that my physical reactions were attraction. Probably because I'd never experienced them before. None of the boys my age interested me. In fact, most of my classmates, male and female, didn't interest me. Books did. They were my companions far more than the people around me.

Dax had changed toward me then, as well. Which made me even more self-conscious because I knew that he saw my crush and was trying to discourage it as gently as he could.

He kept his distance. He'd never been a hugger, but he would occasionally squeeze my shoulder or tug my ponytail when I was younger. Once I turned seventeen, that all stopped completely. He never so much as brushed against me.

He also didn't carry on those easy conversations with me as often. And he made sure that Minerva was always within earshot when he was around me.

I wasn't sure if he was afraid that I would throw myself at him or if he wanted to reassure Minerva that he wasn't going to take advantage of my sudden crush, but it had been so embarrassing.

So, I'd stopped spending time around him. I made sure to vanish whenever he came over. Or bow out of public conversations with him as quickly as possible.

But my crush hadn't died.

Even throughout college, my feelings continued.

Now that I had been back in town for nearly two years since I completed my master's degree, I wasn't as tongue-tied around him, but Dax made sure to maintain his distance.

We'd never resumed our easy friendship. And, somehow, even nine years later, it still hurt.

"It will be okay," he rumbled next to me, pulling me from my thoughts.

"What?" I asked, my head turning toward him.

His dark blue eyes glanced at me before returning to the road. "I said it will be okay. I'll keep you safe."

He thought I was worried about myself. Which made my face heat. I should have been worried about myself and not lamenting the fact that I hadn't had the same relationship with Dax for the past nine and a half years.

Clearly my priorities were all screwed up.

"I know," I replied.

I felt Dax's eyes on me, but he didn't say anything else.

Until we came around a curve and saw a maelstrom of black and grey smoke shot through with arcs of purple lightning. It churned above the road in front of us. Edgar Sommerton hovered in the center.

How on earth had he found me? Had he discovered that I was the key rather than Sela?

Dax slammed on the brakes when that purple lightning shot from Sommerton's hand and tore through the asphalt right in front of the SUV.

The amulet hanging from the rearview mirror flashed with bright white light and an iridescent grid of sparks flared to life over the vehicle.

We were close enough to see Sommerton's expression and the spiderweb of black veins surrounding his eyes.

My heart slammed once in my chest before taking off in a galloping rhythm.

He was using the blackest of dark magic. The kind of magic that was nearly sentient. It infected the user like a virus, multiplying until its motives took over the witch or warlock. Until their personality disappeared and all that was left was evil.

"Stay in the car," Dax said.

He sounded completely calm, as though he were going to shoo a herd of ducks off the road rather than face down a warlock who could use purple lightning to fry him with only a wave of his hand.

I opened my mouth to tell him to keep driving, that Minerva's spell would protect us, but he was already out of the SUV, slamming the door behind him.

I watched in terror as he strode toward the hood of the SUV. His skin took on a light grey cast and his already huge frame grew even larger. Black, leathery wings exploded from his back, arching over his head before extending out to the side.

Thick horns spiraled from his forehead before curving back over his skull.

I gaped at him. I'd never seen Dax shift this much. I'd only ever seen photographs of fully shifted gargoyles, but I knew that he wasn't completely changed.

But this was still the most I'd ever seen him alter his appearance.

He grew another foot in height and his shoulders widened and thickened, as did his arms and legs. His shirt and jeans stretched until I feared the seams would split, but they miraculously held.

Even from behind, he was a terrifying sight to behold.

Yet Sommerton continued to ignore him, his black eyes locked on me in the car.

Somehow, he knew what I was. That I was the key to waking the blood god.

Then again, I shouldn't be surprised because the dark magic he was using could be used in many ways. It could augment a warlock's natural abilities, or it could grant him powers he didn't naturally have. Like the gift of premonition.

Light and smoke shot from Sommerton's hands and slammed against the hood of the SUV again. The iridescent grid threw it back toward him.

Sommerton jerked in the air to avoid the ricochet of lightning, his face twisting into a scowl.

Still, he ignored Dax, who was closing in on him.

At least until Dax reached an arm behind his head and into the neck of his shirt. The hilt of a sword appeared in his hand, as though he'd conjured it out of thin air. In a slow motion, Dax drew out a longsword, the blade flashing with brilliant blue light as it cleared his shirt.

My mouth dropped open at the sight. I knew that he wasn't wearing a sword behind him but somehow, he'd drawn it.

Sommerton's attention turned to him, and I sucked in a breath as the black and grey smoke thickened around him, swirling wildly. I could no longer see the warlock, but I knew he was gathering for a strike.

I couldn't prevent the scream that escaped my lips when the violet electricity burst from the maelstrom, aiming right for Dax.

Dax's skin turned fully grey as the light hit it, absorbing the ferocious attack like dry soil absorbed rain. I gaped at the sight. I'd heard rumors that gargoyles were impervious to magic and that's why they made excellent guardians, but it had never been confirmed. Gargoyles were nearly extinct, and they guarded their secrets as fiercely as they guarded those that earned their loyalty or paid for their services.

Dax picked up his pace, jogging toward Sommerton as though he had all the time in the world. I watched as Sommerton gathered another sphere of magic between his palms, this one nothing but a shimmering ball of amethyst light with no grey smoke mixed in. It was a huge magical attack, and he was going to hurl it at Dax again.

My heart pounded in my chest as Dax began to run full-out at Sommerton, moving faster than I'd ever seen him.

I held my breath when the warlock drew back and heaved the amethyst sphere, aiming for Dax.

Something shifted inside me, like a door opening, and the overwhelming urge to do something, *anything*, swamped me, but I wasn't sure what to do with this sensation. It was like pure energy filling me up from the inside out, swelling until it felt as though I would explode.

Dax didn't even pause as the lightning crashed into him. He just kept moving, rotating the wrist holding the sword in two circles, as though he were warming up his wrist.

Dax lifted the sword, preparing to strike, when Sommerton's eyes widened and an expression of shock and rage took over his face, and he vanished in an explosion of black smoke.

I released the breath I'd been holding. Thank the goddess. The energy filling me drained away as quickly as it had arrived and that shifting occurred again, as though the door inside me was now closed tightly.

I tried to open it again, to reach for that feeling, but it was as if it had never existed.

Dax's shoulders remained tensed as his head swiveled around, letting his eyes scan the tree line on each side of the road.

He waited there for a long time, so long that I was ready to scream again from the tension building inside me.

Finally, after it was clear that Sommerton wasn't going to return,

Dax turned and headed back to the car. His eyes came to me, and my breath stuttered in my chest again. Instead of the usual indigo color, they were pale, ice blue with a hint of grey.

I couldn't look away from him as he reached back and sheathed the sword over his shoulder. I wondered what sort of spell would allow him to do that. Was it a real sword, spelled to a sheath? Or something else?

When he got to the car, his wings had disappeared into the back of his shirt, leaving tatters of the fabric behind. His horns were shrinking, but his skin was still grey, and he was still close to a foot taller than he was in his human form.

Dax gave the trees surrounding the road one last look before he opened the driver's side door and swung his body inside.

The SUV rocked hard when his weight hit the seat. Goddess, in his stone form, he must weigh a ton.

He buckled his seatbelt and put the SUV in gear before he spoke again.

"Are you okay?" he asked.

His voice was so calm. My heart was still pounding in my chest and my palms were sweating, yet he sounded as though he hadn't done anything more taxing than take a stroll down the road.

When I didn't answer, he looked at me, his eyes once again dark blue and nearly purple. "Ally?"

I opened my mouth, but my throat was too tight to speak. I cleared it and said, "I'm fine. Are you okay?"

He nodded, his attention already back on the road.

"You need to call your aunt," he said.

My brain wasn't functioning completely yet because I didn't quite comprehend why I would need to call Aunt Minnie.

"Ally," he repeated my name, his voice soft but firm.

It was a tone I'd never heard before. I turned my eyes to him, blinking rapidly as I tried to focus.

"Call Minerva. She needs to know that Sommerton attacked and that you were his main target. That means he knows that you're now the key instead of Sela."

That gentle tone got through the shock faster than it would have if he started barking orders at me.

I nodded and bent down to grab my purse. I pulled my phone out of the front pocket, trying to ignore the way my hands were shaking, and called Minerva.

"Are you okay?" she asked, her voice breathless. She must have had a vision of Sommerton attacking us.

"I'm fine," I assured her, even though my voice was trembling as much as my hands.

"I think it's safe to say that Sommerton knows what you are," she said.

"He was using dark magic," I blurted out. "And it's already begun to infect him."

Minerva was silent for a moment. "How do you know?"

Her tone was careful, and it made my stomach twist. Had she not seen it in her vision?

"His eyes were black and the veins around his eyes were black as well," I answered.

"Dammit," she murmured. "This is not good."

I knew that, but I wasn't going to say it aloud.

"I'll have to come tomorrow and reinforce the wards around the resort."

I stiffened, which got Dax's attention. "Should I come back home?"

"No, no, no," my aunt replied immediately. "You stay with Dax. I only want to make sure that the wards will handle anything that Edgar might throw at it since he's using dark magic."

"Well, if it makes you feel better, the protection amulet and spell you put on Dax's SUV worked extremely well. Nothing got through."

"That's good," she murmured, sounding distracted. "I'm going to do some research and I'll call you in the morning to let you know when I'll be there." She paused. "Did anything happen during the altercation?"

"I'm not sure what you're asking," I said, even though I had a sinking feeling what she might be referring to.

"Your power, Ally. Did you feel it?"

I took a shaky breath. "I think so, but I've never felt magic before so I'm not sure."

"Describe it to me."

"It was like something happened inside me, a sort of shift, and suddenly there was all this energy filling my body. It was so much, almost too much, as though I was going to explode if I didn't release it somehow."

My aunt's answering sigh was soft. "That was definitely your power," she stated.

"I tried to reach for it again after, but there was nothing. It was like the door leading to that energy was shut and locked tight."

When Minerva didn't reply, I asked, "Aunt Minnie?"

"Yes, honey?"

"Did you have any thoughts? Suggestions? Advice?"

My aunt's soft laugh drifted through the phone. "Sorry, Ally, I was thinking. It sounds like you're blocked somehow. I'm going to do some research tonight and maybe we can figure out what's keeping you from accessing your power. When I come to reinforce the wards at the resort tomorrow, we'll work together for a little bit and see if we can release your magic."

"Okay," I agreed.

"It'll be okay," she said.

"If you say so."

"It will."

I didn't reply. I wasn't going to repeat it and there was nothing else to say.

"I love you, sweet girl. Stick close to Dax and I'll call you in the morning to let you know when I'll be there."

"I love you, too, Aunt Minnie. I'll see you tomorrow."

After we disconnected, Dax slowed the vehicle. I realized that we were at the resort. It was only a ten-minute drive from my aunt's house, but it seemed like it had taken so much longer.

"Did you hear everything?" I asked Dax. Even to my own ears, my voice sounded tired. With his supernatural hearing, he should have been able to hear every word that my aunt said.

"Yes."

"Any questions?"

"No." His hand moved from the steering wheel to rest on my knee, squeezing for a split second before he released me and moved his fingers away again. "Your aunt is right, though. Everything will be okay."

I wondered if he and Aunt Minnie were trying to convince me of that or convince themselves.

CHAPTER
TWO

I was so depleted from the encounter with Sommerton on the road that I couldn't summon any enthusiasm at seeing Dax's cabin.

I'd never been to his house on the resort grounds. When Aunt Minnie told me that I'd be staying with him the day before, I couldn't suppress the thread of excitement I felt at the idea.

Now, all I wanted to do was find the nearest soft horizontal surface and lie down. Even though all I'd done was sit in the SUV while Dax faced down Sommerton, my exhaustion went bone deep.

Dax drove the vehicle past the main lodge, the convention-slash-meeting center, and the various cabins scattered throughout the property. He passed it all, following the road as it veered off through the trees and became gravel rather than concrete.

The main lodge and cottages weren't visible when we stopped in front of a two-story cabin at the very rear of the property.

"Don't get out of the car until I come around and walk you inside," Dax commanded when he turned off the SUV.

I didn't argue, just waited patiently while he got out of the vehicle and came around the hood. His eyes scanned the trees around the cabin, looking for any sign of evil warlocks or rogue lioness shifters.

When he opened the passenger door, I slid out, my purse over my shoulder. Immediately, he hooked an arm around my shoulders, tucking my body against his.

At first, I was so shocked by the action that my feet didn't want to move, until he started dragging me along to the cabin. I realized then that he was using his own body to protect me, something that made my stomach twist painfully.

I didn't like the idea of Dax being hurt because of me, so I hurried my steps to match his long, ground-eating strides.

I also tried to ignore the way his arm felt around my shoulder and his hard body felt against mine. And how small and feminine I felt next to him.

It was too much, a complete information overload. I couldn't process the sensations evoked by being this close to him. Especially since this was the most he'd touched me in nearly a decade.

We entered the house together, me slightly in front of Dax. He released my shoulders, urging me deeper into the house.

"Stay here and I'll go grab your things from the car. Don't come to the door or look out the windows."

I didn't have time to agree or disagree because he turned on his heel and strode out the door, his heavy footsteps echoing on the wooden porch.

He returned a few moments later with my duffel and my laptop backpack. I hadn't even taken the time to look around the living area because I was worried that something would happen to him.

"Let me give you the tour," he said, setting my stuff on the floor next to the front door.

I glanced behind me. The entire bottom floor was open, with only a couple of rustic support beams beneath the loft area. The living area was on the right and to the left was a desk directly in front of the window and bookshelves along the far wall. A small kitchen was set in the back left corner with a tall bar separating it from the rest of the space. Two stools sat in front of the bar, taller than any I'd seen before. I would probably have to jump up just to make it into the seat. A round, four-top table was to the back of the space between the kitchen and a door that seemed to lead to the only separate room on the first floor.

"Everything is open down here, except for the pantry, half bath, and laundry room through the door next to the dining table."

At his description, I immediately imagined a large room with a toilet and sink in one corner, a washer and dryer in the other, and shelves full of canned and dry goods along the walls.

I followed Dax to the area in question and breathed a sigh of relief when I realized that the laundry and pantry were in one general area to the left, but the half bath was closed off by a pocket door.

"The bedroom is upstairs. Let me grab your bag. You can hang up your clothes and put your other stuff away if you want. There's plenty of space in the closet."

My relief over the sight of a private half bath distracted me from his words or I would have realized that he said *the bedroom,* as in singular.

But I didn't.

Instead, I followed him out of the pantry-slash-laundry and took a longer moment to look around while he gathered up my bag.

His house was extremely tidy and uncluttered. Other than the bookshelves near the desk area, there was nothing on the walls. No art. No sconces. No posters. Nothing but white paint and dark wood trim.

Every surface was cleared and shiny from furniture polish. I could still smell the faint lemon scent in the air. There were no photos or personal touches anywhere. Not even a stray sock or cup.

It was as if no one lived here.

Even the resort cabins had more personality than his home. I'd been inside one a couple of years ago, so I knew from firsthand experience.

I followed him up the stairs and froze when I reached the top.

The entire loft was open except for two doors against the far wall. And the only thing in the loft was two nightstands and an enormous bed. A bed big enough for two men the size of Dax. Or at least one fully shifted gargoyle, including his wings. I tried to imagine Dax in full gargoyle form, lying on the mattress, but the image wouldn't come.

It hit me then what he'd said. *The bedroom.* There was only one bedroom. And one bed. I'd never slept in bed with a man before. I eyed the gigantic mattress and decided that it was so big that I wouldn't even know if he was there.

Still, the idea of sharing a bed with Dax set off a swarm of butterflies in my stomach.

I was an adult. He was an adult. We could handle sleeping in the same bed. Right? I didn't have to make it a big deal. And I wouldn't. Decision made. No problem here.

He set my duffel bag on the end of the bed and walked to the door closest to us, distracting me from my racing thoughts.

"The bathroom is through here," he said, opening the door.

I came forward and peered inside. The bathroom was spacious. There was a soaking tub against the left wall, beneath a window, a double sink against the wall directly across from the door, and a big, glass-walled shower was against the right wall. It was a nice bathroom but utterly devoid of any sort of décor or theme. The walls and tile were white. The only touch of color was the finished pine floors and the grey bathmats in front of the shower and tub.

That was it. Even the towels were all white.

"The closet is the other door. There's plenty of space and I have a few empty drawers in the wall system if you want to use them."

He walked away from the bathroom and to the closet. It was a nice-sized walk-in closet with rails, shelves, and built-in drawers, and he hadn't been lying when he said there was plenty of space. It was nearly empty.

Hanging on one of the rails were a few flannel shirts, some t-

20

shirts in white, grey, and black, and one warm winter coat. There were probably eight or nine pairs of jeans next to them, also on hangers. In the shelves next to that rail were two pairs of beat-up sneakers, a pair of scuffed work boots, and a pair of black dress shoes.

That was it.

Other than the flannel shirt, jeans, and work boots he was wearing now, that was the sum total of clothes Dax had in his closet. The rest of the shelves and rails were bare.

"Those drawers are empty," he said, gesturing to a column of four drawers on the other side of the closet.

"Okay," I said, my voice faint. "Thanks."

"Well, I'll let you unpack while I make lunch," he said.

I nodded without looking back at him. Once I heard his heavy steps retreat down the stairs, I opened the drawers to my left. The top two held underwear, socks, and what looked like athletic shorts and pants. The bottom two held nothing. My heart sank as I walked back out into the loft area and looked around. Then, I went into the bathroom.

In the medicine cabinet, he had the basics—deodorant, shave gel, razor, and a comb. Nothing else.

With a sigh, I went back into the loft bedroom and unzipped my duffel, pulling out my toiletry bag. It struck me as sad that, once I unpacked, I would have more stuff in Dax's bathroom than he did.

I knew he'd lived in this cabin for several years, probably close to ten or fifteen, yet it looked like a temporary living arrangement rather than a permanent residence.

I cared about Dax. I had since I'd gotten to know him. I'd always thought he was so much older and more sophisticated than I was, that he had so much more life experience than I did. But this didn't seem like the home of a well-traveled, content man. It seemed like a crash pad.

It made me wonder if Dax was truly living at all.

My chest ached and my heart felt heavy. Dax was a good man... male. He deserved to be happy and to have a full life.

Yet I got the impression that he was merely existing here.

I finished unpacking my clothes, hanging up my pants and shirts in the closet and tucking my underwear, socks, tank tops, and sleep shorts in the drawers.

I wish I'd known that we were sharing a bedroom because I would have packed actual pajamas instead of skin-tight tank tops and tiny boxer shorts. I usually slept in the least amount of clothes possible because I hated feeling tangled up in my nightclothes.

My heart rate sped up again because I remembered that there was only one bed. We weren't just sharing a bedroom, but a bed.

I couldn't think about this right now, because if I did, I'd freak out. I'd have to save the freakout for later. When I had a moment alone.

No, I wasn't going to freak out. I'd already decided we were both adults and I wasn't making a big deal out of this.

Great, now I was in a mental argument with myself. Less than a half hour into my stay with Dax, and I was already on the verge of insanity.

I heard Dax moving around downstairs and smelled something delicious cooking, which made my stomach rumble. Insanity would have to wait until I didn't have an audience.

I finished putting away my clothes and toiletries and tucked my duffel away in the closet. Once I was done, I headed downstairs and found Dax pouring tomato soup into a couple of bowls. The bowls were on plates and there was a grilled ham and cheese sandwich on each one, cut on the horizontal so they made two neat triangles.

Grilled ham and cheese with tomato soup was one of my favorite comfort meals. I always ate this when I wasn't feeling well, or if I was having a bad day.

Considering that I'd already dealt with a warlock throwing around dark magic and finding out there was only one bed in this cabin, I'd say it wasn't the best day so far.

Dax looked up when I paused by the bar. "Done unpacking?" he asked.

I nodded. "Can I help do anything?"

He shook his head. "Everything's ready. Have a seat."

I didn't argue, just parked my butt on one of the stools. Dax brought the plates over before he went to the fridge to grab two cans of soda.

"Lunch looks good," I said when he sat down next to me. "Thanks for making it."

"No problem."

He didn't say anything else, just started eating. Since I was used to his taciturn demeanor, I did the same.

When we were done, I carried my dishes to the sink and started washing up.

"What are you doing?" he asked.

"Washing the dishes," I said.

"You don't have to do that."

I glanced over my shoulder at him. "And you didn't have to make me lunch. The least I can do is clean up after."

"Ally—"

I lifted a hand toward him, interrupting him. "Dax, I already feel like I'm imposing and inconveniencing you. Let me help out."

"You're not imposing on me. Or inconveniencing me," he replied, looking offended.

"So, you needed a roommate?" I asked, going back to washing the plates and bowls.

Dax remained silent and watched as I grabbed the pan from the stove and started scrubbing it, too.

"Let's make a deal," I said, unable to stand his silence. "If you cook, I'll wash the dishes. If I cook, you'll do the same. Does that sound fair?"

There was another beat of silence before he finally said, "Fine."

I finished rinsing the pan, set it in the drainboard, and turned to face him. "What's next today?" I asked.

"I need to go to my office. Poppy is coming by tomorrow. She'll be taking over the running of the resort until your situation is resolved and I need to walk her through what she'll have to do."

I thought of the bookkeeping tasks I needed to do for Minerva and Marjorie. "Okay. I have some work to do, too. I can stay here and finish it up today and tomorrow while you handle that."

Dax shook his head. "You're sticking with me until you're safe."

"I have work to do, Dax," I said.

"Then, bring your laptop and work in my office."

His face and tone said I had no choice in the matter.

"Okay."

This was going to be a long day.

On the upside, being annoyed with Dax distracted me from my internal freakout about tonight's sleeping arrangements.

CHAPTER

THREE

I spent the rest of the day trying to deal with my proximity to Dax and the effect it had on me.

It was one thing I hadn't considered when Minerva insisted that I stay with Dax. I saw him regularly over the years, but never for hours on end. I was always hyperaware of him when I did see him. Even if all he was doing was sifting through paperwork or tapping away at his computer with his huge hands.

An entire day of that hyperawareness was exhausting.

Now, it was nearly ten p.m. We'd watched a movie after we ate dinner and chilled on the couch, but now it was time for bed. Cue the freakout I'd postponed earlier that day.

I'd gone into the bathroom to change into my sleep clothes, wash my face, and brush my teeth, but, at the moment, I was standing in front of the sink, staring at myself in the mirror.

I was nervous about going back into the bedroom. The thought of climbing into that bed next to Dax made my stomach clench, even though the mattress was huge, and I probably wouldn't even be able to tell he was there.

I would *know* he was there. Which meant I probably wouldn't sleep at all.

I realized I'd been staring at myself in the mirror for too long and Dax was probably wondering what in the heck I was doing in here.

With a sigh, I turned away, gathered up my clothes, and left the bathroom. The only light in the bedroom was coming from a lamp on one of the nightstands. The rest of the house was dark and quiet.

Dax came out of the closet just after I emerged from the bathroom. He wore a pair of thin cotton lounge pants and a tight grey tank top. We passed each other, me going into the closet and him going into the bath.

I dumped my clothes in the hamper and moved back into the loft area. It was only then that I noticed the pallet on the floor at the foot of the bed.

There was a long, thin pad with a pillow at one end and a blanket folded on top. I stared at it for a minute, unsure of what I felt.

The door to the bathroom opened and Dax came out. He saw me standing next to the pallet and winced.

"That's for me, not you," he stated.

I frowned at him. "Why are you sleeping on the floor?"

"Because there's only one bed."

"Then, you should take the bed," I said. "Because it's your bed. I'll go sleep on the couch."

He shook his head. "No."

"I'm not kicking you out of your bed, Dax. I already feel bad enough that you're stuck with me until Sommerton and Leona are dealt with. I do not want to feel bad about you sleeping on the hard, cold floor on top of that. The couch is more than big enough for me to be comfortable if I stretch out. I'll sleep there and you take the bed."

He kept shaking his head. "It's not about comfort. If you're downstairs and something happens, I may not have time to get to you. We're sleeping in the same room. Period."

"Then, you take the other side of the bed. You'd be just as far away from me there as you will be on the floor."

"I'm sleeping on the floor," Dax repeated.

"Dax—"

"Ally, go to bed. We're not arguing about this."

I gritted my teeth. "Dax."

He crossed his arms over his chest and planted his feet, making it clear with his body language that he wasn't going to relent.

"Fine," I said, throwing my hands up in the air. "I hope you sleep well on the hard floor."

I turned my back on him and tugged the blankets back from the top of the bed before I climbed under them. When I settled, I saw that Dax had already shaken out his blanket and stretched out on the sleeping pad.

Disappointment and relief warred inside me. I wasn't sure which emotion was the strongest. Okay, that was a lie. Disappointment was definitely the biggest emotion I felt. The relief had more to do with my concerns that I would do something embarrassing in my sleep like try to crawl all over him or have a sexy dream about him and say his name.

Neither of us spoke as I plugged my phone into the charger that Dax must have put there for me (another thing that made me feel shitty about this entire situation because it was a considerate gesture) and turned off the lamp.

The room went dark, only the faintest hint of moonlight peeked around the blinds that were over the windows.

I heard Dax shift under his blanket before he said, "Goodnight, Ally."

I scowled at the ceiling but answered, "Night, Dax."

With that, I turned over on my right side, facing away from the nightstand, and snuggled deeper under the comforter. The bed was a lot more comfortable than I expected.

So comfortable that I fell asleep before I was done being irritated with Dax.

THE CAVE WAS COOL, but not uncomfortable. A fire burned merrily within a circle of big stones and hundreds of candles flickered along the bottom of the cave walls and on top of outcroppings of rocks or freestanding boulders.

This was how the cave always looked when I came here in my dreams.

Though there was a new addition to the floor—an enormous cushion that was approximately the size of Dax's bed. Pillows and furs were strewn across it, piled up into cozy places to curl up or recline. It looked like the orgy pit of some conquering nomadic leader.

I rolled my eyes at the sight, but moved toward it anyway because the air was becoming chillier.

I didn't hear anything, but I knew that he was lurking. I could always sense him, lingering in the shadows and waiting for me to say something.

As usual, I remained silent. I sat next to a tall pile of pillows, crossing my legs and leaning my back against them. I dragged a soft fur over my legs to protect them from the crisp air. The fire wasn't big enough to warm the entire cave.

"You're late tonight," he finally said, his shape emerging from the darkness.

I shrugged, brushing a hand over the fur. "I had something to take care of."

As he drew closer, the candlelight revealed the sculpted bones of his face. I studied him, wondering why I couldn't have found him attractive. He was beautiful, easily one of the best-looking men I'd ever seen. Period.

But other than being able to appreciate his prettiness, I felt not an iota of attraction.

He was nice to look at, fun to talk to, but there was no spark. No chemistry at all.

That didn't stop him from trying to flirt with me when we first started talking. It had taken him a while to let that behavior go. I had a feeling that it was a sort of shield he put up to keep me at a distance.

Now, neither of us were as guarded.

"You look stressed," he said, plopping down on the cushion a few feet from me.

He reclined on his side, resting his weight on his elbow. As usual, he was shirtless, but he wore rough trousers that were held up with a strip of cloth knotted around his waist.

"I am."

"Want to talk about it?"

I sighed. "Not really, but I'm going to because you're here and there's no one else I can discuss it with."

He smirked at me, his black eyes sparkling in the candlelight.

I pulled my knees up to my chest, wrapping my arms around them. "There's a warlock after me. One who is practicing dark magic."

His gaze sharpened and his body tensed. "Why?"

"He wants to wake you and discovered that I'm the key. He tried to attack me today." I shivered, remembering the way Sommerton had looked, hovering in the center of a maelstrom. Sinister was probably the best description.

He moved quickly, sitting up to stare at me. "What?" he barked, his voice even sharper than his stare.

"I'm safe, Talant," I continued. "I'm being guarded by a gargoyle."

His brows rose and his posture relaxed minutely. "That's a good choice. Gargoyles are immune to most types of magic."

It was my turn to stiffen. That wasn't what I'd been told. "Most types of magic?"

"Because of their stone battle form, they are somewhat susceptible to earth magic. Last time I spoke to the gargoyle king, he said they were working to breed that out of their line."

Considering Talant had been sleeping beneath this mountain for the better part of two millennia, I imagined that the gargoyle king had succeeded. Still, I should mention it to Minerva and Dax. Just in case.

"You will have to wake me up at some point," he said. "Why not do it now?"

I laughed, but there was no humor in it. "With what magic, Tal? I've only felt it once and I have no idea how to access it, much less use it."

It was his turn to sigh. "I've offered to help you, Ally. You keep turning me down."

"Because you're impatient and arrogant and I don't want my first magical act to be blowing up this mountain with you in it because you pissed me off," I retorted.

His smirk returned and he flopped back down on his side, looking every inch a god in search of hedonistic bliss.

"So, what are you going to do, then?" he asked. "Live the rest of your life with a gargoyle bodyguard."

If it was Dax, I would happily do it.

Talant leaned forward, just an inch, but his boneless sprawl became something more predatory. His stillness was nearly preternatural, as though he were a statue of a cat that would suddenly come to life and pounce. It was disconcerting when he did things like this. Sudden switches from the amiable friend to the intense predator. It made me wonder if I knew him at all.

"Your expression says that you like the idea," he said.

I scowled at him. Somehow, during our time in my dreams, Talant had learned to read my expressions. Meanwhile, I could never tell what he was thinking because he always hid it behind a smirk or a flirty comment.

I hated feeling so easy to read.

"You like him," he continued.

I shrugged again and looked down at my knees. Inexplicably,

tears threatened to fill my eyes. I blinked rapidly in an effort to hold them back.

Of course, he saw them anyway.

"Why are you upset?" he asked.

When I looked up, the smirk was gone, and he looked as serious as I'd ever seen him.

"I've been in love with him for nearly ten years," I stated. "The gargoyle guarding me."

Talant sat up, bringing his knees up and resting his elbows on them. His hands were clasped between them. "Have you told him?"

I shook my head. "No, he's..." I paused. "A lot older than me. Probably by centuries. I've known him since I was eleven. To him, I'm still that little girl."

"If he agreed to protect you, he must care."

"He cares as a man might care for a little sister," I replied.

By the goddess, it hurt to say it aloud.

"So, make him see you as a woman."

I frowned at him. "What?"

"If he sees you as a little girl, make him see you as a woman." He said it as though it were a simple fact. Something easily done.

"Are you seriously giving me advice on my love life when you've basically been in a coma for fifteen hundred years?"

The smirk returned. "Yes."

I opened my mouth to tell him not to bother, but a low moan filled the cave.

We both moved. I jumped in surprise, but he was on his feet next to the enormous cushion before I could blink, crouched as though he was preparing for a fight.

"What was that?" I asked, my voice little more than a whisper.

He shook his head at me, taking a silent step forward and craning his neck to look into the darkness.

Another moan, followed by a grunt. This time, the sound was familiar, but I couldn't quite place it.

Before I could say anything else, a tugging sensation appeared at the edge of my consciousness.

"Talant, I'm waking up," I said.

There was another grunt, this one louder, and it echoed in the cavernous space. Again, it was familiar, as though I'd heard it before.

"Ally, be safe," he said. A wicked smile curved his lips, but it didn't hide the wariness in his gaze. "I still need you to save me."

"Ha, ha, you're so funny—"

Before I could finish my thought, that tugging sensation became a sharp pull. Darkness swept over my vision, and I opened my eyes to stare at the shadowed ceiling of Dax's bedroom.

There was a rustling sound at the end of the bed, followed by a soft groan.

That's where the sound was coming from and why it sounded so familiar. Dax was moaning and groaning in his sleep. He sounded as though he was in pain.

I sat up in the bed and crawled to the edge. When I peeked down into the floor, I saw that Dax was on his back, one arm thrown over his head, his eyes open and on me. He looked wide awake and alert, as though he hadn't just woken up.

"You okay?" I asked.

"Fine."

"You don't sound fine," I retorted. "You sound like you're in pain. Probably because you're sleeping on a hard floor."

He just stared at me from the said floor, silent.

I rolled my eyes and backed away from the edge of the mattress. "Just get in the bed, Dax."

"No."

"Why not?"

"Because it wouldn't be appropriate."

Seriously? I rolled my head back to stare at the ceiling. Appropriate?

"Two unattached adults sleeping in a bed with three feet of space between them is inappropriate?" I asked, my words all but dripping with sarcasm.

My temper was beginning to twang. I rarely lost it, but when I did, I let it fly. I preferred to talk through disagreements, but he was irritating me more than usual.

"You're so much young—"

"If you say I'm too young, I'm going to strip down to my underwear and streak through the resort so everyone can see how much of an adult I am."

And those words were the exact reason I didn't like it when I lost my temper. I said things I didn't really mean and did things that I regretted. Like streaking through a resort in nothing but a pair of panties. Which would contradict my claim to be an adult because it was a childish threat.

Dax was silent for a brief moment, letting my words hang between us. I knew what he was doing. He was giving me a chance to apologize, but I wasn't going to. While I didn't like losing my temper, his reasoning for not sleeping in the bed was stupid.

Plus, the silence was something he did when I said or did something a little rude when I was younger. Most of the time, I would immediately say that I was sorry. In this case, no way. I wasn't a child anymore and I wasn't going to fall for it.

"I won't be able to sleep knowing that you're in pain on the floor," I said, my voice softer.

"I'm fine."

Okay, then. We would do this the hard way. For both of us.

"Fine." I climbed out of bed and grabbed my pillow. There was a fuzzy blanket thrown across the end of the bed, so I snatched it up as well.

I tossed the pillow on the floor right next to my side of the bed. Then, I shook out the throw and crouched down, putting my ass to the rug.

Holy shit, the floor was cold, even with the carpet beneath me. Shivering lightly, I draped the blanket over my body and put my head on the pillow. I rolled over, hugging the soft material to my chest.

I heard fabric rustling and sensed Dax's eyes on me.

"Ally, what are you doing?" he asked.

I didn't answer because my actions were clear. If he was going to insist on sleeping on the floor, so would I.

He sighed, but I ignored him, keeping my head turned away and my eyes shut.

Was I still being childish?

Probably.

Did I care?

Hell, no.

"Ally, there's no use in both of us sleeping on the floor," he rumbled.

I turned my head and glared at him. He was kneeling at the end of the bed, staring down at me.

"That's the first sensible thing you've said in this entire conversation," I shot back.

His expression never changed but I could sense his disapproval. It was nearly tangible.

"What I mean is there no reason for you to sleep on the floor when I'm already sleeping there," he clarified.

"And there's no reason for you to sleep on the floor either. We're friends, neither of us is a child or involved with someone. If you're so concerned with being appropriate, you can put a row of pillows between us. It'll be like high school again."

"You slept in the bed with a boy in high school?" he asked.

"*That's* your takeaway?" I asked, sitting up on the rug. "Nothing else I said penetrated except that it'll be like high school?"

"Are you going to listen to sense?" he asked, never answering my question.

"If you're sleeping in the floor, so am I," I answered.

Dax sighed again, his eyes going down to the floor. He studied the rug for a moment before he finally looked up at me again.

"Fine. It's three in the morning and I'm not going to spend what little time is left in this night arguing with you about it. Get in the bed."

I crossed my arms over my chest. "You first."

Dax grunted, bent down, and grabbed his pillow. He disappeared around the side of the bed. I heard the mattress creak and the bed move when he laid down. Satisfied that he'd done what I wanted him to do, I took my pillow and got to my feet.

I took a moment to drape the blanket back across the end of the mattress before I slipped beneath the blankets again.

As I said, there was nearly three feet of space between us.

Did the bed seem to shrink now that we were both in it? Maybe, but I was going to pretend that I didn't notice it.

Instead, I pulled the comforter up over my shoulders, turned my back to Dax, and willed myself to sleep.

CHAPTER
FOUR

I woke up feeling incredibly cozy. I was warm and, if it was possible, even more comfortable than the night before when I'd fallen asleep the first time.

I cuddled into the pillow I was curled around, pressing my face deeper into it. It was firmer than I was used to, but it smelled delicious, like pine and snow. Just like Dax.

I cracked my eyes open and stared at the grey fabric in front of my face.

Weird. Dax had white sheets and pillowcases on his bed. His comforter was a light beige, not grey.

Then, I realized the pillow was moving beneath my cheek and there was a thumping sound in my ear.

I sucked in a breath, but stopped immediately, not wanting my sharp inhale to wake Dax up.

Especially since I was all but sprawled over his back.

I opened my eyes the rest of the way, holding the rest of my body perfectly still. During the night, I'd migrated across the bed. Dax was basically hugging the edge, but I still managed to all but crawl on top of him. Exactly what I feared I would do.

Embarrassment washed over me. For all my talk about us being able to share the bed and not even know the other was there, I'd managed to touch him with most of my body.

His breathing was slow and steady, which meant he was still sleeping. That was good.

Now, I just had to figure out how to get off his back without waking him up.

His breaths remained even and soft as I slowly inched back. I tried to ignore the way his body felt beneath mine. His skin seemed to sear mine through the thin material of my tank top. I held my breath as my nipples dragged across the hard plane of his back.

Goddess, this was torture.

I inched backward across the bed until my foot met empty space. I winced as the bed shifted beneath me, but Dax never moved.

Finally, I was off the bed and on my feet, and I hadn't woken Dax.

Moving as quietly as I could, I gathered some fresh clothes and underwear and went into the bathroom to get ready to face the day.

WHEN I CAME out of the bathroom, I found Dax downstairs making breakfast. The scent of coffee and bacon made my mouth water.

Or maybe it was the sight of him in the tight tank top and a pair of loose pants.

With his back to me, I could see a tattoo of what looked like a sword hilt peeking above the neckline of his tank. I wondered if that was where his sword came from yesterday.

If that was the case, the witch who gave him the spelled tattoo must have been incredibly powerful because of his natural resistance to magic.

A spike of jealousy pierced my heart at the idea of another woman putting her hands on his skin, even if it was just to give him a magical tattoo.

Then, I saw the scars on the backs of his shoulders and how they disappeared behind the tank where it covered his mid-back. The jagged, silvery-white lines of the scars made me forget any jealousy I might feel.

Gargoyles weren't just resistant to magic, they were almost impossible to injure. Even in their pure human form, their skin was thick and healed quickly.

To leave scars like that, he must have been severely wounded, lingering on the edge of death. That was the only way his body wouldn't have immediately healed the damage.

At least that's what I understood from the books in Aunt Minnie's library. Yes, yes, I devoured any and all information I could find about gargoyles. Especially when I developed my crush on Dax.

Not that there was a lot of knowledge of their species. They were secretive and, even before they'd nearly become extinct, they rarely allowed other species to live amongst them.

Dax turned from the stove, a spatula in his hand. "Morning. Do you want some coffee?"

"I can get it," I said, moving around the bar.

"I got it," Dax replied, holding up his hand toward me. "Just have a seat."

"Okay. Do you want some help making breakfast?" I offered.

He shook his head and moved to the fridge to pull out a bottle of creamer. As soon as I saw it, I realized that he must have bought it specifically for me since he took his coffee black, and the Italian sweet cream flavor was my favorite.

I gave up and hoisted myself up onto one of the stools on the opposite side of the bar. It was likely for the best. Dax's kitchen was tiny, and we would likely bump into each other every time we turned around if we were both in there at the same time.

After waking up draped over him like a blanket, a little bit of space might do me some good. Even a lukewarm shower hadn't done much to calm the burn of my skin where it had pressed against his back.

"Poppy is coming to the resort in an hour or so," he said. "It'll take a while for her to learn everything she needs to know."

I hated hearing that. Not that Poppy was coming, but that he was giving up his job to keep me safe.

"Don't," he said, distracting me from my thoughts.

"I didn't do anything," I said, watching as he poured creamer into a cup of coffee.

"You feel guilty that I'm going to be taking care of you instead of running the resort."

Yep, he read my mind.

I shrugged, not meeting his gaze when he brought my coffee over to me. He set it on the counter in front of me and leaned forward slightly.

"Look at me, Ally."

I met his eyes. They were nearly purple this morning and a little sleepy. As cheesy as it sounded, my heart skipped a beat just looking at him.

"I want to keep you safe. It's more important than this resort. It's more important than my job. *You* are more important to me than anything else right now."

Even as his words comforted me, they made my throat feel tight because I knew that he wasn't saying them out of the same emotions I felt for him. He was saying them out of affection and friendship rather than love.

And it hurt so badly.

"Thank you," I whispered, hoping that he wouldn't hear the tears in my voice.

I picked up my coffee cup and looked down as I took a sip. I couldn't stand to look into his eyes any longer. I was afraid that he would see everything I was thinking and feeling in mine.

"You don't have to thank me. It's my honor."

The pain grew in intensity, piercing my heart until I had to take a deep breath just to steady myself before I actually burst into tears.

As pathetic as it made me, I would have given anything in that moment to hear him say those words and know that he meant them because he loved me the way I loved him.

But he didn't.

And he never would.

I remained quiet as he finished cooking our breakfast. All my questions about his tattoo forgotten in the face of the pain in my chest.

He made cheesy scrambled eggs, bacon so crispy it was nearly burnt, and toast with orange marmalade. Again, some of my favorite things to eat.

I continued to try and ignore the pain that hammered away at me at his thoughtfulness. I wished that I could have this every day for the rest of my life, just as Talant had joked last night. The idea of having Dax like this on a daily basis for a few decades sounded like bliss.

After we ate, we argued about the fact that I wasn't going to sit in the bathroom while he showered. I refused. No way in hell was I sitting in the same room as a naked Dax. That was a step too far. He must have realized he wasn't going to win because he told me to stay in the house, away from the windows, and that he would be back down in five minutes before he went upstairs to take a shower.

I tidied up the kitchen, loading our plates and cutlery in the dishwasher and giving the pan a quick wash. He was still upstairs with the bathroom door shut by the time I was done. To continue to distract myself from mental images of Dax naked in the shower, I wiped down the stove and countertops.

Dax came back downstairs in just over five minutes, his short hair still damp and his snow and pine scent more intense than usual. I was sitting at the bar, drinking another cup of coffee, and answering work emails. Thank the goddess I worked from home, and I wasn't going to be jobless while I was staying with Dax.

"Poppy will be here in ten minutes. We should go," he said.

I nodded, carried my cup to the dishwasher, and gathered up my laptop and backpack, meeting him at the front door.

As he had yesterday, Dax took my backpack, slinging it over one shoulder, and tucked me into his body as he herded me toward the SUV. My entire body was hot and tingling by the time he helped me into the vehicle.

When he shut the passenger door for me and went back to lock the front door, I took the opportunity to take a couple of deep breaths, trying to calm the sensations rioting within me.

The longer I was in Dax's presence and the more he touched me, the more intense my reaction to him became. I wasn't sure if I was hiding it well or not, but I knew that soon I wouldn't be able to conceal it.

I had to get a handle on it and fast.

Before I threw myself at Dax and he inevitably, but gently, turned me down. And broke my heart completely.

CHAPTER
FIVE

My focus on work was completely shot by ten that morning.

When we arrived at the resort's main lodge, where Dax kept his office, Poppy was already there. She waited in a lobby chair with a travel tumbler of coffee in one hand and her laptop bag at her feet.

As soon as she saw me, she set her cup to the side and immediately came over to hug me.

"You doing okay?" she asked.

"I'm good."

She stared down at me, nearly a foot taller than I was in her high-heeled boots. Then, she smiled. "I'm glad."

And, with that, our discussion about what was going on with me was over. It was one of the reasons I liked Poppy so much. She didn't want to dissect everything that was happening. If I needed to talk about something, she would listen and do it well.

But if I told her that I was fine or that I wasn't upset, she believed me.

She was forthright to the point of bluntness, funny, and one of the strongest women I'd ever met, both physically and mentally.

I also secretly thought that the only reason she wasn't the mayor of Devil Springs was because she didn't want the headaches that came along with it. But that didn't mean that she didn't want things to run smoothly, which was why she and her brother had engineered Daniel Ayres' nomination and ultimate election. And also why she essentially hired herself as Daniel's assistant.

Dax led us both back to his office, which was as ruthlessly clean and impersonal as his home. And just like the cabin, the sight of the sterile office made my chest ache. I didn't completely understand why, but that dull pain throbbed behind my breastbone all the same.

Since Dax and Poppy needed the desk, I set myself up on the couch across the room with my laptop on my lap, eager to get to work and put Dax out of my mind. I knew that once I got my focus and immersed myself in my task list that I would be able to tune him out and concentrate.

Unfortunately, I was as wrong today as I had been yesterday about being able to ignore him.

Every time I would start to sink into my thoughts or a task, the low rumbling sound of his voice when he spoke to Poppy would distract me. Then, I would find myself listening to the things he said. And noting how patiently he would go over information, even if he had to do so two or three times.

And when he pulled out a pair of glasses with thin silver frames, all ability to focus was shot.

Still, I tried to work, even though my speed was glacial. I had to finish Minerva's bookkeeping so I could get to a project I was doing for Marjorie, who owned the local bakery. She wanted to expand and had asked me to do an assessment of her current income and expenses to see if she could afford it. And if she had enough business to support expansion.

I was already pretty sure that she could, but Marjorie wanted concrete numbers and a totally objective assessment. She didn't like to take risks unless she was ninety percent certain about the outcome.

However, at the rate I was going, I wouldn't get to her project until next year because I couldn't think clearly with Dax only a few feet away.

I realized that I was watching Dax and Poppy again and gave myself a mental smack and a silent order to get my shit together. Then, I looked back down at my laptop screen.

Just as I was about to start typing, my cell phone rang.

I managed to resist the urge to beat my head against a wall. It seemed the goddess was conspiring against me today and I was destined to remain unproductive.

I didn't recognize the number on the screen, but that often happened because I often got referrals from my out-of-town clients. Thinking I might have a new client, I tried to put a smile into my voice when I answered.

"Hello, this is Allison Grant."

There was a brief silence on the other end before a low masculine chuckle came through the line.

"Hello, Allison."

The fine hairs on the back of my arms stood straight up at the sound of his voice. I hadn't spoken to Edgar Sommerton often, so I wasn't entirely certain it was him. But who else would call and speak to me like that?

"Sommerton?" I asked.

As soon as I said his name, Dax's head came up, his dark blue eyes pinned to me.

"Yes, dear Ally, it's me. And..." He paused, taking an audible breath as though he were deep in thought. "A friend. You might know his brother?"

What the heck was he talking about? Was he saying that whoever was with him was Talant's brother? Did he have help from someone other than Leona?

"Why are you calling?" I tried to keep my tone calm and questioning. As though I were curious rather than trembling like a leaf.

The timbre of his voice, the way he was speaking, it wasn't right. The dark magic that had infected him was taking hold, twisting him, and changing him in ways none of us would be able to anticipate.

There was another low laugh before he answered me. "Just checking in, Ally. That's what witches and warlocks do when one of their own is getting ready to manifest their magic. So that we can guide you and help you find your purpose among us." He paused. "Especially when they are going to be as powerful as you."

I shivered at his words and the sibilant whisper that seemed to echo when he spoke, as though another voice was superimposing itself over his. Goddess, he sounded almost demonic. Could he be possessed?

"You know that it hasn't," I replied, fighting to keep my voice from shaking as much as my body was. "And you also know that my aunt is the one who will guide me when it does. Not you."

"Perhaps," he whispered back. "Or perhaps you'll realize that you should listen to my advice and instruction. Especially since I know the god's brother."

Oh, shit. That *was* what he meant. Whoever he was dealing with was related to Talant. A thrill of fear ran through me. Was Talant's brother as powerful as he was?

"How do you know him?" I asked.

Another chilling laugh. "Let's just say his power has augmented my own."

Double shit. Dark magic tainted any warlock who used it, but this sounded much, much worse. If he was using a god's magic, would it allow the god to possess him?

"You should let me help you, Allison," he hissed. "It would be much easier for everyone if you did."

"Never."

"You say that now—"

I didn't hear the rest of whatever he said because the phone was plucked from my hand.

I looked up, staring at Dax in shock as he lifted it to his ear, his face set into harsh lines of anger.

He listened to whatever Sommerton said in silence before responded. But when he did, his voice was once again gravelly and rough, like stone grinding against stone.

"You should know that she can't hear you any longer, Edgar," he said.

Unlike Dax and Poppy, I didn't have supernatural hearing, so I had no clue what the warlock's reply was. Only that it succeeded in making him even angrier because his pale skin took on a grayish cast, as it had when he partially shifted into gargoyle form yesterday.

"You'll never get to her, and you know it," he replied. He paused, listening to Sommerton again. "Even if you managed to make it through the wards, your magic is useless against me and my sword. I'll separate your head from your body before I allow you to harm her."

From the look on his face and the quiet violence of his voice, I believed every single word of what Dax said. He would kill to protect me. Even die for me if he had to.

Another tremor wracked my body at the thought. I couldn't stand it if Dax died.

I couldn't hear Sommerton's response, but he must have hung up because Dax lowered the phone, his fingers clasped around it so tightly that it gave an ominous creaking sound. His head was lowered so that he was looking at the ground, but there was tension in every muscle of his body. He seemed poised on the brink of something.

"Dax?"

His head came up and, when he looked at me, his irises were nothing but brilliant blue fire. He was enraged.

"Stay here with Poppy. I'm calling your aunt."

My mouth closed with a snap, and I nodded.

Dax left the office, taking my phone with him. He was so angry that I was afraid what he might do if I asked for it back.

"Interesting," Poppy said.

46

I'd been gazing at the door, bemused, since he left the room, but now her voice brought my attention to her.

"What?"

"It's interesting," she repeated, sitting down in the chair behind the desk. "I've never seen Dax so..." She paused and seemed to be searching for a word. "Unhinged."

Neither had I, but I wasn't going to admit it because it freaked me out more than a little.

"How long have the two of you been seeing each other?"

I blinked at her, confused. "Seeing each other?"

"Dating. Sleeping together." She tapped her nose. "I can smell you on him and him on you."

I shook my head. "Oh, it's not like that. I slept in his bed last night. He took the floor."

Poppy arched a brow at me. Just one. I'd always envied people who could do that because I never could. "Please, don't lie to me. In order to smell so thoroughly of you, he would have had to be touching you all night. Especially since you both showered this morning."

I bit back a sigh. Damn werewolves and their superpowered noses. At least I wouldn't have this issue with Minerva. She wouldn't be able to smell anything.

"He only has one bed and he spent most of the night on the floor, but he was moaning in his sleep and obviously in pain. His bed is enormous, larger than any king-sized bed I've ever seen, so I told him we could just share and neither of us would even know the other was there."

Poppy cocked her head but waited in silence until I continued, her expression stating that she knew there was more to the story.

"And I must have moved across the bed in my sleep because I woke up using his back as a pillow this morning."

A small smile tugged at her mouth. "And he let you?"

I shook my head. "No, he was asleep, too."

Poppy threw her head back and laughed. "Asleep?" she asked,

through her giggles. "There is no way a gargoyle warrior of Dax's caliber would sleep through you even breathing on him much less using his back as a pillow. If he stayed where he was, it was because he let you."

Um...what?

I didn't say it out loud, but Poppy must have seen the question in my face.

"What was he doing when you woke up?" she asked.

"He was sleeping. His breathing was slow and steady, and he wasn't moving. He was completely relaxed," I explained. "I'm pretty sure he wasn't awake. And he didn't wake up when I moved off him and went into the bathroom to shower either."

Poppy started giggling again. "Oh, this is great. Dax let you use him as your teddy bear all night and then pretended to sleep through it. It's priceless."

Heat hit my cheeks and I cleared my throat, trying to clear away my embarrassment as well.

"Poppy, can we stop talking about this? It's embarrassing."

That stopped her laughter. In fact, she was beginning to look a bit pissed off. "Why is it embarrassing?"

"Because I told him that he wouldn't even know I was in the bed and draped myself over his back like a human blanket in the middle of the night!" I snapped. "It's bad enough that he's stuck all but babysitting me until Sommerton is caught and contained, but he doesn't need me all over him in my sleep too!"

Her anger vanished at my words and her face softened. "Ally, I am positive he doesn't view it as babysitting so much as taking care of you. He cares for you a great deal. In fact, I think he would have insisted on protecting you even if no one asked him to do it."

"I just—" I stopped speaking and shook my head again. Yet he had been asked. He hadn't volunteered. It wasn't the same.

Though I never talked about it, I was fairly certain that Minerva and some of my other friends knew about my crush on Dax. Poppy being one of them since her sense of smell was so keen.

"Have you told him how you feel yet?" she asked.

"About what?"

"Him. How you feel about him."

Another head shake. I wasn't sure I'd ever be ready to talk to him about how I felt about him. Especially since he wouldn't return my feelings. Or do anything about it even if he did.

That wasn't Dax. He wouldn't consider it honorable.

Poppy sighed. "Why not?"

I looked away from her patient eyes. They saw entirely too much. "You know why."

"How do you know what he feels for you if you don't share or ask?" she pointed out.

"Because of the way he treats me," I answered.

"You mean how he let you use his body as your pillow last night? What part of that says he doesn't feel anything for you?" she asked.

I frowned at her. "I have no idea what you're talking about."

"Think about it for a second, Ally. You've known Dax for nearly sixteen years. Does he strike you as the type of man who would let you essentially lie on top of him if he didn't want anything to do with you in that way?"

My kneejerk reaction was to tell her that, yes, Dax would let me do it. Then, I realized that he would let *me* do it and I was confident in that. But I couldn't see him allowing Minerva or even Poppy to do something like that.

"Exactly," she crowed, smiling at me.

"It's just that—" I stopped and cleared my throat. "He's never even looked at me in a way that seemed romantic or even like a man looking at a woman."

"How do you know?" she asked. "When you are in the room with him, it's almost as if you're trying to build a wall around yourself so that it's not obvious that you notice every move he makes."

My face grew hot again and I cursed my fair skin because I knew I was blushing.

Before I could ask her if she'd seen anything from him, she waved a hand at me. "He's coming back."

I saved my work and shut my laptop. There was no way I was getting any work done after that phone call.

The door opened and Dax came in, my phone still in his hand and miraculously in one piece.

"Get your stuff together," he said to me. "Your aunt is on her way here now and she's going to meet us at the cabin."

I nodded and shoved my laptop in my backpack. When I got to my feet, Poppy was already around the desk, waiting on me. She gave me another hug.

"I'll see you tomorrow," she said. "Stay safe."

"Thank you," I whispered to her, hugging her back.

"Any time."

By the time she'd released me, Dax had hooked my backpack over his shoulder. He looked at Poppy. "Stay here and I'll be back in a half hour or so. We can finish going over the daily and weekly schedules."

She nodded and waved a hand. "No worries. I have plenty to do and I can figure some things out on my own."

"The housekeeping supervisor and the kitchen supervisor can walk you through some of the day-to-day on their end also."

Without waiting for her to respond, Dax hooked my arm with his hand and hauled me out of his office. I didn't fight his hold, but I did hold my hand out.

"I need my phone back," I said.

He glanced down at me but didn't give me my phone. And he kept walking through the lobby.

"Dax, I need my phone. I have a job and my clients need to be able to get ahold of me."

He tucked me beneath his arm, pressing me into his side as we exited the main lodge and beelined straight for his SUV.

Once we were both inside and on our way back to his cabin, he held my phone out to me. "I blocked the number that Sommerton used to call you, but you have to let me know if he calls you again."

"I will," I responded, tucking my phone in my pocket. "What did Minerva say?"

"She told me not to worry, that she was already coming today to reinforce the wards, and that everything would be fine."

Considering how tightly he was gripping the steering wheel and the tone of his voice, he wasn't happy with the conversation they had.

"If Minerva said it will be okay, it will be okay," I replied, settling back into the passenger seat.

Dax didn't say anything else. But when he tucked me into his side to walk me into the house, I could feel his heart drumming against my shoulder.

He still hadn't calmed down.

That's why I did something stupid when we got inside the cabin. I didn't move away from him when the door was closed. I turned so that my front was pressed against his side and wrapped my arms around his waist.

I tilted my head back so I could look up at him. "Don't let Sommerton get to you. He's always been a horse's ass and isn't worth it."

I gave him a little squeeze with my arms when I said it.

Dax looked down at me, the light reflecting on his glasses so I couldn't see his eyes clearly. He'd been so upset that he'd forgotten to take them off.

I was just beginning to feel awkward when his hand came to the back of my head, tucking my head into his chest.

The drumming of his heart wasn't as loud or hard. He might smell of pine and snow, two things I associated with winter, but his chest was warm and hard, not cold at all. I wanted to stay there the rest of the day, but that wasn't the message I wanted to send to him.

Instead, I released his waist and stepped away, trying to ignore the way his hand felt as it trailed over my hair when I put distance between us.

"What was that?" he asked.

"A hug," I answered, heading toward the kitchen for a glass of water. "You seemed like you needed one."

When I looked back, Dax dropped my backpack off his shoulder and set it on the couch. He was still looking at me with an unreadable expression on his face. Our eyes locked and I realized he was looking at me in a way I'd never noticed before. A way that made me shiver...in a good way.

Before he could say anything, there was a knock on the door.

The spell was broken, and he went to let my aunt inside.

CHAPTER
SIX

I flopped down on the couch, throwing an arm over my damp face.

Who knew that trying to control your magic could make you break a sweat?

"We're done for today," my torturer said.

"I'm kinda wishing I was still fully human," I replied.

My aunt laughed and sat down on the chair to the left of the couch. "Learning to access your magic is much easier when you're younger. It's also easier when you're not blocked."

I peeked at her from beneath my arm. "Any ideas what might be blocking me?"

"Unfortunately, no. Though witches whose power isn't blocked or bound by a spell usually find that their block is caused by repressed emotion."

My only response was to cover my eyes once again.

"Ally, you've been holding back for a long time. Maybe this is a sign that it's time to let go."

My throat felt tight at her words. I had to swallow hard before I could say anything in response.

"There's nothing to let go," I replied.

"Don't lie to yourself or me. You and I both know you've kept your emotions in an iron grip since you were twelve."

I didn't argue with that because she was right. I'd had to. My grief had been so deep and so devastating that I'd had to lock my feelings away just to keep functioning.

The couch depressed next to my waist, and I lifted my arm so I could look up at Aunt Minnie.

"Even if you weren't a witch," she continued. "Shoving all those feelings back isn't healthy for you in the long run. You need an outlet. Someone to talk to or another way to release them. Otherwise, you'll be trapped by them for the rest of your life."

Aunt Minnie ran a hand over my hair as she looked down at me. "And you deserve so much more than to be held prisoner by your emotions for a lifetime."

The tears that had threatened earlier reappeared, welling in my eyes, and trailing down the sides of my face.

"I don't know how," I answered. It was a raw, honest reply.

"How to do what?" she asked, her tone as gentle as her fingers in my hair.

"How to talk about how I'm feeling. I'm afraid of what will happen if I do."

"Afraid of rejection?"

I shook my head. "I'm afraid I won't be able to stop. That if I start, it'll all just pour out of me until there's nothing left. Then, I'll just be empty."

"Or maybe that space will be taken up by happiness," she pointed out.

"I'm happy," I said, but even I could hear the defensiveness in my tone.

"You're content," she argued. "But I want far more than that for you, sweet girl. I want you to experience joy. Bliss. A happiness that transcends time itself."

More tears escaped. I was too tired and too frustrated to control them. "I'm not sure that's possible for me."

A soft smile spread across her face. "I am. I know that you'll have that if you just let yourself *feel*."

"You've seen it? In a premonition?"

Aunt Minnie shook her head. "No. I haven't seen more than a few moments into your future in a few days. Sommerton's attack was the strongest vision I've had. Just like there's a block on your magic, there's a block on my visions. All I know for certain is that you're safest with Dax and that you'll awaken the blood god."

I scooted back and propped my shoulders against the arm of the couch. "What about Sommerton and Leona?" I asked, thinking about my conversation with the warlock today.

I hadn't told my aunt that I was speaking to Talant in my dreams. I knew I should tell her, but I wasn't sure how to explain it. The confession was on the tip of my tongue, but I couldn't open my mouth to release the words.

She shook her head. "All I can see is black when it comes to them. Since Edgar is dabbling in dark magic, I imagine he's found a way to hide himself. And Leona."

"But yesterday—" I started to say.

She shook her head. "It was more a strong feeling rather than an actual vision. As soon as the phone rang and I saw your name, I had a flash of Edgar and a sense of danger toward you, but nothing else."

Crap. That didn't exactly make me feel better.

Minerva got to her feet, smoothing down her skirt. "Now that you're exhausted, tell me how things are going with Dax. Have you made your move yet?"

All thoughts of Sommerton and his claim that he "knew" Talant's brother flew from my mind as I gaped at her. "Made my move? What do you mean?"

"You've been half in love with Dax Tremaine for nearly a decade. Now that you're basically living with him, I thought that nature might take its course."

My mouth opened and closed several times until I finally managed to speak. "But Dax doesn't see me as a woman."

Minerva rolled her eyes. "Ten years ago, you'd be right. He didn't, which was for the best. But now? He's definitely noticed you're all grown up."

My entire body flushed with hot embarrassment. "Aunt Minnie, I'm not talking to you about this."

"Who else would you talk to?" she asked.

"Anyone who's not you," I shot back.

She grinned at me, her eyes twinkling with mischief. "A little birdie told me that you two slept in the same bed last night."

Oh, I was going to kill Poppy. Or, once I figured out how to use my powers, I'd make sure that her wolf tail never went away, even when she was in human form.

"He insisted on sleeping on the floor and he was obviously in pain. His bed is huge, so it was stupid for him to basically torture himself."

My aunt shot me a dry look and I sighed.

"Fine. Fine! Why don't you say whatever it is you want to say so we can get this over with," I relented.

"I want you to open your eyes and really look at Dax the next time you're with him. Pay attention to how he treats you. How he talks to you."

"Why?" I asked, fear creeping into my belly. I was afraid of what I might see if I truly looked.

"Because I think you'll see that you're not the only one who doesn't know how to handle what you're feeling."

"Aunt Minnie—"

She shook her head and lifted a finger to her lips, shushing me. "Just promise me that you'll pay attention. And that you'll take the first step if you see what I think you will. Dax will never do it because he would be worried about making you uncomfortable if you didn't feel the same. It will have to be you."

I scrubbed my hands over my face. Goddess, how had my life suddenly gotten so complicated?

"I'll pay attention," I replied. "I can't promise that I'll make the first move because that's not..." I trailed off. I had no experience with that. I'd never had sex. Or even an actual boyfriend. I'd barely even dated. I'd only gone out with a few boys during college and absolutely no one in high school.

I had no idea how to handle a romantic relationship dynamic, much less sex.

My aunt perched her butt on the coffee table. "Are you still a virgin?" she asked.

I knew my face turned the color of a ripe tomato at her question, which was an answer in and of itself.

"Have you ever kissed someone? Maybe some heavy petting? What about an orgasm? Even if it was self-induced."

"I'm not talking about this with you!" I cried, sitting up straight.

"Why not?" she asked, cocking her head to one side. "I explained sex and all of that to you when you were thirteen. And I answered your questions when you were in high school."

"Yes, but that was mostly about how my periods worked and general sex questions. Not specific things like if I've ever had a freaking orgasm!"

I mean, I had. All self-induced. I even had a few toys, which was something she'd suggested a few years ago. Though I hadn't told her I'd taken her advice to experiment in that way. I wasn't going to discuss this with her. Not now. Not ever.

My aunt studied me in silence for a few moments. "Don't be afraid to ask for what you want, Ally," she said. "Whether it's in or outside the bedroom."

Before I could say anything else, heavy footsteps thudded up the stairs to the cabin and across the porch.

My aunt laid her hand on mine and gave it a pat. "We'll talk more later."

She got to her feet and was facing the door when Dax came inside.

"All done for the day?" she asked.

He nodded, his gaze moving from my aunt to where I was lying on the couch.

"Are you okay?" he asked, taking in my slightly sweaty face, which I was sure was still reddish.

"Fine," I said, leaning back against the couch. "Just recovering from my aunt's brand of torture."

My aunt rolled her eyes at me before she turned back to Dax. "She needs to take it easy tonight. A good meal, quiet evening, and early bedtime," she said. "I'm trusting that you'll make sure all that happens."

Dax nodded. "Of course."

My aunt smirked at me before she leaned down to give me a hug. "Love you, sweet girl. Stay in touch, okay?"

I hugged her back even though I was still exasperated with her. "Love you, too, MinMin. I'll call you tomorrow."

She released me, smiling down at me. "If you don't, I'll call you. You need another magic lesson."

I bit back a groan at the idea and started to get up when she moved away, but she waved me back down. "Stay there and rest. Drink that tea I left for you."

I nodded, relaxing back on the couch.

My aunt went over to Dax, patting his arm with her hand and heading toward the door. "I'll talk to you tomorrow, too, Dax. Keep me updated."

He inclined his head toward her. "Of course."

Minerva walked out the door, shutting it behind her.

"Everything go okay with Poppy?" I asked Dax.

"Yeah. Fine. She's smart and a quick learner. She'll be running this place on her own within the week." He looked around. "Where's the tea Minerva mentioned? You should have a cup."

"On the counter," I said, stretching back out on the couch.

Between the conversations I'd had with Poppy and Minerva about my love life (or lack thereof) and the magic practice, my head was buzzing and foggy at the same time. It was a dizzying sensation that I didn't like. At all.

I closed my eyes, letting my arm fall across my eyes again, blocking out the light coming in through the windows.

A few minutes later, Dax touched my arm. "Your tea is ready."

I sat up and reached for the mug on the coffee table. The steam rising from the cup smelled faintly floral with a hint of something green. I took a cautious sip because I knew from experience that Minerva's teas could sometimes be bitter or noxious.

This one was light and almost sweet with a hint of green herbs. I took a larger swallow, letting the warmth of the liquid wash over me.

"How does soup sound for dinner?" Dax asked from behind me.

"Perfect," I answered, drinking more of the tea.

The warmth in my abdomen washed out into my limbs, bringing a sweet lassitude throughout my body. Wow, this stuff was potent.

My muscles relaxed and I felt as though I were about to sink through the couch. Still, I wanted more tea, so I finished the cup in two swallows.

After I set the mug to the side, my eyes narrowed. I realized that my aunt had snuck something into that tea to make me sleep. Granted, I probably needed it since my head was still buzzing uncomfortably, but I also felt less guarded. Looser.

I felt myself wobble and laid back down on the couch on my side. My eyes closed despite my efforts to keep them open.

"You okay?" Dax asked, his voice much closer than before.

I pried my eyelids open just enough to look up at his face where he leaned over the back of the couch. "I'm mad at MinMin," I slurred.

I didn't register the surprised amusement on his face because I was focused on fighting the effects of the damned tea.

"Why?" he asked.

"Stupid tea. She put an herb in it to make me sleep and something else…" My eyes were beginning to drift shut.

"Something else?"

"Truth serum or something," I answered even though I didn't plan on it.

Yep, definitely a truth serum or something of the sort.

My damn meddling aunt was determined for me to open up, whether I liked it or not.

"Good thing you're going to sleep, then," he murmured. "Otherwise, we'd have to play truth or dare."

The last thing I remembered was laughing at his joke.

WHEN I WOKE UP LATER, I could hear Dax moving around in the kitchen and I smelled cooking meat and onions. He must have been making the soup he mentioned earlier.

I smiled a little when I remembered the joke he'd made right before I'd gone to sleep. I'd forgotten how funny Dax could be. His sense of humor was dry and sometimes it took me by surprise when it snuck out.

I was also surprised I hadn't dreamt of Talant. I usually did, even if all I took was a short nap. Whatever Minerva put in that tea must have put me down so deeply that I didn't dream.

Cautiously, I sat up, running a hand over my hair. It was still light outside, so I hadn't slept too long. There was also a light blanket draped over my body. Dax must have laid it over me while I slept. It was a sweet gesture, one that caused my chest to squeeze.

"You're awake."

I looked over my shoulder to find Dax standing at the bar, looking at me. His glasses were nowhere in sight, which made me a little sad because I liked the way he looked in them.

"How long was I out?" I asked, stretching my arms above my head and leaning from side to side.

"About thirty minutes. How are you feeling?"

I took stock of my body and realized the fuzzy, overwhelmed

feeling in my head was gone. As was the urge to blurt out every thought in my head.

Which reminded me...

"I feel good," I answered, reaching into my back pocket to grab my phone.

It wasn't there. I stood up and took a moment to search the couch. It had fallen out of my pocket and between the cushions. As soon as I plucked it out from between them, I opened up the app for my text messages and clicked on my aunt's name.

What in the hell did you put in that tea?

Three dots immediately popped up, so I knew then that she was waiting by the phone for me to wake up.

Just something to relax you and help you sleep.

I could sense the smirk she must have been wearing when she sent her answer. My thumbs moved furiously over the on-screen keyboard.

Not cool, Minnie. Don't ever give me something like that again. I felt like blurting out every single thought in my head. The only reason I didn't is because I fell asleep on the couch before I could. I know you want me to open up but forcing it on me isn't okay. At all.

There was a pause before the dots popped up again. It took a while before her answer came through.

I'm sorry. That wasn't my intention. You must have reacted to the relaxation potion in an unexpected way. I promise I won't ever do it again. All I wanted was for you to rest and I was afraid that you wouldn't, and you'd end up fainting and scaring the hell out of Dax. Please don't be mad at me.

I sighed, my shoulders drooping as the anger drained out of me. I knew she wasn't lying because my aunt never lied to me. She always told me the truth, even when it was incredibly uncomfortable for both of us.

Unlike me, who hadn't told her the entire truth about my dreams. Nor had I told her what Sommerton said when he called earlier about Talant's brother. Mostly because I'd already lied by omission in not telling her about Talant at all.

Which only compounded the guilt I was feeling.

Even though I never manifested my magic as a teenager, my aunt still educated me in some of the basics of magic, potions, and teas. Living in Devil Springs meant that I needed to understand how magic worked. Especially when I used to work at her shop in high school. I needed a knowledge of herbs and how they would aid in certain spells and potions, or the other uses they might have. I also had to understand how semi-precious stones and crystals affected magic. Though I couldn't utilize power, I probably knew as much about magic as any other witch my age. Except how to release and use my power.

I understand and I'm not mad anymore. And I promise that I'll rest if you tell me I should. Especially after a magic lesson.

Her response was immediate this time. *I love you.*

I love you too. We'll talk tomorrow. No magic lesson though. My brain still hurts.

I would tell her about Talant and how I met up with him in my dreams then. And about Sommerton's claim to know Talant's brother. Then, we would figure out what to do.

Sure thing, sweet girl. Be sure to practice for a little bit tomorrow though.

Will do.

I put my phone down and walked into the kitchen. Now that I was awake, I was thirsty.

Dax was still watching me. Usually, I would have tried to ignore the way he was looking at me, but this time I paid attention. Because of my conversations with Poppy and Minerva, I realized that my usual tactic for dealing with Dax was avoidance and disconnection. And because of that, I was unaware of a lot of things about him and how he interacted with me.

Now that I was focused, I noticed that his eyes followed my every move.

Hm. Interesting.

I got a glass out of the cabinet and filled it up at the sink. No one here drank bottled water in Devil Springs because it couldn't beat what came from the tap. The water here came from a natural spring that ran beneath one of the mountains. That was how the town got its name. The mountains here weren't very high, but there were some rock formations. The one closest to the entrance to the underground spring resembled the horns often drawn on a devil in religious illustrations.

Considering so many of the residents of Devil Springs had horns in their natural forms, it had become a sort of joke that had eventually stuck.

I drank half the glass before I lowered it and asked, "What kind of soup are we having for dinner?"

"Vegetable beef," he answered.

Another of my favorites. Especially the way he made it.

"Cornbread too?" I asked, my mouth watering.

He nodded and turned back to the stove, stirring the contents of the pot. "It's in the oven. This will be done in twenty minutes."

I moved around the kitchen, getting out bowls and cutlery. I loved Dax's cooking, but I didn't like feeling like a burden.

"I can make dinner tomorrow," I offered as I set our places at the bar.

Dax looked up from the pot. "You don't like my cooking?"

There was a teasing edge to his voice, so I knew he wasn't offended, but I explained myself anyway.

"I'm living in your house while you're protecting me. I should help out while I'm here, not be a burden."

"You're not a burden," he rumbled. "And we've already discussed this."

I lifted my eyes from where I'd been fiddling with the silverware. He was staring at me. Now that his eyes weren't hidden behind his glasses, I saw the intensity in them. He didn't look angry exactly, but neither did his expression contain the patience it typically did.

"I know, but I'm also not used to being idle. I need things to do, or I'll sit and stew on the fact that I can't go anywhere or be alone for goddess knows how long. So, how about we take turns making dinner and breakfast?"

"Okay," he agreed, turning back to the stove.

I smiled a little because that was Dax. He seemed to understand me better than anyone else. Sometimes even better than Minerva did.

For the first time since my aunt informed me that I'd be staying with Dax for an undetermined amount of time, I felt lighter. The weight of the guilt I'd felt at the idea of inconveniencing Dax, Minerva, and everyone else lessened.

CHAPTER

SEVEN

The next morning, I woke up feeling just as warm and cozy as I had the day before.

I knew before I opened my eyes that I'd moved in my sleep again and I was cuddled up to Dax.

Except this time, he was on his back. My head was on his shoulder and my leg was thrown across his thick thigh so that I basically straddled his leg. I was pressed to him from head to toe. Well, my toes, not his, because he was so tall that I couldn't reach his feet with mine.

I'd been almost shocked last night when Dax got ready for bed and climbed right in without us having to discuss it or argue.

I also dreamed about Talant again. I told him that my aunt was trying to help me access my power and how she said I was blocked. He'd practiced with me for a little while, helping me feel my magic and hold it.

When we first started, it felt as though I was trying to grasp grains of sand. By the time we were done, it was more like thick slime. I could feel it and touch it, even hold small amounts of it, but it would eventually slide out of my grip.

Still, it was an improvement from my practice with Minerva.

And my brain didn't hurt the way it had earlier. I only felt tired.

When Talant told me that we were done, I'd started to argue but he'd just waved a hand and sent me away, saying, "I'll see you tomorrow night. You need rest."

He sounded just like my aunt.

And just like my aunt, I hadn't told him what Sommerton said about his brother.

Goddess, I hated lying, yet here I was keeping secrets from everyone. That was the problem with lies. Even by omission. If you had one, then another followed shortly after to hide the first. Then another. And another. Until you were buried beneath the weight of them all.

My sleep was dreamless after I left Talant until I woke up plastered to Dax's body.

I took stock of my position and tried to figure out how to move away without waking him. I also realized that he had one arm wrapped around my back, his hand resting against my ribs, and his other palm rested against the leg I'd thrown over him. My shorts had ridden up during the night and his hand against my bare thigh felt like a brand.

As soon as I started to inch away, his hold on me tightened.

"What were you dreaming about last night?" he asked, his deep voice even more gravelly than usual.

I could feel it vibrate throughout my entire body since I was pressed against him. I suppressed a shiver. Then, my brain focused on his question and my heart started to race. I knew he could probably feel it, maybe even hear it.

"I don't remember. Why? Did I move around a lot or something?"

He didn't buy it. I knew it before he even spoke.

"Who's Talant?"

Just when I thought my heart couldn't pound any faster, it went from racing to approaching Mach 1.

"I don't know. Why?"

In a blink, I was on my back, staring up at Dax's hard face. He didn't look pleased with me. At all. I tried to move away, but he rested more of his weight against me, pinning me down.

I pushed at his shoulders, trying to create some space between us, but he was immovable.

"Dax, what are you doing?"

"You're lying to me, Ally. You know exactly what I'm talking about. What I want to know is why you won't tell me."

In the early morning light, his eyes were no longer dark blue or even purple, they were the color of sapphires, brilliant and gleaming with the same cold light as a gemstone would.

I took a deep breath, suddenly very aware of how my breasts were crushed against his chest and his hips were wedged between my legs. All the thoughts flew out of my head. I shifted beneath him, trying to put an inch of space between us.

"Who's Talant?" he repeated. "You said the name several times last night and the night before, too."

"I did?"

"Yes, it sounded like you were carrying on quite the conversation last night."

Dear goddess, had I been talking in my sleep since I started dreaming of Talant?

"I don't remember," I insisted.

I didn't want to talk to him about this. When I'd first started dreaming of Talant a few months ago, I thought he was a figment of my overactive imagination. Then, when I realized he was real, I hadn't wanted to admit my ignorance to anyone, much less Minerva. It had taken me over a month to understand that I was actually dreaming of a real person. I'd felt stupid and it didn't seem like that big of a deal, so I'd kept it to myself.

I'd thought it was a latent magical talent, a minor one. I hadn't understood then what it meant. Or who Talant was.

Then, when Minerva explained that my power would be the key to unlocking the spell holding back the blood god, I'd realized who I was speaking to and why I was able to communicate with him.

He and I had a connection. One I didn't fully comprehend. And it was up to me to free him from his rock prison.

And, now, because I'd kept the secret of Talant for months, I had another secret—the blood god had a brother and it was very likely that Sommerton was feeding on his power and likely becoming a host for the god himself. One secret had multiplied into two. And I was keeping them from everyone, not just my aunt or Dax.

"Stop lying," Dax said, leaning closer and interrupting my train of thought.

Since I couldn't make any more space between us, I did the next best thing. I turned my head and covered my face with my hands. If I couldn't escape him physically, I would shut him out.

I didn't know how to explain it to him. Or to Minerva. Not without them thinking I was crazy. My connection to Talant was something special. Something just for me. He was my friend, even if he was incredibly powerful, obnoxiously arrogant, and oblivious. And I'd already kept him a secret for so long that it would be nearly impossible to explain why.

Dax grabbed my wrists, pinning my hands above my head with one of his, revealing my face.

"Tell me," he insisted.

I kept my face turned away until his fingers clasped my chin. I didn't fight the pull. Instead, I stared at him, tilting my chin up.

"By the goddess, I forgot how stubborn you can be."

He sounded irritated but also a little amused.

"Why won't you tell me?" he asked.

"Because I don't think you'll understand." I answered him honestly this time.

His expression softened and his gaze moved over my face. "I don't have to understand in order to listen."

"I also don't feel like being lectured," I snapped.

"When have I ever lectured you?" he asked.

I glared at him in response this time because he was right. He never had lectured me. Even when I did incredibly stupid things like wandering off into the woods behind Minerva's house without anything but a book. I'd gotten lost, cold, and scared. It was just after I'd come to live with my aunt, and I'd still been walking around in a fog of grief.

But he'd found me and carried me home, flying above the treetops. Now, Minerva had given me a talking to, right before she'd wrapped me in the tightest hug I'd ever received and burst into tears.

"Tell me," he repeated again.

I sighed because, even though he said I was stubborn, he was more so. He could be as unyielding as the stone his skin turned into when he changed into full gargoyle form. He wasn't going to give this up or let it go until I told him the truth.

"A few months ago, I started having dreams. At first, they were short and not very often. Usually about a man sleeping inside a stone. Then, he started to wake up around the time Bethany died."

Dax nodded. Bethany had passed a little while ago. She owned the local mercantile and was one of my clients. Her great-niece, Cari, now owned the store and was mated to Daniel Ayres, the mayor.

"At first, I thought I was just dreaming. But..." I stopped and took a deep breath. "I started to realize that he wasn't some crazy figment of my imagination. He's a real person, er, god."

"Why didn't you tell Minerva?" Dax asked.

"This is the part I don't think you'll understand. I'm scared she won't either."

"Your feelings are your own," he replied. "I don't have to understand them to accept them."

Goddess, this was why I loved Dax. He was wise and compassionate. And accepting.

"I didn't know who he was until Minerva told me that it was my destiny to wake the blood god. And, when I understood, I kept it to myself because I was embarrassed. It took me over a month to even realize that Talant was a real being, not just a figment of my imagination. And even when I did know what he was, I never thought anything would come of it. My time with him was mine. Something I discovered on my own. I knew that if I told Minerva, she would get excited and want to push me. And I was worried that this connection to Talant, these dreams, were the only magic I would ever possess. I never thought I'd have a reason to tell her about it. She never said anything negative when I didn't manifest my powers as a teenager. She never seemed to love me any less. But—"

I stopped talking because my throat was closing up. I cleared it before I continued.

"But I knew she was disappointed that she couldn't share her knowledge and her skill with magic with me. I didn't want to disappoint her again."

"But you know differently now," Dax pointed out.

"Do I?" I asked. "I still haven't manifested. Minerva says I'm just blocked, but what if it's more than that? What if I don't have the kind of power she thinks I have? What if all I can do is talk to Talant in my dreams?"

"Your aunt has never been wrong in her visions nor has she been disappointed in you," Dax said, his voice patient. "None of us have. It doesn't matter if you're fully human, fully witch, or something in between. We will all love you just the same."

Though I knew he wasn't saying he was in love with me but that he cared about me, a thrill still ran through my body.

I couldn't suppress my shiver and I knew Dax felt it because his hand tightened slightly on my wrist. Awareness fizzled along my nerve endings, settling between my thighs with a throb.

My mouth was suddenly dry, and I licked my lips.

Dax's gaze moved from my eyes to my mouth and his fingers tensed on my chin. His body moved over mine, shifting a scant inch closer.

Reflexively, my thighs squeezed his waist.

In a blink, Dax had released me and was on his feet next to the bed. As he turned away, I saw the tented front of his pajama pants.

My eyes widened, but Dax didn't see because he was striding into the bathroom, his back to me. When the door shut behind him, I looked up at the ceiling.

While I might be a virgin, I knew what I'd just seen. Dax had an erection. A rather large one. My heart pounded in my chest and my palms dampened with sweat.

Holy crap. I didn't know if I was excited or terrified. I might not have had sex with an actual man, but I did have a couple toys. However, none of them were as large as what I'd just seen. Well, I did have one that was close, but not quite.

I blinked rapidly at the ceiling. Did he have an erection because of me? Or just because it was morning?

Damn. I had no answers because I'd never woken up with a man before him. Nor was this something they covered in health class in high school.

There was only one person I could ask, and I needed to talk to her anyway.

I picked up my phone, my thumbs moving rapidly over the screen.

Are you up?

My aunt replied within seconds.

No, but I'll open my eyes for you.

I had to roll my eyes at that. She was an early bird like me, often rising before the sun. I couldn't figure out what to say, so I decided to just come out and ask.

Do men always have an erection in the mornings?

I heard the shower come on in the bathroom and knew I'd have a little time before Dax emerged. Still, she was taking too long to answer.

Finally, her answer came through, but it was actually a question.

Why are you asking?

I wasn't sure how to respond because everything that had happened this morning was complicated.

I settled on partial truth.

I lied to Dax this morning when we woke up and he sort of rolled on top of me and pinned me to the bed until I told him the truth. Then, he stared at my mouth for a second until I moved my legs, and he jumped out of the bed like it was on fire. But he had an erection when he did. But I don't know if it's because of biology or if it was because he was close to me.

The three little dots danced for a very long time. So long that I was afraid that Dax would finish his shower before she replied, and I wouldn't get a chance to read it.

It was because of biology and you. Did you snuggle up to him again last night? And did he let you? Because if he did, that means I'm right about how he feels about you.

I made a face at my phone. She was going to be a pain in the ass about this. I just knew it.

Yes, I cuddled up to him in my sleep and yes, he let me. Which reminds me, there's something I need to tell you that doesn't have to do with Dax. Can you come by this evening?

Of course. About Dax though...

I waited. The shower shut off and I mentally urged Minerva to hurry.

Take the risk. Make a move and see what happens. The worst that can happen is that he lets you down easy.

That wasn't exactly true. The worst he could do was disappear from my life completely. It would be difficult in a town the size of Devil Springs, but not impossible. If he didn't want to see me, he wouldn't. And there would be nothing I could do about it.

I'll think about it.

Her reply was immediate. *You do that. I'll see you tonight.*

Tonight.

I shut down my screen and set the phone aside just as the bathroom door opened. Dax came out wearing nothing but a bath sheet. On me, the bath towels were huge, covering me from my arm pits to my knees.

On Dax's huge frame, it looked much smaller. The towel barely reached all the way around his hips.

"We should get going," he said, heading toward the dresser. "Poppy will be at the resort in an hour."

His voice was cold, aloof. I'd heard him use this tone before. But never with me. He hadn't even looked at me.

The fragile hope that had blossomed after my texts with my aunt withered and faded within a split second.

I'd misread the entire situation. He wanted to keep his distance and he was letting me know without actually saying it aloud.

Without a word, I climbed out of bed, gathered my clothes, and went into the bathroom to shower. Maybe the hot water would warm up the cold that had settled around my aching heart.

CHAPTER
EIGHT

The day went much like the day before.

We met Poppy at the main lodge, and we all worked in Dax's office.

Just before lunch, I received a text from an unknown number.

How's my girl?

I frowned before typing, *Who's this?*

A picture came through of Sommerton's face. I nearly dropped my phone at the sight. He hadn't been an ugly man before, but now he was terrifying. His eyes had turned completely black, with only a sickening violet oblong pupil in the center. The black veins that had surrounded his eyes only two days before were now all over his cheeks, forehead, and snaking down his neck.

He wore a massive grin that made my skin crawl. I felt as though I was being watched, and as I stared in horror at the picture, it winked at me.

I did drop my phone then, lunging to my feet.

Dax was at my side in a split second, looking at me for the first time since he'd rolled off the bed that morning. "What is it? What's wrong?"

"S-S-Sommerton texted."

Dax scowled. "I thought you blocked him."

"I did!" I exclaimed, running a shaky hand through my hair. "I'm not sure how he got through."

Dax picked up my phone and looked at the screen, his scowl turning into a grim, stony expression. I imagined that he wore that face into battle back before the gargoyle civil war. I knew he'd been a part of the gargoyle army based on a few things that he'd said in passing over the years.

At the moment, he looked as though he was ready to murder someone in a single stroke of a blade. Preferably Sommerton.

"I'm taking your phone," he said.

"No! You can't!" I lunged for it, but he yanked it away, moving too fast for me to see.

"He's upsetting you, getting into your head," Dax said, his voice tight but still patient. "It's best if we don't give him the opportunity anymore. It's feeding his need to manipulate you into doing what he wants."

"I have to have my phone, Dax," I said. "I have clients. I need to talk to Minerva."

I couldn't stand the thought of having no one to talk to but him because he was currently freezing me out. I'd go crazy if I had to sit in that house in silence while he ignored me.

I kept talking, keeping my eyes resolutely on his chin. "I also need to be able to call for help if something happens. I can block him again and keep blocking him."

"He's not going to stop," Dax said.

I chanced a glance up at his eyes, grateful I couldn't see them because of the glare from the light on his glasses. I couldn't stand to see that distant expression on his face again.

"I know. I can handle it."

"You were terrified a few seconds ago," he pointed out.

I gestured toward the screen of my phone. "Did you look at that picture? Wouldn't you be terrified if that was suddenly on your phone screen?"

Dax shook his head, which made me snort. Of course, he wouldn't. No, he'd be reaching for his sword and turning to stone before he tried to decapitate the warlock.

"I can handle Sommerton. Especially now that I know what he's up to and that he can still get in touch with me when I block him. Plus, there's not telling if he'll slip up and mention more things we need to know. Like saying that he was with Talant's brother."

Dax stiffened. "Talant's brother? When did he say that?"

His tone was dangerous, which made me freeze. Shit, I'd forgotten that I hadn't told him about that. This was why I hated lying and secrets. Because it was too easy to screw up and say the wrong thing.

I shrugged. "Yesterday. I didn't know if he's telling the truth or not, so I didn't bring it up. But that's what he said."

His brow furrowed. "Have you told Minerva? And why didn't you tell me?"

"I didn't tell you because I thought he was probably lying. I'm going to talk to Minerva about it tonight because I thought it was a conversation best had in person." I held out my hand. "My phone please."

Dax stared down at my palm. For once, I could read his expression. He was torn between what he thought best and not interfering with my free will.

After a few tense moments, he sighed and put the phone in my hand. I noticed he was careful not to touch me when he did.

Still, the fact that he didn't outright deny me access to my phone surprised me. I thought I'd have much more of a fight on my hands.

"You'll let me know when he gets in touch with you," he rumbled, his voice once again gravelly.

I was hearing that timbre more often over the past few days and I was beginning to understand that it was how he sounded when he was frustrated. Something he rarely seemed to feel around me in the past.

"I will," I agreed. In fact, I would probably complain about Sommerton's attempts to get under my skin if they continued.

Now that I was over my surprise at the sight of the warlock, I was annoyed. Sending me that picture reeked of frat bro behavior, which had been a huge reason why I hadn't dated in college. Half the guys I'd talked to, whether they were in a fraternity or not, acted like I should be ecstatic they were deigning to speak to me. That arrogance was obnoxious and off-putting to me.

I took a moment to block the number that Sommerton had used to text me and tucked my phone back into my pocket. "See? I blocked him. If he texts me again, you'll be the second person to know." I paused. "Well, the third since Sommerton is one and I'm two—"

I had to bite back a grin when Dax grunted and turned on his heel, stomping back over to his desk. As soon as he leaned down to type on the keyboard with an index finger, Poppy winked at me over his head.

A small snort escaped my mouth, but I made sure to look busy when Dax looked in my direction.

The rest of the day was uneventful. I informed Dax over lunch that my aunt was coming over after work and he insisted she stay for dinner.

I half wondered if he was trying to limit our time alone and that suspicion grew when he stayed much later at the office than he had the day before. It was only when Poppy declared that she'd been here long enough and took off that he started to shut down his computer and tidy his desk.

Since I offered to make dinner, Dax disappeared outside almost as soon as we arrived at the cabin.

I tried to ignore the ache in my chest as I scrounged through the fridge, looking for ingredients for the meal. I wasn't quite as good a cook as Dax, but I wasn't horrible either.

In the end, I decided to make chicken enchilada casserole. It was one of Minerva's recipes that I'd tweaked and made my own. Every time I made it over the years and Dax was over for dinner, he would eat nearly half the pan by himself.

Since he'd been making all my favorite foods over the past couple of days, I decided to return the favor.

I had the chicken simmering in a pan with onions and peppers when the thought of going outside hit me. I tried to shake it off. Dax was out there, and it was clear he was avoiding me. I didn't want another awkward encounter with him.

I was also enjoying the first time I'd been alone in over forty-eight hours. At least that's what I told myself.

Once the chicken was done, I assembled the casserole and slid it into the oven, ignoring the thought circling in the back of my mind that I should walk out the front door.

Just as I was about to set the timer, the thought became more insistent, almost painful in its intensity. I *needed* to go outside. I went to the window and peeked outside. There was nothing there but trees. I didn't even see Dax.

I tried to shake off the thought and went back to the counter where my phone sat. I needed to set the timer, but my feet kept going, carrying me around the bar and through the living room.

I tried to stop, to turn around, but it was as if my body no longer belonged to me. By the time I reached the door, I was no longer trying to stop myself. The urge to walk out of the cabin and into the trees nearby was unrelenting and irresistible.

My steps were slow and measured as I crossed the porch and went down the steps. I skirted the SUV in the driveway and walked into the forest, going away from the lodge and the cabin. The farther I went from Dax's house, the less I was concerned about staying inside. Or Dax. Or anything.

All I could think about was getting to the edge of the property. There was something special waiting for me there.

I heard a whooshing sound above me, but I didn't lift my head to look up. No, I needed to keep going. The edge of the resort was beckoning me.

Something heavy landed to my right but my vision narrowed until all I could see were the trees in front of me.

Almost there. Another hundred feet and I'd reach my prize.

I felt something around my wrist, and I tried to shake it off. It tightened until I hurt, but still I fought to get free. I cried out in pain and the manacle around my wrist released.

Smiling, I turned back toward my destination. My freedom. That word echoed in my mind, melodic and soothing like a song that consisted of a single word.

Freedom.

There was pressure on my face, around my cheeks, and my body collided with a hard, warm surface. I tried to move around it. When that didn't work, I tried to shove it out of the way.

I had to get to the edge of the forest. To my freedom. It was worth fighting for. Worth dying for.

Suddenly, a pair of brilliant blue eyes filled my vision, the sapphire irises shot through with silver. They were beautiful and familiar.

I was caught for a moment, trapped by their beauty.

Then, the siren's song of freedom called to me again. I had to keep moving. To reach my destination.

I tried to sidestep the obstacle in front of me, but the pressure on my face increased and those eyes got closer.

There was a pressure against my lips. I opened my mouth to insist on leaving, but warm breath ghosted over my skin and there was a warm, wet touch on my lower lip.

My body abruptly belonged to me again. I lifted my hands and touched the wall in front of me. It was warm and hard. My fingers curled, digging into fabric and flesh.

The pressure on my cheeks lifted my face, tilting my head back and to the side. I realized the touch of wetness on my lip was a tongue just as it slipped into my mouth. The smell of snow and pine invaded my senses, breaking through the whispered words echoing in my mind.

I whimpered, clutching at Dax's chest, and opened my mouth. All that mattered was that he was kissing me as I sometimes dreamed he did. Like he couldn't get enough of me. Like he never wanted to let me go.

His lips were hot and soft, and his tongue was in my mouth, stroking mine. My legs shook, growing weak, and I all but collapsed against him.

Dax released my face, and his arms went around my waist, holding me up. But he kept kissing me, his mouth insistent as it moved against mine.

I moaned, lifting my arms to twine them around Dax's neck. My entire body tingled and there was a relentless throb between my thighs. I needed more than a kiss. I needed his hands on me. His skin against mine.

His kiss woke something inside me, a fire that had lain dormant until now.

When my hands clasped the nape of his neck, Dax shuddered against me, his arms all but crushing me against him. He lifted his head slowly and I rose on my toes to chase his lips. I realized I'd closed my eyes at some point and opened them.

Dax stared down at me, his eyes still that bright, bright blue shot through with silver that seemed to sparkle in the early evening light. He was breathing hard and still holding me so close that I could barely move.

"Thank all the gods," he whispered, his voice so deep that it nearly hurt my ears. "I thought I wouldn't be able to stop you without hurting you."

I stared up at him. "What happened?"

"You were walking toward the edge of the wards. Why?"

I shook my head. "I...don't know. All I remember was thinking that if I got there, I would be free."

I blinked when I saw Dax's wings flex above his shoulders,

arching high above us. They were enormous, which they would have to be to carry his weight in full gargoyle form.

"Hang on," he rasped, bending his knees slightly.

I barely had time to wrap both my arms and legs around him before he launched us both into the air. I sucked in the air to scream, but no sound emerged because it all became trapped in my lungs.

Dax hadn't carried me in flight since I was a child. And never holding me like this.

I made a sound of distress in my throat and locked my ankles together behind his back, squeezing as hard as I could. The iron bands of Dax's arms adjusted around me, one moving beneath my butt and the other across my upper back. He skimmed the tops of the trees as he headed back toward his home.

The flight back to the cabin was short. Dax landed lightly, his wings flaring behind him before disappearing into the back of his torn shirt.

But he didn't put me down. He held my weight with a forearm under my butt and carried me up the steps, across the porch, and into the cabin.

He still didn't release me once we were inside. He kicked the door shut behind us and walked straight to the couch. Dax shifted me, his other hand going behind him to my ankle. I loosened my legs, and he turned me so I sat sideways across his lap as he lowered himself to the couch.

My head rested against his shoulder. I could feel his heart pounding through his shirt. His body shuddered again but he remained silent.

"I'm okay," I assured him.

"I left you here alone," he replied. "I shouldn't have done it. I can't lose—" He abruptly went quiet again.

"I'm right here. You stopped me from walking out of the ward's protection."

He didn't reply.

After a few moments, I lifted my head and looked at him. His eyes were once again such a deep, dark blue that they were nearly purple, the silver streaks gone. A question trembled on the tip of my tongue, but I was afraid to ask.

No, I wasn't afraid to ask. I was afraid of the answer. But if there was ever a time to be brave, it was now. Dax had given me mixed signals all day and I needed clarification.

"Why did you kiss me?" I asked, forcing myself to hold his stare. Aunt Minnie had suggested that all I needed to do was watch him to see how he felt about me. So that's what I was going to do.

But, goddess, it was fucking hard.

His gaze jumped to my mouth before he caught himself and met my eyes again. A dull pink flush spread across his cheeks. His right hand was still resting on my knee and his fingers flexed around it.

And I understood then what my aunt meant.

All these years, I thought Dax viewed me as his little sister. Or a family friend.

But that wasn't true.

He saw me as woman. And, whether he wanted to admit it or not, he was attracted to me, too.

"Dax?" I pressed.

"I..." He didn't finish his thought.

I saw his jaw clench and all but heard his back molars grind before he finally answered.

"You reacted for a moment when you saw my face, but it didn't last. My only options were knocking you unconscious or kissing you and..." He paused, his eyes moving away from mine. "I couldn't hurt you."

My heart immediately started to race at his words, and I knew Dax heard it because his gaze shot to mine again.

"Ally—"

I lifted my hand from where it had been resting on my lap and touched his cheek. "I'm glad that was your choice."

For the first time since I realized how I felt about Dax, I had enough confidence to tell him what I wanted.

"But I want you to do it again."

His swallow was audible, but he didn't move. With our faces so close together, I saw his eyes change, the deep blue melting into silver and sapphire and sparkling in the dim light inside the cabin.

"Ally, I don't think—"

I shook my head. "I don't want an excuse or a flimsy reason why it's a bad idea. Do you want to kiss me?"

Once again, his eyes flicked down to my mouth and stayed. His hand on my knee tightened and his arm around my back pulled me an inch closer.

And I had my answer.

Keeping my eyes open and on his face, I leaned forward until I felt his breath against my mouth. Dax didn't move. He was barely even breathing.

I stopped just before our lips touched, giving him a chance to pull away. When he didn't, I closed the distance and laid my mouth against his.

I hated that I hadn't been fully aware for our first kiss, but I was now. I felt the soft warmth of his lips and the rapid pounding of his heart.

I affected him just as deeply as he affected me. He was just better at hiding it.

Dax took a deep breath and pulled me closer, the hand at my back moving up through my hair to the base of my skull. His palm cradled my head, tilting it backward. His hand burned like a brand against my scalp, and I gasped at the sensation.

Then, I lost all ability to breathe because his tongue slid into my mouth, tangling with mine.

I didn't remember moving my hands, but they were suddenly fisted in his short hair as he deepened the kiss.

Shocks of electricity arced through me, raising goosebumps on my skin, and pebbling my nipples.

This kiss was even better than I'd ever imagined it could be.

I turned into Dax, shifting restlessly on his lap. I wanted to touch him. Everywhere. Or for him to touch me. No, it was more than want. It was need. I needed his hands on me, just as I had earlier.

Before I could tear my lips from his to tell him what I needed, or beg for it, there was a knock on the door.

Then, the front door opened, and my aunt sauntered inside.

When she saw us on the couch, both gaping at her in astonishment, she beamed at us.

"Took you two long enough," she said.

CHAPTER
NINE

Once Aunt Minnie arrived, Dax lifted me off his lap and gently set me on the couch. He mumbled something about checking the perimeter of the ward. Then, he disappeared outside.

Minerva sighed after he was gone, shaking her head. "His head's a mess."

His wasn't the only one.

Between the kisses and how Dax went hot and then cold on me, my thoughts were a jumble.

Aunt Minnie turned toward me and really looked at me, then her eyes widened. She came over, her hands cupping my cheeks. She tilted my head back and from side to side.

"That's some nasty spellwork," she murmured.

She ran her thumbs over my eyebrows and whispered a few words, her voice too soft for me to hear them. My head began to clear.

Maybe the residual spell was what had clouded my mind.

I thought about the kisses I'd just shared with Dax and my thoughts grew clouded again. Nope, not entirely the spell.

"Why don't you tell me what happened while I make you a cup of tea," she suggested.

I scowled at her. "Magical tea like what you gave me yesterday or *tea* tea?" I asked.

My aunt gave me an arch look. "Tea from Dax's cabinet. Unless you want the tea I brought with me now?"

I shook my head. "Herbal tea will do just fine."

Minerva snorted and continued into the kitchen.

I moved from the couch to the bar, settling on one of the stools. Then, I smelled the enchilada casserole. Before I could say anything, Minerva opened the oven, peered inside, and hummed.

"I think dinner is ready."

She was probably right. I hadn't had a chance to set the timer, but I wasn't sure what time I'd been forced to leave the cabin.

"Just close the door and turn the oven off. It should keep until we're done talking."

My appetite was non-existent right now anyway.

My aunt began the process of making tea, moving around the kitchen as though she'd been here many times. I knew she hadn't because Dax liked to keep to himself. Other than Daniel and maybe Garrett, I don't think anyone else had ever been here either.

"So, what happened?" she asked, putting the kettle on the stove, and lighting a burner.

"I was making dinner when I had this thought of going outside. It seemed to come out of nowhere. I tried to ignore it, but the thought just kept popping up. Then, the word freedom kept repeating in my mind, over and over. I was still fighting it until my feet just seemed to carry me outside. The farther I got from the cabin, the less I could control myself. It was like I lost control of my body first and then my brain. I didn't even see Dax when he came to stop me. I kept moving. Even when he grabbed my wrist, I pulled away until I hurt myself."

I lifted my hand to rub my wrist. Now that I was talking about it,

I noticed the pain throbbing there. I looked down and saw the skin was already turning purple. I was going to have a bruise.

"When he leaned down and put his face close to mine, I hesitated. Something about looking into his eyes broke through for a second. But then, the thought came back. I had to walk away, to get to the edge of the forest. I would have kept moving if he hadn't—"

I fell silent. This was where things got complicated.

"Until he what?" Minerva asked.

"Until he kissed me. But it didn't break through right away. It still took a few seconds," I finally answered.

"But his kiss interrupted the spell?" she asked.

I nodded, still staring down at the bruise coming up on my wrist and rubbing a thumb absently over it.

Minerva came over to the bar and took my hand, lifting my injured wrist.

"I don't have any healing balm with me, but it won't help much now that the bruise is already forming."

She waved a hand over it and a pale blue light emitted from her palm. Immediately, the pain dulled to a mild twinge. The bruise faded slightly, but there was still a dark smudge on my wrist. My aunt must have used a lot of magic today because she could usually heal such things easily. Guilt jabbed me. I hated that she might be exhausting herself in order to keep me safe.

"That will help with the pain," she said.

My aunt leaned over and kissed my forehead.

"I do have something that will protect you from spells like that," she said, moving back toward the stove to get the whistling kettle.

"How was the spell able to affect me, anyway?" I asked. "I thought the ward around the resort would deflect magic."

Minerva sighed as she poured hot water into two mugs that she'd already put tea bags into.

"It should have, but dark magic is tricky. It changes the witch or warlock using it. Changes their power. It's insidious and deceptive.

There was only so much I could do in terms of the ward without the blessing of the coven for a full blood spell. Dax's blood in the spell should have helped deflect the attack on you, but if Edgar has accessed stone magic somehow..." she trailed off. "There are a number of ways he could have gotten the spell through the ward. Unfortunately, I can't see him in my visions. For the first time in years, everything I see of the future is all a grey and black fog."

"It's happened to you before?" I asked. "Not being able to see what's coming?"

She brought one of the cups over and set it on the counter in front of me. "Yes, it has. Usually before something significant happens in my own life. The last time was a few days before your parents..."

She didn't finish the sentence, but I knew what she meant. The last time she'd been unable to see the future was right before my parents died and she'd become my guardian.

This also meant that something was about to happen to her. The thought made my stomach clutch painfully.

I couldn't lose Minerva. She was the last of my family. Beyond that, she was my closest friend. She'd become my touchstone in a world where I'd been set adrift at the age of eleven.

As usual, my aunt seemed to know the direction my thoughts had taken, and it had nothing to do with the fact that she was a witch. She'd always understood me. She said it was because I was so much like my mother and, being sisters, she'd understood my mother better than anyone else.

Minerva came over and laid a hand on mine. "Nothing is going to happen to me," she said. "I'm not leaving you for a very, very long time."

I turned my palm over, clutching her fingers. "Swear it."

"I vow that I will not leave you."

I noticed that she didn't say she wouldn't be hurt or anything else. Only that she wouldn't leave. Still, I didn't call her out on it.

For the first time, I could feel the power snap in the air when she said the words. They were magically binding, as vows were in Devil Springs. There was magic in the air here and promises made were promises kept. Or else the magic would take its due.

My aunt released my hand and picked up her tea, taking a sip. "What did you need to talk to me about when you messaged this morning?" she asked. "Other than Dax having a hard-on."

I scoffed. That was just like her. A sneak attack to change the subject, along with an outrageous statement to throw me off balance. She was sneakier than any fox.

Goddess, this was more difficult than I thought it would be. It was the first real secret I'd kept from her, and the guilt was a razor's edge cutting at me.

"I've been having dreams the past couple of months," I admitted. "About a man."

She leaned forward and rested her elbows on the counter. "About Dax? Were they sexy?"

I shook my head. "No, about a man named Talant. I thought, at first, that my imagination was working overtime because I was stressed or bored or something. Because, when I first started dreaming about him, he was sleeping inside a stone prison. But, around the time Bethany died, he started to wake up. And he talked to me."

My mouth was dry, so I took a sip of my tea. The warm liquid soothed my throat, and the floral scent of chamomile calmed me somewhat.

"It wasn't until Sommerton kidnapped Sela that I realized he wasn't a figment of my imagination. He was real." I took a deep breath. "And then, when you told me that I was destined to wake the blood god, I realized that's who he was. That we had a connection." I took a deep breath, preparing for the most difficult part. "I kept it a secret because I was embarrassed that it took me so long to realize what was happening and..."

"And what?" Minerva asked. She didn't sound angry, only curious.

It made the tightness in my chest ease a little.

"And I thought that's all my power would be—talking with Talant in my dreams. I didn't think it was anything special or world changing."

Minerva stared at me, an astonished expression on her face. She set her mug to the side. "That's why didn't you tell me about this when you realized what was going on? Because you were afraid I would judge you?"

I shrugged. "I don't know. Maybe. I've been so confused about it and a little scared."

See, that was the tricky part. I talked to Minerva about nearly everything, but this was a difficult conversation because it made me much more vulnerable. And I didn't want to hurt her feelings or have my feelings hurt either.

"Ally?" she pressed.

"I thought that it was the only magical ability I would have. And I didn't want to disappoint you again."

Minerva looked confused. "Disappoint me again? I don't understand. I don't think you've ever disappointed me."

I had to keep going, even though I didn't want to.

"I know you were disappointed when I didn't manifest during puberty or high school." I lifted a hand when she opened her mouth and said, "Let me finish."

Minerva closed her mouth and crossed her arms at her waist, nodding.

"You never said anything, but I know that you wished I'd manifested. I was excited at first when I realized I had power. Until it hit me that this might be it. My dreams about Talant might be all I was ever capable of. And I knew you'd be disappointed again."

Minerva shook her head, her eyes filling with tears. "Sweet girl, I was never, ever disappointed that you weren't a witch. And I'm so sorry if you thought that. The only thing I ever worried about was how *you* would feel about being a human in Devil Springs. There aren't many humans here and I worried that you might feel unwelcome or as if you didn't belong here. I was terrified that you wouldn't come home after college, but I never said anything because I only want you to be happy." She sniffed, wiping away one of the tears that fell. "That's all I've ever wanted—for you to be happy and healthy and have everything you've ever dreamed of."

A lump settled in my throat. "But what if I don't have any more magic than this? Nothing other than being able to talk to the blood god in my dreams?"

Minerva sniffled and then laughed. "Oh, Ally, this is why I wished you'd come to me. I could have explained to you that you have a very special ability. One that many witches would love to have."

Um. What?

She continued as though she'd heard my silent question.

"It's called dreamwalking. It's an extension of telepathic magic. In sleep, you can make a connection to others and either walk into their minds or bring them into yours."

I could bring someone into my mind? Wow, that was nuts.

But it also brought up another question.

"Why haven't I heard of this before?" I asked. "You've taught me all about witches and the different types of magic. Why not this one?"

Minerva smiled at me. "Because I've only met one other dreamwalking witch in my lifetime. It's a very rare ability. One that has its dangers and requires a great deal of training. It never even occurred to me that your power might be something so rare."

"But I've only been able to talk to Talant," I said.

"As I said, it requires training. All mental magic does. You've connected to Talant because it's your destiny to wake him and he's quite powerful. But, with some time and practice, you'll likely be able to make a connection with anyone you wish as long as they don't have a protection spell in place." She paused. "And if you're strong enough and have the training necessary, you might even be able to get through their protection spells."

Minerva came over to the bar. "And even if this wasn't case. Even if the only person you were able to dreamwalk with was Talant, I wouldn't care. I would still work with you and train you if you wanted, or, if you didn't want to train, let you be. It's up to you what you do with your power."

"But you just said I'm supposed to wake the blood god."

"That may be," my aunt replied. "But I would never force you to do something like that. If you want to, I'll work with you and help you figure it out. If you don't want to do it, then I'll focus my efforts on tracking down and containing Sommerton and Leona. You are what matters to me. Not my premonitions."

That damn lump was back in my throat. I cleared it and said, "I want to help Talant. We've been talking for a while now and he's become a friend."

"Then I'll keep training you until you can access your power," she replied. "Have you been practicing?"

"Yes. I practiced with Talant last night."

Minerva grinned. "See? There are already benefits to dreamwalking with the blood god. He's teaching you how to use your magic." She paused. "Then again, that may be a bad thing. Gods are notorious for not caring about what happens to humans."

"I think he cares about me. He promised to help me." I cleared my throat. "But Sommerton said something yesterday when he called that worries me."

She cocked her head but didn't speak.

"He said he was with Talant's brother," I continued.

Her brows rose. "His brother? As in, another god?"

I shrugged. "I didn't get a chance to clarify much before a pissed off gargoyle took my phone out of my hand."

"Hmmm." She hummed, her eyes narrowing.

"Does that change things?"

"Maybe."

"Do you think he was telling the truth?"

It was Minerva's turn to shrug. "Possibly. I've read histories of witches and warlocks siphoning power from a god. It never ended well or without bloodshed. And I've also read about gods possessing witches and warlocks who call to them. But all of these stories are so old that they're considered legend, and I don't know how accurate they are. There's a lot of hyperbole in legend and sometimes outright lies."

"So, what do we do?" I asked.

For the first time in my life, my aunt said, "I don't know."

"Well, if Talant is actually the brother of whatever entity Sommerton is gaining magic from, he should be able to protect me, right?"

My aunt looked relieved. Well, more like slightly mollified but she did relax.

"That didn't happen tonight, did it?" she asked, answering my question with a question of her own.

She had a point there. We hadn't even discussed it, but there was little doubt that Sommerton (or whatever was possessing him) had been the one to cast the spell to draw me out of the protection ward. As far as we knew, no one else wanted to harm me. Or in his case, use me.

"I'll talk to Talant about this the next time I dreamwalk," I said.

"Good. Keep me apprised. And I'll do what I can, too." She cleared her throat. "Just stick close to Dax."

I nodded, trying to ignore the anxiety swirling inside me. I picked up my cup and sipped my tea, letting the warmth wash through me again.

"Now, tell me more about the kissing I interrupted," she insisted, leaning over to rest her elbows on the counter, her face awash with curiosity.

I nearly choked on the tea I was drinking at her abrupt change of subject. Oh, yes. Aunt Minnie knew exactly how to catch me off guard. I only hoped that one day I'd be able to return the favor.

I lowered the cup. "I told you. Dax had to kiss me to break through the spell that Sommerton cast on me."

She frowned. "I interrupted your first kiss?"

No, she hadn't.

Aunt Minnie must have read the answer on my face because her frown disappeared. "So, I interrupted a different kiss?"

I groaned, leaning over to cover my face with my hands. "I don't know what to do, Aunt Minnie. He kissed me the first time, but I kissed him when we were sitting on the couch. And he let me. But I can already tell by how he ran out of here that he's going to come back and pretend it didn't happen. Just like he walked around all day pretending this morning didn't happen." I lowered my hands and looked up at her. "I don't know what to do. I told him what I wanted, which is how we ended up kissing on the couch, but he's so closed off. I'm not sure he'll be willing to do that again."

"You're right. Dax is extremely closed off. With everyone except you," she said. "I think you've noticed by now that I'm right about how different he is with you. He's had a very long life, Ally. And it's been a hard one, full of loss and grief. I think that's why he was able to get through to you when I brought you here after your parents passed. But that's also why he's resisting how he feels now." She sighed and straightened from her position leaning over the counter. "You two are so alike, I'm not sure how you'll be able to work through this unless one of you is willing to open up and be vulnerable first."

My chest tightened at her words. Just the idea of taking that risk, of giving Dax more power to hurt me, it made it difficult to breathe. And I wasn't sure what I feared the most—being rejected or getting what I wanted only to lose it at some point in the future.

"Ally."

Minerva's voice cut through my thoughts, bringing me back to the present.

Her expression was somber when I focused on her once again. She gestured to the amulet I wore.

"I didn't tell you this, but I included a birth control charm on your amulet. Because I thought something like this might happen if the two of you were together for more than a day or two."

I had no idea what to say to that. My mouth opened and then closed.

"He's not going to touch you unless he knows for sure that you're ready. And the only way he'll believe it is if you show him. As frightening as it is to be vulnerable like that, I promise that the reward is worth the risk."

Before I could formulate a response, the front door opened, and Dax came inside. It had begun to rain at some point because his grey t-shirt was plastered to his body.

Aunt Minnie didn't say anything else, just gave me a look. One that I knew well. It clearly said that she expected me to be the one to take the risk.

Based on how Dax wasn't even looking at me, I knew she was right that the first step would have to come from me.

Minerva picked up our mugs and carried them to the sink to rinse them out. Then, she turned to face Dax.

"I'd love to stay for dinner, but it seems that I have a protection amulet to make. The full moon is tonight, and though the clouds will interfere a bit, magic is still strongest at moonrise, so I need to get to work."

She came around the counter to give me a hug. "Love you, sweet girl. See you tomorrow with your new amulet."

I squeezed her back, relishing in the scent of lavender and rosemary that clung to her. "Love you, too."

She released me and approached Dax. "Don't let her out of your sight until I get the amulet to her. She'll be vulnerable until then. I should have planned for something like this."

Dax nodded but didn't speak.

Minerva patted his arm. "I trust you to keep her safe. That's why she's here with you."

He didn't respond at all, his face shutting down until it appeared to be hewn from stone.

Aunt Minnie gave me a wave and walked out the front door. Dax followed, standing in the doorway to watch her progress to her car. A little of the fear that had iced my heart melted at the sight. It also made me realize that Minerva was right.

The reward would be worth the risk.

As long as Dax didn't outright reject me.

CHAPTER
TEN

I climbed to my feet as Dax shut the door, locking it.

Then, he surprised me.

I believed that he wouldn't bring up the kiss, that he would act like it hadn't happened at all. And I was wrong.

When he faced me, Dax immediately said, "We need to talk."

"About?"

His wince was visible, but he answered, "When we kissed."

My legs trembled beneath me because I wasn't sure what he was going to say. His expression was still locked down tighter than a vault and his entire body seemed tight.

"I'm guessing you have something you want to say."

"It can't happen again."

Okay, so instead of pretending it hadn't happened, he wanted to shut it all down.

"Why?" I asked.

His lips tightened. "Because it isn't right."

"Why?" I repeated.

Now, his jaw was flexing. My questions were getting under his skin. I studied him, looking closely at his body language. His demeanor screamed that he didn't want to have this conversation and he wanted to get it over with as fast as possible. Was that for my benefit or his own? I was betting it was for himself.

"Ally..."

"Why isn't it right, Dax?" I asked, keeping my voice soft and even.

Now that I was watching him, actually looking at him instead of trying to avoid him in an effort to hide my feelings, I could see more of what my aunt saw. What Poppy saw. I affected him.

"Because I'm several centuries older than you and I've known you since you were a child," he answered, a snap in his words.

"Daniel is several centuries older than Cari and she's less than a handful of years older than me."

He crossed his arms over his chest. "Again, I've known you since you were a child."

"Do you still think I'm a child now?" I asked, gesturing to my body.

His eyes moved from my face, down my chest and abdomen to my hips. I saw his fingers flex against his biceps as he looked me over. I could practically hear his teeth grinding before he looked away. Oh, yes. I affected him. The realization gave me courage to keep pushing him.

"No," he answered.

"Then, I don't see how either of those things is relevant as to why you can't kiss me." I paused. "Or I can't kiss you."

The deep blue of his eyes began to swirl and change, becoming lighter. I was beginning to understand what that change meant.

"Your aunt trusts me," he argued. "She said it before she left. I won't break that trust by...by..."

I started laughing then, which made him fall silent.

"I don't see what's so funny," he finally said when my laughter didn't abate.

I swallowed back a giggle before I answered, "While you were gone, my aunt asked me if you'd made a move yet. In fact, she's been encouraging me to make the first move, rather than waiting around on you."

As I spoke, I took a few steps forward, getting closer to Dax.

For the first time since we started speaking, I could read his facial expression clearly. He looked shocked. "What?"

I was within arm's reach now. When I took one more step forward, he backed up. I smiled and took another step. He retreated again. This big gargoyle, who wasn't afraid of a dark warlock throwing magic around, was backing away from me and how I made him feel. He might not be willing to admit it, but he wanted me.

His back hit the front door.

"My aunt, who trusts you to keep me safe, also expects for you to have sex with me. In fact, she encouraged me to approach you about it. Would you like to see the text messages?"

It was the first time I'd ever seen Dax rendered speechless with disbelief. He didn't talk a lot to begin with, but his mouth was hanging open as he stared at me as though a second head had popped out on my shoulder.

"You're joking," he finally rumbled.

I shook my head.

That was when he pulled out the big guns. "But you're untouched."

I paused then. How did he know I was a virgin?

"Why do you think that?" I asked.

"I don't think it," he answered. "I know it."

My confidence wavered until I saw him swallow hard as a single bead of sweat ran down his temple to his jawline, disappearing into the stubble that covered it.

It was just another excuse. Another reason he was giving me because he was afraid. This huge, almost invincible gargoyle was scared—of me, a human who was nearly two feet shorter than him and maybe a quarter of his weight. Minerva was right. I was going to have to make it crystal clear to him that I wanted him. I was going to have to push through my reticence. It was the only way I might get what I wanted.

So, I moved closer again until my face was only inches from where his arms crossed over his chest. He couldn't back up any further because the door was behind him, but I swear he tried.

"I'm not sure if I'm still a virgin," I said. "I mean, I've used sex toys on myself, so technically I've had a penis inside me. It was fake but—"

I could not believe I was saying these things to him. Then, again, now that I could see how I affected him, it wasn't as difficult as I thought it would be.

"Stop," he said.

A dull flush worked its way across his cheeks, and he swallowed hard again, his eyes glued to my face. I watched his pupils dilate as he looked down at me, his eyes a lighter blue shot through with silver.

I didn't stop. I could tell I was getting to him, as much as he got to me all these years. I lifted a hand and put it on his arm. His skin was burning hot beneath my fingers.

I continued, "So, in technical terms, I've had sex. Just with a dildo instead of a man."

His hand moved from his bicep to clamp down over where mine rested on his arm. Then, he shocked me again.

He took my hand and lowered it, pressing it down on the bulge behind his zipper. "I don't want to hurt you. And I'm not a small male. I will."

He made a pained noise when I gave him an experimental squeeze and he tugged my hand away.

When I smiled up at him, he looked terrified for a split second.

"You're not much bigger than one of my toys," I said.

A low noise escaped his throat, but he remained silent, holding my hand in his against his chest.

I inched even closer until my body brushed his. "I trust you, Dax. I trust that you won't hurt me like some of my friends were hurt their first time. I can't think of anyone who would take better care of me than you."

My other hand was free, so I lifted it and cupped his cheek, my thumb running across his bottom lip. It was so soft, but the flesh beneath the softness was firm.

"No one would dare hurt you. I would kill them," he said.

My thumb moved with his lips when he spoke. My eyes were locked on his face and, for once, I could read him clearly. His resolve was weakening.

"But you're okay with another man being the first to touch me?"

His jaw flexed again, and I was close enough to hear his teeth grind together.

"No," he answered.

I moved my hand from his cheek to the nape of his neck, tugging his head down toward me. He didn't resist, his gaze moving from my eyes to my mouth.

The words came out easily now because I could see that he was on the precipice. He wanted me, maybe as much as I wanted him.

It was time to tell him what I wanted. No beating around the bush. I needed to lay it out for him.

"I like how it feels when you kiss me. I want you to do it again. And I don't want you to stop this time," I whispered, my mouth brushing his as I spoke.

That same low noise came from him as he uncrossed his arms, his hands going to my waist.

I wasn't sure who started the kiss, but he took over completely within a breath.

He lifted me off my feet and reversed our positions until I was against the door. I wrapped my legs around his waist, locking my ankles together behind him. His mouth opened over mine and I matched him movement for movement. His tongue slid past my lips, and I moaned.

Dax pressed me against the door, the hard ridge of his cock

almost exactly where I needed it. I shifted against him, moving my hips, and it was his turn to groan.

He tore his mouth from mine, his face flushed and his eyes more brilliant than I'd ever seen them, the silver in his eyes shimmering like molten metal.

"Are you sure about this, Ally?" he asked.

"Yes," I whispered, leaning forward to press my lips against his neck. "Don't you dare stop."

He turned and carried me toward the stairs.

My heart was pounding hard and fast as he took them two at a time, carrying me as though I weighed nothing.

I nipped the skin of his throat with my teeth, and he stumbled, his hands clutching me tightly.

"Dammit, Ally," he said, his voice lower than I'd ever heard it and gravelly, like stone grinding against stone. "You're going to make me drop you."

I moved my mouth to bite him again, going for the place where his throat met his shoulder. Then, I sucked the flesh into my mouth.

When I released him, I said, "Then, you should hurry up."

He hit the top step a moment later and carried me to the bed. "Just remember I'll bite you back," he said.

I shivered and I knew he felt it because his fingers dug into my waist just a bit after.

"But maybe you like that idea," he murmured. His hand went from my waist to my ankle at the base of his spine. "Let me go."

I did as he said and removed my legs from his waist. He lifted me a few inches until I stood on the bed. Even then, he was still taller than me.

I released his shoulders, my hands moving to the hem of his shirt. I managed to slip my palm beneath it before his fingers clamped around my wrists.

"What are you doing?" he asked.

I glanced up at him. "Seriously?"

A smile tugged at his mouth but never truly appeared.

"We're doing this my way," he said.

When I opened my mouth to argue, he continued, "You said you trust me with this, so you're going to let me be in charge."

Damn, I had said that.

I nodded.

"Take off your pants," he murmured, his fingers dipping beneath my shirt to skim the waistband of my jeans.

My heart picked up speed, thumping against my breastbone, but I didn't hesitate. I wanted this so badly. I'd dreamt about having Dax this way. I wasn't going to give him a chance to change his mind.

My hands shook slightly as I dropped them to the button of my jeans. It popped free and then I lowered the zipper, the sound seemed so loud in the quiet of the house. Then again, so did the beating of my heart.

I shoved my pants down my legs. When I wobbled, Dax grasped my hips to hold me steady and then plucked me off my feet.

I gasped when he released me, and I was falling. I was lying on the edge of the mattress, staring up at him as he shoved my jeans to the side and knelt down. I couldn't take my eyes off his face as he wrapped his hands around my hips, his thumbs rubbing a spot just inside my hipbones. My nerve endings flared to life, and I shifted restlessly against the comforter.

He flattened his hands on my abdomen and slid them up, gliding beneath my shirt against the skin of my belly. My muscles quivered beneath his fingers as his hands went higher, taking the t-shirt with them.

His fingertips traced the bottom edge of my bra before skating up over my breasts, barely touching me. My t-shirt rose higher.

"Lift your arms," he whispered.

As I did what he said, he whisked the shirt over my head, leaving me on the bed in nothing but my bra and panties.

When his hands returned to my body, he traced the top edge of my bra with his fingers, his eyes going to my chest. I looked down and shivered again at the sight of his hands on my skin and how

103

his palms barely ghosted over the light pink cups that held my breasts.

His fingertips were just a little rough, as though he had calluses, but not quite. They were almost the texture of stone without the sharpness.

"Take off your bra," he said, his eyes never leaving my chest.

This time, I did hesitate. I'd never been naked in front of a man before. I wasn't exactly shy about my body, but this was different. This was Dax.

Dax's gaze moved up to my face when I didn't immediately comply. "Do you want to stop?"

I bit my lip and shook my head.

"Then, take off your bra," he repeated.

I sat up, reaching behind me to unhook it, and tugged the straps down my arms. I tossed it over the edge of the bed, keeping my eyes on Dax's chin.

He nudged my chin up with his hand until I met his gaze.

"You're beautiful, Ally."

I fiddled with the neckline of his shirt as he stared down at me, his eyes trailing from my face to my breasts.

"I want to see you, too."

The finger he'd used to lift my chin traced the skin of my throat, skating back and forth across my collarbone, and then moved lower. One finger became all five as he followed the upper slope of my breast down. My nipples tightened, anticipating his touch, but his hand moved to trail around the curve on the side of my breast.

"Take your shirt off, Dax," I demanded, my voice breathy, barely a whisper.

He paused before his hand left my body and he tugged off his shirt. As soon as he pulled the fabric away from his torso, my hands were there. I pressed my palms against his chest, eager to touch as much of him as I could. His skin was hot and smooth. I ran my hands lower, my fingers running over the bumps of his ribs. I felt a rough patch of skin on his side. It was like stone, rough and porous. The light coming in through the blinds was muted, so I couldn't see what I was touching clearly.

When I tried to look down, Dax grabbed my wrists, taking my hands from his chest and pinning them behind my back.

"Dax—"

He kissed me, cutting off my question and fogging my mind. I leaned into his kiss until my breasts touched his chest. He pulled me closer, plastering my body to his, and all I could think about was the scalding press of his skin against mine and how he tasted.

He kept my wrists pinned to my lower back with one hand and the other traveled up my spine to my nape. He took a handful of my hair and gently tugged my head back, releasing my mouth to trail his lips over my throat.

When his teeth nipped my skin, I jumped. They were sharper than mine and the quick bite sent an arc of electricity through my entire body, straight to my nipples and between my legs.

He used his arms to cradle my weight as he tugged my hair back a bit more, arching me over the mattress. I was caught and off-balance, I could only let him position me as he liked. His lips followed the same path his fingers had taken earlier, ghosting over my collarbone and down my chest to my breast.

My breath caught in my chest, and I gasped when he traced his tongue across the upper slope, around the outer curve of my breast. It was rougher than it had been moments before when he was kissing me and textured.

"Dax, your tongue, it's—"

Before I could finish what I was saying, he stopped teasing me and ran his tongue over my nipple before he sucked it into his mouth.

My back arched hard at the sensation. It was almost too intense. He released my hands when I yanked at his hold. With my hands free, my fingers clutched at his hair as he suckled, tugging hard.

He released my nipple with another lick, leaving me breathless and gasping in his arms. Dax laid me back on the bed, releasing my hair, and running his hands down my sides. He hooked the waist-band of my panties with his fingers, pulling them down. My nipples tingled and throbbed, my clit echoing the sensation.

As soon as he removed my underwear, Dax grabbed my hips and yanked me to the edge of the mattress. His hands ran down my thighs until he reached my knees. I didn't have time to react when he pushed my knees apart, high and wide, leaving me open and bare to his gaze.

A strangled sound of shock escaped my throat, turning into a moan when one of his hands ran down my inner thigh until his fingers brushed lightly over my clit.

"Are you ready?" he asked.

Ready for what?

Before I could voice the question, Dax lowered his head and licked me, his tongue running from my opening to my clit. That strangled noise escaped me again, especially when his textured tongue circled my clit lightly and repeatedly.

I clutched at the comforter beneath me as sensation coursed through my body. The pressure of his tongue increased, causing my hips to jerk.

Dax made a low growling sound against my pussy, the vibration shooting straight from my clit to my nipples. My hands flew from the comforter to his head, holding him close. His mouth became more voracious as he slipped a finger inside of me, pressing deep.

My hips arched when he sucked my clit into his mouth and flicked it rapidly with that grooved tongue. He added a second finger to the first, stretching me wider. He hooked them, rubbing a spot inside of me that made white burst behind my eyelids.

My eyes flew open as my body tightened, my hips rocking in time with the rhythm of his lips and tongue. I gripped his short hair, my thighs clamping around his head. Dax pressed a palm to the inside of my thigh, pulling it away from his head and holding it down to the mattress to keep me spread wide.

Dax added a third finger inside of me, the stretch nearly painful.

A choked moan escaped my throat as he filled my pussy and flicked my clit repeatedly with his tongue.

Tension built between my legs, making my muscles lock down on his fingers inside me. Dax made another growling sound against me, and the vibrations sent me over the edge.

Wave after wave of pleasure pulsed through my body, dragging cries from my throat. My thighs trembled and my back arched as he didn't let up, pushing my orgasm higher until it bordered on piercing.

"Dax!" His name was nearly a scream as my entire body spasmed on the mattress.

His mouth softened against me, his tongue moving slower. His fingers were still deep inside me, stretching me wide.

As the last tremor wracked my body, Dax lifted his mouth, pressing his lips to my lower belly.

My fingers unclenched from his hair, cupping the back of his skull as he pressed a line of kisses up to my belly button.

His thumb barely brushed my clit, making me shudder one more time.

"You're so tight," he murmured against my skin. "Did I hurt you?"

I was floating on a cloud of bliss, so the answer tumbled from my lips without a thought. "Absolutely not."

Dax withdrew his fingers, and I realized how wet I was when he lifted them to his mouth. I couldn't tear my gaze away from his face when he slipped them between his lips.

I was boneless, my limbs too heavy to move.

As Dax licked his fingers clean, his eyes wandered over my body, but he didn't touch me. I'd never imagined that he would look at me with that heat in his eyes. Or that I would be sprawled out naked on his bed.

"Dax?"

He didn't answer. His eyes still roving from my breasts to my hips. He cupped my inner thighs, his thumbs tracing over the lips of my pussy as he stared down at me. Then, his hands moved up my body, one long, firm stroke from my hips to my breasts.

"Dax?"

"Hm?"

I lifted my upper body, resting my weight on my elbows. The change in position pushed my breasts deeper into his palms. He ran his thumbs over my nipples, making me shiver.

"Are you going to join me on the bed?" I asked.

His gaze jumped to mine as he played with my nipples. "Not tonight."

I sat up further, gripping the back of his head with my right hand. "What?" I asked, bringing my lips to his.

"I told you. If you want me to be the first man to touch you, we're doing it my way," he said.

"Why not tonight?" I asked. His words stung.

"I don't want to hurt you, so we're going to take this slowly until I think you're ready."

I frowned at him. "Until you think I'm ready?" I repeated.

It sounded like another excuse to me. Another reason he wasn't going to make love to me.

His thumbs dragged across my nipples again, bringing my attention back to the way my body was still humming from my orgasm.

"And when might that be?" I asked, a bite in my voice.

Dax's eyes warmed and crinkled at the corners, but he didn't smile. "I don't know."

"How about an estimate?" I pushed.

This time, his grin was wide enough to show his teeth. "I don't know. How big is your toy?"

Dax had never teased me like this before, but I didn't appreciate it all that much because I felt like he was just putting me off, giving me a little but not everything.

"It's in my bag," I answered. "Do you want me to go get it so we can do a comparison?"

His eyes grew hot. "You brought it with you?" he asked.

"Well, I didn't know we'd be sharing a bedroom," I answered. I sounded huffy, but I couldn't help it. I *was* huffy. "Or how long I would be here, so I thought I might need them."

"Them?"

Oh, shit. I'd basically told him that I'd brought more than one sex toy with me.

"I'll tell you what," he said, not waiting for me to answer. "Why don't you go get everything you brought with you, and we'll see how it goes."

I swallowed hard, staring up at him. It was on the tip of my tongue to say no, but I also wanted more.

Dax ran his hand over my side, down to my hip, his eyes following the path of his touch. I liked the way he was looking at me, as though he couldn't get enough of touching me. Decision made, I pushed him back and headed to the closet where my duffel bag was still lying on the floor.

He seemed surprised that I wasn't going to fight with him, but what he didn't know was his time was limited.

I already decided that I would give him two days. If he hadn't made love to me by then, I was taking matters into my own hands.

CHAPTER

ELEVEN

Much later, after several orgasms, I was asleep and in Talant's cave. He was helping me practice my magic. I'd dropped the brother bomb on him as soon as I arrived, telling him about Sommerton's claim to know his brother. I'd also shared that I was certain his "brother" was slowly possessing the warlock and taking control.

Talant remained silent for a long time before he finally said that he would handle it and protect me. He wouldn't say much else, even when I asked and pushed, which was infuriating. Still, I hadn't refused when he insisted that we practice gathering my power. Because I knew that I would need the power and the control to free him from this mountain.

We'd been working for at least an hour now and I was struggling.

"Ally, magic is like a muscle. The more you use it, the stronger it gets," he said, walking around behind me as I tried to gather a ball of light into my palm.

He called it basic magic, but it felt like freaking difficult magic to me. My power responded a bit better than it had the night before, but it was still sluggish and thick rather than smooth and fluid.

"You sound like Minerva," I grumbled, a bead of sweat dripping down my temple.

"Your aunt?" he asked.

"Yes," I murmured, focusing all my attention on the ball of light in my palm.

"She sounds like an interesting witch. I'd like to meet her someday."

"Well, if I can ever figure out how to make my magic respond like it's supposed to, you will," I answered.

With my attention split between Talant and the ball of light in my hand, the magic began to dissipate. The bluish-white glow faded, and the ball disappeared.

"Dammit!"

Talant put a hand on my shoulder. "You're doing fine, Ally. Getting frustrated will only slow the process down. You must remain in control of your emotions in order to master your magic."

"If that's the case, then how do all these damn teenagers manage to harness their power when they're practically emotional basket cases," I grumbled.

Talant chuckled behind me. "It's a little different then because a young mind is a malleable one. While their emotions vary more wildly than an adult's, they also have no concept of boundaries or limits, so they're able to adapt to those bursts of magic more easily. As an adult, your brain has set pathways that it likes to take. Adding new pathways takes a lot more time and effort. Now, try again."

I dropped my hands to my sides and groaned. "Talant, I'm tired. I need rest. Can't we continue this tomorrow? Or the next day?" I asked.

I'd discovered that practicing my magic when I dreamwalked with Talant wasn't as exhausting as doing it when I was awake, but it still took a toll on me. I was tired when I woke up, as though I hadn't slept much.

"I wish we could, Ally," he answered. "But my brother won't wait. He has a plan, and it involves using you and your magic if you haven't learned enough to wake me yourself. I fear what he might do to you during his quest to bring me out of my slumber."

And there was the confirmation I needed. His brother was taking over Sommerton. Great. Just one more problem to face. One more thing that Dax and my aunt would have to protect me from.

I sighed. "Okay. One more time."

A little while later, I'd finally managed to pull a ball of magic into my hand, the blue light pulsing with white. I cradled it in my palm, feeling how the power danced against my skin.

"I did it, Talant!"

"Excellent job, Ally. Now, I want you to look at that boulder over there," he said, gesturing to a big rock in the corner. "Imagine it shrinking to the size of a pebble, something small enough to fit into your pocket. Keep that image, that thought, in your mind and hit it with your magic."

"You're kidding," I said.

"No. You've harnessed your raw power. That means you can use it for whatever means you wish. Tonight, we're going to start with shrinking a boulder. Tomorrow, we'll move on to something a little more difficult."

Difficult? Shrinking a two-ton boulder wasn't considered difficult?

I bit back a smartass comment about gods and their impossible standards and stared at the boulder. In my head, I saw it shrinking until it fell onto the ground, so small that I would have no trouble picking it up and sticking it in my pocket.

I tried to keep it in my mind as I threw the ball of magic at it.

I realized as soon as the magic left my hand that it was going to miss the boulder. I'd never been very good at throwing things. Or aiming. Or anything sports-related. At all.

The ball of magic seemed to hover as it approached the boulder. It was clear that it was too high.

The image of the boulder shrinking was still in my mind, though. Clear as a bell.

At least until the magical ball I'd tossed stopped right above the rock before it dropped straight down, the bluish haze of light suddenly expanding to encompass the entire boulder.

I gaped as the boulder began to shrink rapidly. So rapidly that I nearly missed it when a tiny pebble fell in its place.

"Very good," Talant said.

I'd done it! But how?

"How did I hit the boulder? It should have missed."

He patted my shoulder as he walked around behind me. "Intent is the most important part of magic. If your intention is clear, the magic responds." He grinned at me. "I think it's safe to say that your intention was more than clear since the magic did exactly what it should."

He walked over to the pebble and picked it up. Talant came over to stand in front of me. He took my hand, turned it palm up, and dropped the small rock into it.

"Keep this as a reminder that your intentions should not only be clear in magic, but good."

I stared down at the pebble in my palm. "Thank you, Talant," I said.

He shook his head. "Don't thank me. I'm completely selfish. I want you to learn your magic so you can wake me up and get me out of this rock prison."

I knew he was full of crap, but I didn't call him on it. He might want out from under this mountain, but he wasn't completely selfish. I just wrapped my fingers around the rock, cradling it in my palm.

"Either way, you're teaching me and I'm grateful for that, Talant."

He opened his mouth to answer, but the cave seemed to shake.

"What—"

My question was cut off when the cave went dark and vanished. I gasped and opened my eyes.

Dax loomed over me in the darkness of the bedroom. He looked angry, a rare expression on his face.

"What's wrong?" I asked. "Did something happen?"

"Were you with Talant again?" he asked, his voice so low.

I blinked up at him. "Yes. He was teaching me how to use my magic."

I couldn't believe it, but he looked even angrier. His brows lowered over his eyes as he glared down at me.

"You're talking to another male while you're lying in my bed?"

Well, when he put it like that, it did sound terrible.

"It's not like that, Dax. You know it's not," I answered. "He's more like an annoying big brother than anything else."

"It doesn't matter."

Okay, so he had a point there. If our roles were reversed, it would bother me. So, I pointed out something else he needed to know.

"I can't control it," I stated. "Every night, I dreamwalk with him. It's not intentional and there's nothing I can do to stop it."

Some of the ire drained from his face.

I cupped his cheek. "Even if I could stop it, I wouldn't."

He scowled at me. Any other time, I would have been discouraged by his anger, but he'd spent another hour wringing every ounce of pleasure he could from my body before bed, and I couldn't bring myself to feel anything but relaxed. He still hadn't made love to me, but he'd brought me to orgasm over and over with his hands, his mouth, and the toys I'd packed in my duffel bag.

"I'm learning how to use my power," I said. "I'm learning how magic works. There's only so much that Aunt Minnie can show me, but Talant has been around for thousands of years. He's the best chance I have at learning what I need to learn to protect myself."

"I hate knowing that you're in my arms, but that you're also somewhere else. With someone else."

He no longer looked angry but agonized.

I understood it because the thought of our roles being reversed made my stomach hurt. So, I did something that scared the hell out of me. I told him exactly how I felt about him.

"It's only you," I admitted. "You are the first man to touch me like this. The first man I've wanted to touch me. The only one."

He stared down at me, the silver glint appearing in his eyes and shining through the shadows of the bedroom. I moved my hand from his cheek to his neck to pull his mouth down to mine. He kissed me back immediately, no hesitation, and I relished in it. Even after the first time he'd made me come with his mouth, it had taken him a couple of moments to respond to me when I kissed him.

I shoved at his shoulders, urging him to roll over onto his back, still kissing him. Dax shifted, taking me with him. His hands settled on my hips, lifting me to straddle his body. I wore nothing but a pair of panties and I rolled my hips back until the ridge of his cock pressed against my center.

All that separated us was the thin shorts he wore and my panties.

He ran his palms up my body to cup my breasts as I sat up. It was the first time I'd had a real opportunity to touch him back. I ran my hands over his chest, his skin smooth but there were places of roughness. Leaning forward, I ran my lips over his pectoral, flicking his nipple with my tongue. There was another rough spot on his ribs, running around his side. It felt like a sliver of stone spliced to his skin.

I realized as my fingers traced it that it was a scar. My hands moved down his ribs as I kissed his chest and there were more scars, some long and thin, others short and wide. His torso was covered in them.

I was distracted from my exploration by Dax. His hands moved to my hair, gathering it in his fists and tugging my head away from his chest. He pulled me forward to capture my nipple in his mouth.

My hips jerked as he sucked hard. He'd been gentle with me up until now, his hands and mouth never too forceful. My body didn't know how to handle the intensity of the sensations.

I whimpered, rolling my hips again, feeling empty and desperate.

Even after the orgasms Dax had given me, I wasn't satisfied. Not completely.

Dax released my nipple, his mouth slipping over the inside curve to my breast. I pushed myself to my feet, standing over his body on the mattress. I shoved my panties down my legs and kicked them away.

He stared up at me, his eyes glinting silver and blue in the shadows. When I knelt over him, I scooted back and grabbed the waistband of his shorts.

"Ally, what are you—"

I tugged them down, revealing his cock, and the words died in his throat. My mouth went dry when I saw the size of his erection. I understood now why he'd been so concerned he would hurt me. He was bigger than the toy I'd purchased, a toy that, in my more hopeful moments, I'd assumed would be just as big as he was.

I was wrong.

Though Dax had spent time learning my body earlier, he hadn't given me the chance to touch him much. But I was going to touch him now. I left his shorts halfway down his thighs and ran my hands up his legs, directly to his long, hard cock.

As soon as I touched him, wrapping my fingers around him, his legs tensed beneath me. I tightened my fingers around him and then stroked, and a ragged breath escaped his lips. As I continued to stroke him with one hand, I lowered my other, cupping his balls before I squeezed gently.

"Fuck!"

Suddenly, our positions were reversed, and I was flat on my back with Dax hovering over me.

"Did I hurt you?" I asked, my voice breathy.

He shook his head, his jaw muscles clenching.

"I wanted to touch you," I complained.

"Later," he murmured.

His mouth was on mine, and he shoved my knees apart with his, settling on me. I gasped against his tongue when the hot length of his cock prodded me, pressing down on my clit as he gave me more of his weight. His hips rocked, creating friction that sent sparks shooting from my clit through the rest of my body.

My back arched as I tried to move with him, but his weight was pinning me to the mattress, holding me down. I lifted my legs, locking them around his waist and shifted.

The head of his cock slipped lower and nudged the entrance of my pussy. Dax froze, lifting his head to look down at me.

I wiggled, trying to line our bodies up, but he leaned back so he was kneeling over me and clamped his hands on my hips.

"Ally, wait."

I shook my head. "I want to feel you inside me, Dax," I said, lifting my hips. "I need it."

His face flushed as he looked down at me and his body tensed. "I don't—"

"You're not going to hurt me. Or, if you do, it will only be for a second," I insisted. "I want this. I want you," I insisted.

He looked torn, staring down at the juncture of my thighs for a few moments. Then, he seemed to come to a decision.

Using his grip on my hips, he rolled over onto his back, bringing me with him so I was once again straddling his body. His arm reached out, grabbing the lube from the nightstand. I'd packed it with my toys before I'd realized that I wasn't going to have the privacy to use it.

I watched as he popped open the cap and poured a small amount in his palm. He replaced the bottle before he began rubbing the liquid over his cock.

"Lift up," he murmured.

I lifted off his body and inched forward. His hand came between my legs, slick fingers gliding over my clit before rubbing the liquid all around my entrance. When two of his fingers slid inside me, I gasped, and my body clenched around him.

His other hand lifted to my breast, capturing my nipple between his thumb and index finger and tugging. My body rocked against his hand as he slipped another finger into me, stretching my body further.

Unlike the first time, it didn't sting at all, only left me feeling full. But it still wasn't enough.

Dax removed his fingers from my pussy, reaching between our bodies.

"Scoot back," he murmured.

I rose up on my knees and felt the head of his cock nudge me. The fingers on my nipple moved down to my hip, around to my lower back.

"Tilt your hips," he instructed.

I did exactly as he said, gasping when the head of his cock slipped just inside of me.

I shifted back, taking a little more inside of me, until his hands clamped down on my ass, holding me still.

"Hang on," he said.

His fingers slid down my ass, trailing over the crease down to where he was barely penetrating me. He spread my body wider and I felt myself opening up even more.

"Can you take more of me?" he asked.

I nodded eagerly. His hold on me loosened minutely and I rocked back onto his cock.

I gasped as he slipped further inside of me, my body stretching around him. As the stretch took on the edge of pain, I stopped, my muscles clenching and relaxing around his girth.

I rocked my hips forward just a little before I shifted back again, sliding further down his length. The lube eased his way, but he was still thicker than the toy I was accustomed to. A lot thicker.

I moaned as my body opened up even further, taking him deeper. There was no more pain, just pressure, but it eased with each rise and fall of my body. I looked down and saw his eyes locked on my face. His jaw was tight, and the corded muscles of his neck were standing out.

Still staring into his eyes, I repeated the motions, rocking back and forth, working him deeper inside me until I was filled completely.

I hadn't quite taken all of him, though. I gave one more experimental rocking motion and the last inch of his cock slid home. All the air left my lungs as I settled on his hips, shuddering.

"Goddess," I sighed. "I-I..." I couldn't think of the words for what I was feeling. I had no idea what I wanted to say. The sensations coursing through my body were overwhelming.

Dax growled low in his throat, his hands flexing on my hips. "When you're ready—"

He choked on the words when I moved my body, rolling my hips against his. His fingers dug into my ass, but he didn't try to stop me from moving.

It took me a few moments to find my rhythm, rising and falling on his cock, having him fill me over and over again.

The tension built within me, bringing me to the edge of orgasm, but I couldn't quite go over the precipice.

As though he was reading my mind, Dax took my hand and brought it between my legs. "Touch your clit for me."

My nipples tightened further at the way he was looking at me, the way he pressed my finger against my clit.

I took over, circling the bundle of nerves. Dax's hands went back to my hips, helping me move on him, bringing me down a little harder than before.

I moaned, my head falling back as the pleasure built. I could feel it coming, my body pulsing around his cock, the muscles growing tighter.

"Ally," he groaned. "You're close, I can feel it."

"Yes," I hissed, all my attention focused on the sensations building between my legs.

The pleasure narrowed, winding tighter and tighter, until it finally snapped. I cried out, my hips jerking as I rode out the orgasm.

My hand left my clit, and I braced my palms against Dax's chest, my head snapping forward. I opened my eyes and stared down at him as he began to slam me down on his cock, rougher and faster than before. My orgasm swelled, going on and on, until another cry was torn from my throat, this one nearly a scream.

Dax slammed my hips down on his one last time and released a guttural groan, deep and gravelly.

As we shuddered together, he reached up, fisted my hair, and pulled my head down to kiss me, his teeth nipping my lips before he plunged his tongue in my mouth.

His kiss gentled as my orgasm waned and my hips stilled. Little tremors still wracked my body when I collapsed on top of him. His other arm wound around my lower back, holding me securely against him.

Finally, he released my mouth. I tucked my face into his neck, pressing my lips to his throat for a brief kiss. We were both still breathing hard and dewed with sweat.

The enormity of what just happened washed over me. I'd had sex for the first time, with the gargoyle I'd loved for close to a decade. I knew, deep in my heart, that I would never be able to have this with anyone else. I would never even want this with someone else.

The realization was terrifying. If Dax rejected me, I would be alone for the rest of my life.

Dax ran his fingers through my hair, stroking from my scalp to the ends in one slow, smooth stroke. The motion distracted me from my frightening thoughts.

He was still hard inside me and I could feel his heart thumping against his chest. Whatever was happening between us, he felt it, too. I had to remember that.

I couldn't worry about the future. I could only think about what was happening now. And right now, he was here with me. Holding me and stroking me as though he treasured me.

I nuzzled his throat as our breathing evened out, letting myself relax against him and enjoyed being held as I'd dreamt about.

For once, reality was far better than a dream.

Dax abruptly stiffened beneath me, startling me.

I lifted my head to look down at his face and his eyes were no longer silver, so I couldn't see them in the darkness. "What's wrong?"

"I didn't wear a condom," he said, his voice sounding shocked.

"It's okay," I said. "I—"

"It's not okay," he interrupted, sitting us both up. "I could have gotten you pregnant."

The movement dislodged his softening cock from my body. I winced at the minor ache between my legs, but he didn't seem to notice.

I reached up and grabbed his face with both hands, bringing his attention back to me. The intensity of his gaze nearly burned.

"I have a birth control amulet," I said. "You didn't get me pregnant."

His body relaxed beneath me, and he released a relieved breath. I tried not to let it get to me. I wasn't ready to have a baby. I didn't want to get pregnant right now.

Still, his palpable relief stung. As though the idea of getting me pregnant were a catastrophe.

For once, Dax didn't seem to notice that he'd hurt me. Instead, he lifted me out of bed, setting me on my feet next to it.

"Are you sore?" he asked, changing the subject completely.

"More tender than sore," I answered.

And it was the truth. My pussy felt a little raw, but it wasn't painful.

"A hot bath will help anyway," he said.

He swept me off my feet and carried me into the bathroom. I could feel the distance he was trying to establish between us. The way that he was holding himself and the way he was holding me.

When he sat me on the edge of the tub, I said, "I'll only take a bath if you're in it with me."

He glanced at me when he bent to turn on the taps, but his answer surprised me.

"Okay."

I studied him as he adjusted the water until the temperature was to his liking and then he walked over to the cabinet beneath the sinks, opening one and pulling out a bag of bath salts. I looked closer when he returned to the tub. The salts were unscented and labeled for muscle soreness.

I bit back a smirk as he poured a handful into the steaming water. I had trouble imagining Dax soaking in the huge tub, but it was clear that he did because the bag was half empty.

"Get in," he said, turning to return the bag to the cabinet.

I climbed into the tub, wincing a little at the heat of the water, but I sank down into it. It barely came to my waist. A few moments later, Dax returned to the tub, a washcloth in one hand and my body wash in the other. He set them on the edge before he climbed in behind me. The water level was suddenly much higher.

Now I understood why he climbed in before the tub was full. If he'd waited, our combined body weights would have displaced too much water, and it would have gone all over the floor.

His arms reached around me to turn off the water when it reached my upper chest. Then, he leaned back, his hands going to my shoulders to pull me back against him. I reclined on him and released a long breath. The hot water and his big body surrounding me instantly removed the tension from my muscles.

I relaxed against Dax, letting my hands drift down in the water to rest on his legs where they surrounded my hips.

His arms came around me, one hand stroking down my belly to cup between my legs and the other spreading across the base of my neck, his long fingers resting on my collarbone and his thumb against the side of my throat.

His touch was proprietary, not meant to incite a reaction. At least until his fingers stroked over me, parting the folds of my pussy.

"Dax," I whispered.

"Are you sure I didn't hurt you?" he asked, his lips brushing my ear.

I understood the hold then. He wanted to see for himself that I was okay, and he was going to hold me in place until I told him the truth.

"I'm sure, Dax."

"I wasn't gentle in the end," he murmured.

I shifted my hand so that it rested on his between my thighs. "I liked it," I admitted, my voice soft. "A lot."

His finger flexed against me, nudging my clit. For the first time that night, my body didn't react with a jolt. I was finally satisfied.

Not wanting him to withdraw from me again, I continued, "I want to do it again."

His low chuckle against my temple made me shiver. "Let's give your body a chance to recover first."

"All right. You have twelve hours, but you should know I have a list."

His fingers had been lightly stroking my collarbone until I said that. They stilled before he asked, "A list? Of what?"

"Things I want to try. Positions, for one. And blow jobs. I've never given one and I'm curious what it's like."

His hand at my throat spasmed, gripping me for a moment. But it was the hand between my folds that got my attention. His fingers tensed and one slipped inside my pussy, just a little.

"Is this list written down somewhere?" he asked.

"No, it's a mental list," I answered, wondering why that was his first question.

"Maybe it should be."

It was my turn to ask, "Why?"

"I told you that if we do this, we do it my way. And that means all of it, so I'll be the one to choose what we mark off on your list."

I tensed against him. "I thought—"

"That I only meant tonight? No." He lowered his head, his lips moving from my ear to my throat. He spoke against my damp skin, bringing goosebumps up on my arms and making my nipples harden.

"I meant every time, Ally. Every time I touch you." His tongue

123

came out to draw a line down the side of my neck. "Every time I fuck you. It will be my way."

I shivered and felt him smile against my skin.

"And I promise you will enjoy every second of it."

"But I want—"

"You'll get what you want...." He nipped the muscle where my shoulder and neck met. "Eventually."

While my body was heating up, my brain was churning rapidly. Did that mean I couldn't touch him when I wanted to? That everything had to be on his terms?

That was when my stomach sank. He was going to give me everything I wanted, but no control.

Which meant I wouldn't have what I truly needed—his heart.

CHAPTER

TWELVE

The next day was Sunday, Dax's only day off for the week. When I woke, I was shocked to see that the sun was already fully up and he was lying next to me, still sleeping.

I stared at his face in the bright morning light, taking in the angles of his cheekbones and the heavier ridge of his brow. His face was relaxed in sleep. He didn't look younger, but there was a peacefulness that I rarely saw from him.

"You're staring," he said, his voice rougher than usual. I loved the sound of it. He sounded sleepy. And sexy.

"I am," I agreed.

"Why?" he asked, not opening his eyes.

I didn't want to admit I'd been gazing at him with longing and love, so I quipped, "Just wondering if you were okay since the sun's up and you're still in bed."

Dax opened one eye to look at me, the dark blue iris looking brighter in the morning light. "As I recall, I was up half the night, checking some things off your list."

I bit back a laugh. After our joint bath, the darn gargoyle had actually tracked down a piece of paper and pen and made me write down my list. Then, he'd checked off a couple of items, such as trying cowgirl position and oral sex because we'd already accomplished that. When I'd protested and tried to explain that I meant giving oral sex, not receiving it, he'd ignored me.

So, I'd snatched the pen away from him and written GIVE A BLOW JOB in all caps at the end of the list. Which had made him laugh. Something I always loved to see.

Dax didn't laugh a lot, but he did laugh the most with me. Sometimes with Minerva. But I rarely saw it with anyone else.

Now that I was paying attention, I saw another way that Minerva was right. He treated me differently. He was more open with me. More human. He expressed emotion. It simultaneously warmed my heart and hurt it at the same time. I hated that I was the only person he lowered his guard around. But I also loved that he felt safe enough around me to do it.

"Where'd you go?" Dax asked, interrupting my thoughts.

I blinked and focused on him again. "I was just thinking of things to add to my list," I lied.

He smirked. "It's not long enough?" he asked.

"At this rate, we'll have checked everything off within forty-eight hours."

I succeeded in shocking him. "Forty-eight hours? I'm a gargoyle, not an incubus. There's no way I can help you get through it in two days."

I couldn't hold in my laugh any longer. When he realized I was only teasing him, he rolled on top of me, pinning me to the bed.

"I think I have an item to add to the list," he said.

I merely raised my eyebrows in response, which made him smirk again. "I'm not sure I should let you add items to *my* list. But I'm willing to hear you out."

"Have you ever heard of orgasm denial?"

My mouth fell open and I smacked his shoulder with my free hand. "You'd better not! That's definitely not going on there!"

It was Dax's turn to laugh again. When he did, his hips shifted, and I felt his hard length against my thigh. I wriggled beneath him, trying to line our bodies up so that I could feel it where I wanted it, but he pulled away slightly.

"No, you need to give your body some time to recover."

I scowled at him. "For the last time, I'm fine. I'm not sore. And I will chain you to this bed if you try anything like orgasm denial."

"Hmmmm." His eyes narrowed at my words.

"What?"

"I'm thinking that if I chain you to the bed, then you won't get a say at all in what we check off the list."

I shuddered at his words, but not from disgust. Dax seemed to know that he'd piqued my interest because his eyes began to turn silver and I felt his cock harden further against my leg.

"You like that idea," he growled.

I nodded, unable to speak because my mouth was suddenly dry.

"Then, we'll give it a try," he murmured, lowering his head to kiss me. When he ended the kiss, he continued, "But later because you need to give your body a break."

It was my turn to growl at him, which only made him smirk again. He bent his head and nipped my lips before he rubbed the tip of his nose against mine. Then, he released me and rolled out of bed.

I watched as he walked into the bathroom, shutting the door behind him. He hadn't noticed how my breath caught in my chest at his affectionate gesture. Or how my heart started racing.

I tried to tell myself that I was reading too much into his behavior, but my poor, foolish heart couldn't help it. I rolled over onto my side, facing the door to the bathroom, and tugged the blanket up over my body. Though it was spring, the mornings could still get chilly.

A few moments later, Dax emerged from the bathroom, still naked, and I forgot all about my hopeful heart and my thoughts were now fully directed by my hopeful pussy. I squeezed my thighs together to soothe the sudden ache between them and watched as he walked toward me.

"Stop looking at me like that," Dax demanded.

My gaze jumped from his cock to his face. His expression was tight, and his eyes were beginning to turn silver again. I would forever associate silver with his eyes. They only looked like that when he was thinking of kissing me. Or he was kissing me. Or touching me.

The ache between my thighs intensified and I bit back a moan.

Dax made it to the bed in a blink and jerked the blankets off me. "You're hurting," he stated.

"Yes," I said.

"Dammit, Ally, I told you—"

I rolled over onto my back, trailing my hand over my breast and down. Dax fell silent, his eyes locking onto the movement of my fingers like a laser beam. I bent my knees, planting my feet on the bed, and spread my legs.

Yes, I was tender, but there was another ache there. One that only he could satisfy with his hands, his mouth, or his cock.

Encouraged by the flush on his cheekbones and the way his cock was beginning to harden, I dipped a finger down, rolling it over my clit the way I had the night before when he was moving inside me.

Dax groaned and fell to his knees beside the bed. "Are you hurting for more?"

"Yes," I whispered.

His hand curved over my knee and pulled, turning me around so I laid sideways across the mattress. He nudged my hand to the side before he lowered his head and fastened his mouth over my clit.

He shoved my knees up and to the side, leaving me wide open for him. And he gave me what I needed.

AN HOUR LATER, I was sitting on a barstool downstairs, wearing nothing but a pair of panties and one of his flannel shirts. My wet hair hung down my back, drying quickly from the heat of the woodstove. Dax had lit a small fire as soon as we came downstairs because he saw me shivering.

After two orgasms courtesy of Dax's lips and tongue, he'd still refused to have sex with me, though I had added and checked off another item from my list. I'd watched him masturbate in the shower, watching how he touched himself, what he liked. I wanted to know how to drive him as wild as he drove me. I wanted to make him feel the way I did when he touched me.

Now, we were in the kitchen, and he was making us breakfast. I tried to help but he just picked me up and sat me back on the stool.

I decided that if I was relegated to spectator, I was going to enjoy it, so I made him take off his t-shirt. He hadn't argued but his eyes twinkled when he stripped it over his head and handed it to me.

It was the first time I was able to see the tattoo of the sword on his back clearly. It was a true work of art. The hilt rested just below the base of his neck and the blade extended down his spine to the waistband of his pants.

"How does your tattoo work?" I asked him as he made us both coffees.

He glanced over his shoulder at me. "It's a spell."

I rolled my eyes. "I know that. But you're a gargoyle. I thought you were resistant to magic. How can you carry a spelled tattoo on your body?"

He hesitated before he answered. "She used a special needle. There isn't much that can harm a gargoyle. But there is a type of alloy, one my people created, that is able to pierce our skin, even in our fully stone form. It's infused with obsidian and magical fire."

I gaped at him. "So, it burns?"

"Like hellfire, yes," he said, nodding.

"And you *let* someone use a needle made of this on your body?"

His face shut down, but he did answer me. "I needed a weapon that wasn't immediately visible. Something I could carry with me always. At the time, I believed this was my only option."

It was my turn to remain quiet. The jealousy I had felt toward the witch who gave him the tattoo faded now that I knew how painful it must have been for him.

"Thank you for telling me," I murmured, sipping my coffee.

He nodded with a grunt and went back to pulling things out of the fridge. Since I'd made dinner last night, he insisted on making breakfast this morning.

After a few moments of silence, I decided to change the subject and hopefully dispel some of the tension in the room.

"Do you need to go into the office today?" I asked.

He shook his head. "The assistant manager is here today. She can handle anything that comes up and it would be good for Poppy to get used to working with her." He glanced at me. "Do you need to work today?"

I shook my head. While I didn't have a set schedule, I usually worked five or six days a week, but I always tried to reserve Sundays as my day off. Now, I was glad because it meant that I didn't have to do anything but spend the day with Dax.

"What are we going to do all day?" I asked.

"Considering it's nearly eleven, I'd say half the day is gone."

He answered my question without answering, so I decided to give him a nudge.

"How about we each choose one thing to do?"

This time, when he glanced at me, his expression was knowing. And heated. He understood exactly what I was talking about when I said that.

Then, he surprised me.

"All right. But I choose first. After we eat."

I grinned at him. "Deal."

Unfortunately, I underestimated his sneakiness.

After breakfast, he announced, "I know what we're going to do first."

My blood started to hum in my veins when he came closer. "What's that?"

He stopped right in front of where I was still sitting at the bar and leaned down, his face only inches from mine. Our mouths were a breath apart. I licked my lips, anticipating what he might say.

"We're going to get dressed and you're going to practice your magic," he stated.

I blinked up at him for a second, completely confused. Then, his words penetrated the fog of lust in my brain, and I made a sound of disgust.

That infernal smirk was back. "What did you think I was going to suggest?"

I rolled my eyes. "Stop messing with me, you evil man."

"I think you mispronounced gargoyle."

I nudged him back with my elbow and stood up. "Well, let's get this over with so we can move on to what I want to do," I groused.

I ignored his laugh as I skirted around him and headed for the stairs.

Two hours later, I made Dax carry me back into the house because my legs were trembling with exhaustion. It was crazy how difficult it was to manipulate my magic in the real world rather than when I'd dreamwalked the night before.

Dax had been quiet and watchful the entire time I worked, standing at the edge of the clearing he'd taken me to, his head moving slowly as he scanned the trees. Occasionally, his wings would appear, and he would take to the sky to scan the forest and the resort from a higher vantage point.

I hated to admit it, but his presence was distracting. I was so aware of his every movement, his every breath, that I had difficulty focusing on my intention for my magic.

It had taken me those two hours just to gather a ball of magic in my hands the way I had the night before with Talant. I hadn't even tried to shrink anything or change it. Just gather my power.

"You're doing well," Dax said as he carried me through the woods in his arms.

I laughed, but the sound was more sarcastic than humorous. "Sure. Great. I can barely gather my magic, let alone cast it."

"I've been around a long time, Ally. I've seen witches who have just manifested their magic. It's a very dangerous time, not only for a witch or warlock, but for everyone around them. Your magic is tied to your emotions and most witches are much younger than you, which means they don't have the control that you do. I've seen the damage that can be wrought from a witch or warlock who lost their temper or was overwhelmed by an emotion. It can be lethal."

I settled into silence for a moment before I said, "It makes me wonder..."

"What makes you wonder?" he asked after my words trailed off.

I cleared my throat before I continued because it felt tight. "Just, well, if maybe my parents' dying is why I never manifested. I was in so much pain that I eventually went numb after they were gone. I didn't feel much of anything."

His arms tightened around me as he carried me through the trees.

"It wasn't until you started coming around that I woke up a little. But it still took a long time. Over a year," I murmured, mostly to myself. "So, I've been wondering if I was so shut down that my magic couldn't come through. I tamped all my emotions down for so long that it's almost impossible for me to express them anymore. Except with Minerva and you."

I yelped when he clutched me so tightly that my ribs compressed.

"I'm sorry, Ally." I almost didn't hear his apology because his voice was so low.

"It's okay. You didn't hurt me."

"No, I mean—" He sighed. "I'm sorry about a moment ago, but I'm also sorry about before, when you were younger. I know what it's like to lock a part of yourself away because the pain is too much to bear. And I hate that you had to do that. But, if there's anything I've learned in the centuries I've been on this earth, it's that we do what we must to survive. Even if it hurts us to do it."

Minerva had told me that Dax's past was a hard one. I suppose that was why I responded to his presence as a child. I recognized a kindred spirit in him. I still did.

We were silent the rest of the journey to the cabin. I leaned my head against Dax's chest and listened to the steady thump of his heart, letting it comfort me with its mere presence, just as the gargoyle managed to do fifteen years ago when I first came to Devil Springs.

CHAPTER
THIRTEEN

We never got to do what I had planned for the day because Dax laid me on the couch as soon as we walked into the cabin, tucking a blanket around me with the admonishment to rest.

That was the last thing I remembered until he woke me up to eat dinner.

After I scarfed down the cheesesteak sandwich and potato chips Dax piled on a plate for me, he surprised me yet again.

He stretched out on the couch with my back to the rear cushions and he was on his back. My head rested on his shoulder and my arm was thrown over his waist. Then, he turned on the TV and pulled up a streaming app.

"Have you seen Schitt's Creek?" he asked.

I blinked a few times before I answered because that was not a question I was expecting.

"Um, just the first season, but it's been a while."

"Want to watch it?"

"Sure," I answered.

"We'll start with the first episode."

As the show began, Dax tucked me deeper into his side before his hand went to my hair, trailing through the strands.

Before I noticed it, I was completely relaxed against him, thinking of nothing at all. I realized that I'd been tense for days now, stressed about everything happening with Sommerton and the fact that I was struggling to access my power.

I also wondered what it would be like to have nights like this with Dax all the time. Dinner and watching TV on the couch together. When I was younger, my fantasies were much more romantic—he would take me out on dates or for picnics in the forest. Maybe a trip somewhere like a beach or the mountains but always secluded.

Now that I was older, I understood that moments like the one I was experiencing now were more important to me. While a picnic in the forest sounded like fun, this was more precious. Simple, everyday moments that could make up a lifetime. This was what I wanted for my future.

"Feel better?" Dax asked me quietly when the second episode ended.

I tilted my head so I could see his face. "Yes." I raised my eyebrows. "So, all this was to make me feel better? Do you even like Schitt's Creek?"

His expression was solemn rather than impassive. I wasn't sure if he was showing me more of what he was thinking and feeling or if I was finally learning to read him more easily.

"I do like the show. I thought it might help you stop thinking about everything that is going on."

"It did," I answered. "I mean, it is. But so is this."

"This?"

My heart rate sped up at the idea of blurting out what I was thinking, but Minerva's words were haunting me. For whatever reason, Dax wasn't in a place where he could meet me halfway. I was going to have to take a risk and let myself be vulnerable with him.

"Being here with you. Cuddling on the couch after dinner. It helps."

He stared at me for a moment before the hand stroking my hair cupped the nape of my neck to pull me forward. His lips were light and gentle as he kissed me.

When he released my mouth, he pressed my head back down on his shoulder. I snuggled back into his side as the next episode began.

Dax didn't speak, but his lips had said it all.

Hope bloomed in my chest. Maybe Dax and I were building something here. We hadn't discussed it, and I wasn't ready to bring it up. Though he was softer with me and becoming more open, I sensed that he would shut down if I brought up the future and how it pertained to us.

~

WHEN I OPENED my eyes inside the cave, I was surprised to find it was dark. Usually when I dreamwalked to Talant's cave, he had a fire and hundreds of candles lit.

This time, the rough walls were completely dark, save the flickering light given off by a single oil lamp.

There was also a chill in the air, sharp enough that it stung the bare skin of my arms. I wrapped them around my waist, hugging them to stay warm. Even though the cavern was shadowed, I could see the plumes of my breath as I exhaled.

Why was it so cold? While Talant's cave was always cool, it was never this frigid.

"Talant?" I called, craning my neck, and trying to peer through the darkness.

Something skittered behind me, like talons clacking on rock. I whirled, my hands up to shield my face, but there was nothing there. From my left, there was a slithering sound, and whatever was moving had to be large because it was much louder than if it was a small animal.

I glanced in that direction, but again, I couldn't see anything.

"Talant, this isn't funny!" I yelled.

"Why do you call for my brother, little witch?"

The deep voice echoed in the open space, even though the words weren't loud.

I turned in another circle, looking around wildly, but all I could see was darkness.

"Sommerton?" I asked.

There was a low laugh. "You know that isn't my name."

"Then, what is your name?"

A heavy pause followed my question.

Finally, he answered, "I don't think I should tell you, witch. Names have power you know." He paused again. "That's how I called you here after all, *Allison*."

I flinched when he said my name. The word felt like claws, not against my skin, but on my psyche. How could my name hurt when he said it?

My brain worked feverishly, trying to figure out what I should do next. I needed more information about whoever this entity was. More information about his plans and how he thought I fit into them.

"Why did you call me here, then?" I asked.

I heard footsteps to my right. I didn't spin around, though I wanted to. I turned slowly to face that direction. One of the shadows moved, separating from the darkness in the shape of a man. I couldn't see his face, but I got a general idea of his size. He was tall, as tall as Dax, but not as bulky. His shoulders were broad, narrowing down to his waist and hips. That was all I could ascertain.

"How is my brother?" he asked, meandering in a circle around me.

I turned with him, keeping him in my sights. Dax always told me never to turn my back on a threat and every instinct inside me screamed that this being, whatever he was, was a threat.

"Talant is fine." I chose my next words carefully. "He doesn't want you to hurt me."

There was another chilling laugh, low and dark as the shadows in the cave. It echoed and seemed to grow louder rather than fading away.

I winced but remained facing him without covering my ears. Finally, the laugh faded.

"I have no intention of hurting you, witch. I need you. Unlike my *brother*," he drawled the word. "I don't break my toys."

It was on the tip of my tongue to snap that I wasn't a toy, but I knew it wouldn't make any difference. Whoever he was, this being didn't see me as a person. He didn't care about my feelings or my safety. To him, I *was* a toy. Or a tool to be used. Nothing more than an inanimate object. Though he claimed not to *break his toys* as he said Talant did, I instinctively knew that was a lie. He wouldn't hesitate to hurt me, even kill me, after I'd served my purpose.

"Then, why did you call me here?" I asked, working hard to keep the impatience out of my voice.

"Because I have a bargain for you," he murmured.

Though he didn't appear to be any closer, his voice sounded next to my ear, as though he was right behind me.

When I glanced over my shoulder, I gasped and jumped back, my bare foot landing on a rock and rolling my ankle. I bit back a cry of pain and forced myself to remain standing, even though the joint immediately began to throb.

There was a man standing not two feet from me, but his body was formed out of black smoke and shadows. His features still weren't discernible in the darkness of the cave. Nothing except for his eyes. They gleamed with the same purple lightning that Sommerton had wielded just days ago.

"Would you like to hear my offer?" he asked, his voice tinged with amusement, as though he enjoyed frightening me.

"Sure," I lied. I had to keep him talking until Dax either heard me talking in my sleep and woke me or I woke up on my own.

There was another deep laugh.

I shivered, hoping by the goddess that he didn't do that again. It hurt me to hear it.

"Though I know you're merely humoring me, I'm still going to share my bargain with you anyway," he said. "You see, I need you to wake my brother. Your power is the key, but it's a key that only works once—at the moment your power truly manifests. Too early or too late and the door will remain locked, and my brother trapped."

I interrupted him. "But my power already has manifested," I said. "I used magic just last night."

He shook his head. "No, no, that wasn't a manifestation. A power like yours, a magic as strong as yours, leaks through. That's what you're using now, the surplus that escapes the binding. When that barrier between you and your magic breaks down, you won't be able to contain the first rush of power. It will pour forth from you like a geyser. That's what will free my brother. I can sense it rising in you, little witch. I'm sure you feel it too. A moment where your body can't contain itself. Like your skin will split in two. The higher the magic rises, the more often you will feel that sensation, as though you'll burst if you don't release it."

I shook my head. "I haven't felt that yet."

Not to the extreme he was describing, anyway.

"You will," he whispered. "The power will pulse from you, a little here, a little there, as it grows. Like the small tremors in the earth that precede a volcanic eruption."

"How will I know when it's just a...pulse as you call it or my power manifesting?" I asked.

"You'll feel it."

I barely refrained from rolling my eyes. Lovely. He'd been so clear until now.

"My bargain is this, witch," he said. "If you wake my brother and free him from his prison, I will give you your heart's desire."

"My heart's desire can't be given to me by you," I replied,

thinking that the only thing I wanted was for Dax to love me the way I loved him. To want to be with me the way I wanted to be with him.

"But I can, Allison. The gargoyle may be immune to much of my magic, but not in this. His heart is just as susceptible as a human's. Especially when it's clear that he already cares for you in his own way."

I tried to hide my wince, but I knew I failed, even before he spoke.

"Surely you know that he can't give you what you want on your own?" he asked, prowling closer to me. "It won't matter what you say or do, the gargoyle has built a wall around his heart. Even one as powerful as you won't be able to scale it alone. You'll need my help."

"I—"

Suddenly, he was right in front of me, leaning down so that I looked directly into his eyes. My heart hammered in my chest because he'd moved so quickly, I hadn't been able to react at all.

He looked a great deal like Talant, but his beauty was cruel and cold. His face was molded from sharp lines and deep shadows. My imagination couldn't have conjured up a better visage for an evil god. He was breathtaking...and terrifying.

"You should know, Allison." He leaned even closer. I could smell him then, woodsmoke and spice. It would have been a wonderful scent had I not already longed for the aroma of pine and snow. "You would not need to bespell me if you chose me. I would be more than willing to give you anything and everything you want."

My entire body froze. Was he...

His cheek brushed mine as he brought his mouth to my ear. "We would be unstoppable together. In every way."

Yep, he was hitting on me.

Chills erupted on my arms and legs. Dear goddess, I did not want this being to have the hots for me. No way, no how.

The urge to flee gripped me. It was so strong that I took a step back before I could control my reaction. The need to escape was all-consuming.

And when I did, the floor dropped from beneath me and I fell into the pitch black of an abyss.

I couldn't even draw the breath to scream as my body plummeted straight down. I scrambled with my hands, trying to grab onto something, anything, to break my fall. I didn't want to hit the bottom. It would kill me.

Suddenly, my descent slowed. There was a light beneath my feet, golden and soft. I willed my body to slow down even more, and, to my utter shock, it did.

The light flickered and I realized it was from a fire or maybe candles. A hole appeared beneath me, and my body floated through it. As soon as I passed through, I realized that I was in Talant's cave.

But it was clear he wasn't expecting me. He was sprawled on his back in the center of his circular bed, a fur blanket draped over his hips, but his chest and exposed leg were bare.

I drifted down from the ceiling of the cavern until my feet touched the stone floor. When I landed, his eyes opened, glowing reddish-amber, and he sat up in the bed, one hand out in front of him with a crackling ball of red and gold magic gripped in his fist.

"By the gods, Ally!" he yelled, lowering his hand quickly. "How did you get here?"

I looked around me, completely confused. "I have no idea."

"I didn't even feel you approaching!" he snapped, jumping to his feet.

I yelped and turned my back to him when the blanket fell away from his body, showing me that he wasn't wearing a stitch of clothing beneath it.

"Holy shit, Talant! I did *not* need to see that!" I yelled, throwing a hand over my eyes.

"By the hells, woman, if you don't let me know you're coming, I can't make sure I'm clothed!" he yelled back.

"I don't know how to let you know that I'll be here!" My voice was pitched higher, almost a screech. "So, I don't know what you're talking about."

There was some shuffling behind me but no way in hell was I going to turn around yet.

"You don't know that you're communicating with me before you arrive?" he asked.

"No!" I heard footsteps closing in behind me. "You better have some damn clothes on!" I screeched.

Talant was grinning when he walked around me and, yes, he wore a pair of pants that rode too low on his hips, but at least all the important bits were covered. He never wore a shirt anyway, so the sight of his bare chest didn't bother me.

"Are you always so...prudish?" he asked.

Judging by the heat in my cheeks, my face was glowing like a stop light and probably twice as red.

"You're like a big brother to me and I don't need to see my big brother's dangly bits."

His grin widened, revealing two dimples. "Dangly bits? Do you mean my—"

I held up a hand and snapped, "Shut up!"

He outright laughed. "Your visits are always so entertaining. Even more so when you're uninvited."

I growled at him. "It's not funny, Talant. The only reason I'm here is because I was running away from your *brother*." As I said the final word, I used my fingers for air quotes.

The laughter faded from his face immediately. "What?"

"Your brother, who refuses to give me his name because it will give me power over him, pulled me into his dreams tonight to give me an offer I couldn't refuse."

Talant's hand shot out and gripped my bicep. His fingers were so tight that they pinched.

"Talant!"

"Tell me exactly what happened," he demanded.

It was the first time, in my eyes, that he truly resembled the god he was. His muscles were drawn taut and stood out in stark relief.

His eyes glowed like amber and ruby fire. He suddenly seemed huge, as though he loomed over me.

I stammered. "I-I-I woke up in a cave, but it was dark and really cold. There was only an oil lamp so I couldn't really see anything. Then, he moved around in the shadows, freaking me out for a few minutes, before he finally talked to me."

Talant's fingers tightened around my arm to the point that tears sprang into my eyes.

"You're hurting me," I whispered.

He glanced down at where his hand was gripping me and released me as though I burned him. "I'm sorry, little witch," he said.

I took a step back. "You sound like him."

He looked sickened. "What?"

"He called me little witch, too."

Talant scrubbed his hands over his face in a rough motion. "I'm sorry, Ally. Come sit down and tell me what happened."

I wanted to tell him there was no way I was sitting on the bed where he'd been lying naked moments before, but my body was beginning to shake, and my teeth were chattering.

"Please, Ally. Come sit."

I let him lead me to the edge of the sleeping pit and wrap a soft blanket around me. It wasn't the fur he'd been using earlier, so I didn't complain.

He took my hand in his. "What happened with my..." He swallowed before he completed his question. "Brother?"

"He offered to reward me if I made sure that I woke you. He said that he would give me my heart's desire and that he didn't like to break his toys the way that you do."

The fire was back in Talant's gaze, flickering madly. Where his brother was full of black smoke and violet electricity, Talant was flame and gold—glittering with beauty but still deadly.

"And he knew what I want, deep down. He said that he could make Dax love me and want to be with me. I didn't believe him at first because gargoyles are immune to magic, but he said that Dax's heart was susceptible to magic and that he would get it for me."

As I spoke, my words ran over each other in a rush. I hated admitting all this out loud, giving Talant all my secrets, but I was beyond frightened. Whoever this being was, whether he was Talant's brother or not, he scared me more than being vulnerable.

Talant's expression was thunderous by the time I was done. He scowled down at the floor, the muscle in his jaw ticking madly.

"Is it true?" I asked.

"That he can make your gargoyle love you?" Talant shook his head. "Not the way you want him to love you. He would be bespelled, which never works out in the end. At some point, the magic would twist him and this 'love' that he felt for you. It would become dangerous, maybe even lethal, for him. And for you."

Tears pooled in my eyes and, for once, I didn't try to fight them back. "I was going to tell him no, but then he...he..."

Talant's fingers squeezed mine gently. "He didn't touch you, did he?"

I shook my head. "No, but he, well, he hit on me. He said that he would give me anything and everything I wanted. It was *creepy*." I winced and glanced at him. "I know he's your brother, but it was creepy. I don't know him, and he attacked me with magic a few days ago and now he's decided he wants to be my boyfriend? It doesn't make sense."

The ghost of a smile crinkled Talant's eyes. "It's because he's my brother that I know what you mean and, you're right, it is unsettling when he does things like that. Which is exactly why he does it. He wants to keep people off balance. It gives him the upper hand and makes it easier to manipulate people into doing what he wants."

That made sense because it had definitely thrown me off balance.

"It was right after that when I stepped back and the floor just disappeared. I was falling really fast, but I eventually started to slow down. There was a light below me and when I fell through the hole, it was your cave. And you know what happened since then."

Talant asked, "When you were falling, did you think about slowing down?"

I nodded. Then, I remembered, "Oh! I forgot. He said that the power I've been using isn't my actual power. He said I still haven't manifested yet and that the magic I'm harnessing is like surplus and is leaking through the binding on my magic. He said that the closer I get to manifesting, it will get worse. That it will pulse and expand, but I don't know what that means."

Talant sighed. "I know what it means but I fear you won't appreciate the answer."

"I still need to know," I argued.

"Yes, you do." He released my hand and got to his feet, pacing in front of me. "When any of our anointed witches come into power, they send out a call. The call is one of power that resonates with ours. It is so we can find them and guide them through their initiation into magic. That's the pulse he mentioned. It's when your power swells until it explodes out of you. It's like a giant bell tolling, calling the gods to you."

"Gods? As in more than you and your brother?" I asked.

His answer wasn't comforting. "I've been slumbering for a very long time, Ally. I don't know who is still lingering or who has moved on. When I settled down for my rest, there were many of us. It has been millennia since then."

Well, that didn't make me feel any better.

"Whatever happens, Ally, I promise you that I am here to help you. No matter what. If you are unable to wake me, I will still be here if you need me. You are one of the Anointed and it is my duty to teach you."

"What does that even mean, that I'm Anointed?" I asked. "And why didn't you tell me before now?" My voice was getting louder as I asked my questions.

Talant came to sit on the sleeping platform next to me. "I'm going to tell you, but I want you to promise me that you won't freak out and run away when I do."

My eyes bulged. "Is it dangerous? Am I some kind of blood sacrifice?"

He shook his head. "By the gods, Ally, no, of course you're not. Where would you get an idea like that?"

"You're trying to make me promise not to freak out and run away when you tell me, which means I probably won't like the answer. Plus, you haven't mentioned this in all the time we've been talking," I replied. "So, the worst-case scenario is what came to mind."

"No one is going to sacrifice you," Talant said. "But the information I'm about to impart can be overwhelming. Especially if you've spent the bulk of your life not only ignorant of what it means but also thinking you have no magic at all. That's why I didn't tell you before now. You were already struggling to accept the fact that you were a witch. I feared you would shut me out completely if I told you that you're so much more."

I didn't admit it aloud, but I knew he was right. I probably wouldn't have handled the news well.

"What does it mean, Tal? Just tell me already because whatever it is, it can't be worse than what my brain is coming up with."

"The Anointed are what we call witches and warlocks with the potential to ascend and become what we are."

My entire body locked up. I couldn't breathe. Or blink. I think even my heart stopped beating. Just when I thought I was going to pass out, my heart exploded into a wild rhythm, and I sucked in a hard, ragged breath.

"What did you say?" I choked out. Before he could answer my question, I answered it myself. "Because I thought you said that I would become a goddess."

Talant scowled at me. "See? This is why I didn't tell you before now." He sighed. "I said you had the potential to become a goddess. Not that you would. It is a possibility, not a certainty."

"How is that even possible?" I asked. "And why haven't I heard of this before now? This is important for witches and warlocks to know!"

Talant raised his hands. "Slow down, Ally. I'll answer your questions the best I can, but I can't tell you everything you need to know in one night. I promise I will help you with whatever you need. I won't leave you alone and I will protect you."

I realized I was hyperventilating and took a moment to control my breathing. I forced myself to inhale slowly and then exhale one small stream of air. My lungs wanted to expand again, but I waited until they were empty. Then, I did it again.

Once I had my breath under control, I spoke. "Why haven't I heard of this before now? My aunt is a walking, talking encyclopedia on the history of witches and warlocks, magic, spellwork. She's the ultimate witch. I don't think I've met anyone else with as much knowledge about the origins and inner workings of magic as her, not even scholars who have won awards and published books on the subject. If she knew about this, she would have told me."

"I'm afraid I don't know the answer to that question, Ally. I haven't been in the world for over a thousand years. Time has moved on without me and I don't know why the knowledge of the Anointed has been abandoned."

I knew he was right and that I shouldn't expect him to have all the answers, but at the same time, he was a god. He should be able to answer some of my questions.

"How would I become a goddess?" I asked. "I mean, I'm not sure I would want to be, but, either way, I should know so I can either make sure to do or not do whatever it is."

Talant gave me a rueful look. "I'm afraid that's one of those questions that I can't answer in one night. Remember how I told you that intent was the most important part of magic?"

I nodded.

"Well, this is similar. If your intent is to gather and grow in power, to ascend to godhood, then the magic follows your lead." He sighed. "But I will warn you there is always a heavy price to this. And it is usually that which we love the most. Only those whose intentions are pure and for the good of mankind ascend without paying that price. And, even then, it's because they have sacrificed of themselves in some way. They take the burden of payment onto their own soul rather than passing it to another. They are truly selfless and that is merely another type of sacrifice."

I swallowed hard. Nope, I didn't think I wanted to be a goddess. Especially if it meant that I might live for thousands of years. I didn't know what the gargoyle lifespan was, but I was pretty sure that it wasn't as long as Talant's.

"You're right, that is a lot of information," I finally said.

"It is," he agreed. "But you aren't in this alone. I will help you."

I started to nod, to say something else, but my chest was suddenly tight. I lifted a hand and pressed it against my sternum. The tightness increased, then spread to my abdomen. I looked down, expecting to see my belly expand, but I looked normal.

"Talant?" I whispered, my voice harsh. "What's happening?"

He seemed to know exactly what I was experiencing. "Just breathe, Ally. Your power is spilling out. Remember the call I told you about?"

I managed to nod.

"You're about to put out your first call. If you wake, don't fight it. Let it happen and it will be much less painful."

The pressure was becoming excruciating, but I couldn't respond to him. I could feel myself falling away from the cave, which meant I was about to wake up.

"I'm here, Ally. Even if you can't see me."

His words echoed in my head as my eyes popped open and I jerked into a sitting position on the bed, yanking myself out of Dax's arms.

CHAPTER

FOURTEEN

"Ally, what's wrong?"

I could hear Dax, could hear the concern in his voice, but my chest and abdomen were so full that there was no room for air. I tried to gasp it in anyway, but nothing happened.

I had to get outside. I needed the night air, the stars above me, and the trees around me.

I ran to the steps, my feet barely touching them as I sprinted down them and unlocked the door.

"Ally!"

Dax's hand slammed onto the door, keeping me from opening it. The pressure was building, and I knew I only had moments before it exploded. I had to get out.

"Out, I need out," I rasped. "Dax, let me out."

He stared down at me. My body spasmed and I nearly fell to my knees. If I could breathe, I would have screamed at the pain.

"I need the air," I whispered, the words sounding as though they were torn from my throat.

I writhed again as another pain wracked me. I needed to be

outside before I released all this pressure. I had to or something terrible would happen.

Dax unlocked the door and threw it open before he swept me into his arms and carried me out onto the porch.

"The trees," I choked out. "Take me out there."

He sprinted down the steps, past his SUV, and out into the woods.

"Further."

I couldn't scream, but there was a horrific sound escaping my throat as I fought the tension building within me. I had to wait. Had to.

When we were out of sight of the house, I could take it no more.

"Put me down and run," I panted. "My power. It's building and I have to release it."

"Your power can't hurt me," Dax said.

I wanted to argue, to warn him that I was no normal witch, that I was different, but there was no time.

"Down," I said.

Dax knelt on the ground, lowering my legs and buttocks to the grass. He cradled my upper body against his chest. "Let it go, Ally. You're hurting yourself."

I had no choice in the matter any longer. I threw my head back and screamed as the pressure within me burst, exploding outward in a wave of white light. It shot out through the trees like a shockwave, shaking limbs and blowing over smaller saplings, until it hit the edge of the ward.

There was a low rumble before the entire sky above us lit with the same white light, arcing over the trees like a lacy dome.

I collapsed against Dax, my body shaking violently. My chest and throat burned.

He cradled me closer, lifting me off the ground and into his lap. His hands stroked my back as I turned my face into his neck. I sobbed into his throat, grasping at his biceps with my hands.

"It's okay, Ally. You're safe."

"I could have killed you," I cried.

He hugged me closer. "I'm immune to magic, remember?"

"Not my magic. I'm different and so is my power. It can affect you."

His hands stilled on my back. "What?"

"I'm Anointed," I sobbed. "Talant said that I have the potential to become like him."

"Imprisoned?" Dax asked, his hands smoothing my hair away from my face.

"No, a goddess."

His fingers froze in my hair. "What?"

"He said that I could become a goddess if I was willing to pay the price. But I don't think it's worth it. I don't want to lose anyone I care about for that."

I had no idea what I was saying, only that the tears and words were pouring out of me unchecked.

"Shhh." Dax shushed me.

I continued to shiver, feeling a chill down to my bones now that the power had escaped me.

"I'm going to lift you and carry you back to the house," he said.

I nodded, my forehead rubbing against his throat.

Dax slipped an arm beneath my knees and another around my back before he rose to his feet.

"Hang on to me," he said.

I wrapped my arms around his neck and held on tight. There was a whoosh, Dax squatted down, and then we were in the air.

He was silent as he flew through the night, carrying me close to his chest. My breath trembled as I tried to calm down, but the tears kept coming.

He dropped lightly to the ground, barely making a sound when he landed. Then, he spoke.

"Ally, look up."

Fear spiked through me, and I lifted my head. But the sight before me wasn't one of destruction. The white light that curved over the resort, shimmered and shifted, the patterns of the lace twisting and turning, as though the magic danced to music that no one else could hear.

"What is that?" I asked.

"I think it's the ward," Dax murmured. "It reacted to your magic."

He stood in the yard in front of his cabin, holding me in his arms, and we stared up at the lights dancing in the sky.

Until I shivered again.

Dax looked down at me. "Let's get you inside where it's warm."

As he had earlier, he carried me up the steps and into the cabin, straight to the couch. Dax settled me on the cushions, covering me with the blanket that I'd left on the back of the couch after my nap, and headed straight for the woodstove.

Once the fire was started, he came back to the couch, scooping me up before he sat back on the cushions, holding me in his lap.

He tucked the blanket around me before pressing my head into his chest. I shivered for a bit longer until the heat of his body and the fire began to warm me.

"Can you tell me what happened tonight?" he finally asked.

I hiccupped. "I can, but it's a long story."

"I'm not going anywhere."

"Just...don't ask too many questions until I get through the entire story, okay?"

"Okay."

I took a deep breath and told him about waking up in the dark cave and the entity that claimed to be Talant's brother. Though I left out the part about him offering me my heart's desire. And his offer to give me anything and everything I wanted if I gave him ace to a lot more than my magic. I had a suspicion that Dax would lose his shit if he found out about either of those things.

I also told him how I managed to escape to Talant's cave and how Talant warned me what to expect when my magic pulsed.

True to his word, Dax listened to everything I said. He didn't ask any questions. He merely held me close, stroking my back or my hair as I talked.

When I finished by telling him that some instinct inside me was screaming that I had to be outside and away from the cabin before I released my magic, he pressed his lips to the side of my head.

"That's everything that happened until the moment when you woke up."

He remained silent.

Worried, I asked, "Do you have any questions?"

"Not so much a question, more like a request."

I tilted my head back to look at him. "What's that?"

"Ask your aunt to stop you from dreamwalking. I'm sure there's something she can do."

I stiffened in his lap. "What?"

"You're not safe when you dreamwalk. I can't protect you if I can't follow you."

I sat up, leaning away from him. "I need to dreamwalk, Dax. Talant is going to have to train me to use my magic. He understands what I am and how my power works. He's the only one who can help me."

Dax scowled at me. "It's not safe."

"I understand that, but it doesn't mean it's not necessary," I argued.

"Ally, you need to stop. At least until we capture Sommerton and whoever it is that's possessing him, and make sure he can't harm you."

I jumped out of his lap, whirling to face him and propping my hands on my hips. I was no longer cold. "Dax, you don't understand. If I don't receive some kind of training in my power before I manifest, I may hurt someone. Even kill someone. I may be in danger from Sommerton and Talant's creepy brother, but *everyone* around me is in danger from me until I know how to control my magic!"

He got to his feet, his jaw working, but he didn't argue. Probably because it would be difficult to refute what I'd just said.

The sound of Dax's cell phone ringing interrupted the tense silence between us. It was still upstairs in the loft.

He ignored it, still staring at me with indigo eyes.

"Dax, you need to answer it. It could be important."

His cell phone stopped ringing and mine started. I knew then that it was likely my aunt. I wondered if she'd had a premonition.

I turned on my heel and headed toward the stairs, but Dax beat me to it. His wings expanded and he swooped up to the loft with one powerful leap.

By the time he made it, my cell had fallen silent and his was ringing again.

Definitely my aunt. She wasn't going to give up until she got ahold of one of us.

I heard Dax's rumbling voice as he answered. I ran up the stairs in time to see him turn toward me, the phone to his ear.

"She's okay, Minerva. Just shaken up." He stopped and listened to whatever she was saying. Then, he replied, "I think you should. There's something I want you to do." Another silence. "Okay. See you soon."

When he hung up, he tossed his cell on the bed and headed toward the closet. "Your aunt is on her way. When your magic hit the ward, it woke her up. Apparently, she included some sort of warning in the spell so she would know if it was attacked or breached."

Dax disappeared into the closet and, when he came back out, he was pulling a t-shirt over his head.

"I won't ask her to suppress my dreamwalking ability," I stated, planting my feet, and crossing my arms over my chest. "And I can guarantee you that she won't do it once I tell her everything that Talant explained to me tonight."

Dax stopped at the end of the bed and put his hands on his hips. "You're not going to ask her. I am."

His comment enraged me. My tenuous hold on my temper snapped and I felt the heat rising from my chest, up my neck, and into my cheeks. Even my scalp tingled and burned with the force of my ire. I dropped my arms and stalked forward, poking him in the chest with a finger.

"*You* have no right to ask her to do anything to me or my magic. My body and my power belong to me. You have no say in what I do with either of them."

He bent down, looming over me with a fierce frown on his face. "I do when I'm in charge of keeping you safe."

"If you try to force this, I will pack my shit and take my chances staying with Minerva, no matter what her premonitions say. This is one boundary you don't get to cross."

Dax rose to his full height, his skin taking on a greyish tinge and his muscles swelling as though he was about to take on his gargoyle form.

"If I'm guarding you, there is no boundary there. You do what I say when it comes to keeping you safe because that's my job and I understand it better than you."

"And this is my body and my power, and I understand it better than *you*," I hissed, leaning forward. "When I tell you that I need Talant to train me because I could end up killing someone, including you, with my magic, you do what I say!"

I was yelling now. By the goddess, I was so fucking *angry*.

I stared up at him, breathing heavily. I wasn't going to back down on this. I needed Talant's help. There was so much I didn't know or understand.

Dax, being Dax, didn't rise to meet me with anger. He went stone cold. "I'm not going to argue with you about this. We'll give Minerva the facts and let her decide. You should probably get dressed. I'm going to call the clerk on duty at the front desk tonight and make sure that our guests aren't freaking out about the light show or magical shockwave that just went through the resort."

He snatched his cell phone up off the bed and headed downstairs.

I watched him go, my eyes narrowed. What he didn't understand is that Minerva would most likely side with me in this. She understood how dangerous uncontrolled magic could be and the damage that I could do if I wasn't properly trained. She would also understand that she wasn't the right person to train me if she didn't know what an Anointed witch was.

I stomped over to the closet and grabbed a pair of sweatpants off one of the shelves. I needed to do laundry soon or have Minerva bring me more clothes. I was running out of things to wear.

Then again, if Dax kept fighting me on the dreamwalking, I wouldn't be here much longer anyway. I'd been telling the truth when I told him that I would leave if he tried to force me to suppress my ability to dreamwalk.

I jerked my pants on, grabbed a sweatshirt off a hanger, and pulled it over my head. Then, I left the closet and went straight to the dresser, grabbing a pair of thick socks from one of Dax's drawers. My feet were still frigid from being outside without socks or shoes.

I dropped onto the bed to yank the socks on and grabbed my phone before heading downstairs. Dax was pacing in front of the woodstove, the phone to his ear.

Figuring that he was still on the phone with the night clerk, I stomped to the kitchen and set about making tea. Goddess knew I could use some. My emotions had run the gamut of terror, concern, exhaustion, and anger in less than an hour. I needed something to soothe my nerves.

By the time the water was boiling, Dax was off the phone. He had stopped in front of the woodstove and was staring at it, his hands on his hips.

Though I was still irritated with him, I made three cups of tea. Minerva would likely be here any moment.

The tea had just finished steeping when there was a knock at the cabin door, and I knew it was my aunt by the sound of it.

I gathered up the cups and carried them into the living room while Dax opened the door. As I suspected, it was my aunt.

She rushed inside, her eyes bouncing from Dax to me and back

156

again. When she saw that neither of us was severely injured, her posture relaxed.

I set the mugs on the coffee table as she headed toward me. I knew what was coming next.

She wrapped her arms around me, yanking me into a tight hug. "Goddess, Ally, I was so worried about you when the ward alarm woke me up."

"I'm okay," I whispered against her shoulder.

"Tell me what happened," she insisted, releasing me.

I glanced over her shoulder at Dax, who was still lurking by the front door, his arms crossed over his chest and a thunderous expression on his face.

"Maybe we should sit down. It'll take a while."

WHEN I WAS DONE, my aunt's teacup was empty, and she was staring at me with wide eyes as she flopped back against the back of the sofa.

"You're going to become a goddess?" she asked.

I shook my head. "Not if I can help it," I answered honestly. The more I thought about it, the scarier the idea was. I didn't want that kind of power, that kind of longevity. At least I didn't right now. Who knew how I would feel once my power actually broke through the binding.

"Why not?"

"Because Talant said that ascension comes with a price and that it's usually whatever we love most." As I stared at her, I realized that I'd assumed I would lose Dax, but that she would have been another possible payment for that kind of power. "Or we must sacrifice of ourselves. I'm not prepared to do either of those things right now and probably won't ever."

Minerva's silence was her only response.

Dax interrupted our quiet moment. "Minerva, after what

happened when Ally dreamwalked earlier, we decided it might be best if you prevented her from dreamwalking in the—"

It was my turn to interrupt. "There was no we, Dax. *You* decided. I told you that it was best if I don't have that power bound. I told you that I needed Talant to train me in how to use my magic. That he is the only one who knows what I am and how my power works."

Minerva's gaze once again bounced between the two of us.

"Ally—" Dax's voice was deeper and gravelly, stone grinding against stone, when he said my name.

Minerva held up a hand, which made him shut up.

Huh, I wondered if that would work for me.

"Dax, I respect you a great deal and understand that your first responsibility here is to her safety, but Ally has already made her feelings clear to you and now to me. I would never bind a witch's power without their consent or unless they were a danger to themselves or others."

"But she is a danger to herself if she ends up dreamwalking straight into Sommerton's arms!" Dax roared.

I jerked back. It was the first time I'd ever heard him yell like that and it was shocking. His body swelled and his skin shifted to a grey undertone. Two lumps appeared on his forehead, probably the beginnings of his horns. His eyes morphed from dark blue to straight silver, shot through with white light. He looked more like a monster than I'd ever seen him before.

Minerva got to her feet and walked right up to him. "As I'm sure my niece has already told you, she is different. Special. I am not equipped to teach her and guide her now that she is coming into her power. Talant is. He has already promised to help her and protect her."

Dax opened his mouth to continue to argue, revealing fangs, but Minerva shook her head and continued.

"Ally is one of the smartest people I know, Dax. She knows what's best for her. Even if I didn't already agree, I wouldn't intercede against her wishes."

Dax's mouth closed with a snap.

"Now, with that settled, it's nearly three a.m. I need to head home and get some rest so I can open the shop tomorrow morning," she said, brushing her hands down her loose sleeping pants.

I got to my feet, careful to keep my distance from Dax. Minerva turned and gave me another hug.

"You call me any time day or night if you have questions or you just need to talk, sweet girl," she said against my hair.

"I will, MinMin."

She gave me another squeeze and released me, stepping back with her hands on my biceps. I winced at the sharp pain in my arm, and she frowned.

"Are you hurt?" she asked.

I pulled my sweatshirt up and threaded my arm out of the sleeve. When the material was shoved away, I saw that there was a reddish-purple bruise glowing on my bicep. I lifted and turned my arm this way and that and realized the mark was shaped by Talant's hand.

Dax sprang forward, a growl emerging from his mouth. "Who did this to you? Was it Sommerton?"

I sighed. "No."

"It was Talant?" Minerva asked, sounding shocked.

"Yes, but it was an accident."

Neither of them looked like they believed me.

"He grabbed my arm to keep me from falling and then I gave him the bad news about Sommerton's...uh, possessor, or whatever you want to call it. That the entity inside Sommerton claims to be Talant's brother. As soon as I told him that he was hurting me, he let me go and apologized."

Minerva rubbed her hands together until a pale blue light began to glow between them. Then, she curved her hands around my bicep over the mark. A few moments later, the throbbing pain was gone. The bruise was still visible, but just barely. Minerva must have recharged her power somewhat today.

"I think perhaps Talant and I need to have a conversation," she murmured.

"If I could arrange it, I would. He's already said he wants to meet you," I replied.

Dax said nothing, only hovered behind Minerva, his eyes still locked on my now unmarked arm.

"Well, be sure to tell him that if he ever marks you against, I'll turn him into a eunuch, god or not," she retorted.

The gargoyle looming behind her only growled again. She turned and patted his arm lightly. "Don't worry, Dax. I would let you have him after that."

I sighed but didn't roll my eyes as I wanted to. "I'll tell him, but I don't think it'll intimidate him at all."

Minerva shrugged. "Some males have to learn the hard way."

She leaned over to kiss my cheek before she brushed past Dax and headed toward the front door. "I'll talk to you both tomorrow."

With that, she opened it and went outside.

"I'll be right back," Dax rumbled, hurrying to follow her.

I didn't respond. As my aunt as said, it was nearly three in the morning. I was exhausted. I grabbed the mugs and carried them into the kitchen to load them into the dishwasher.

By the time I was done, Dax was back inside and locking the front door. I didn't wait for him to say anything.

I yawned and said, "I'm going back to bed."

"Ally, I wish you would listen to me about—"

I lifted my hand, and what do you know, he stopped talking. Either that or he saw the expression on my face and knew I wasn't in the mood.

"We can argue until we're blue in the face tomorrow. All day if you want. Right now, I just need some sleep."

I lowered my hand and waited until Dax nodded. Then, I walked upstairs and stripped off my sweatshirt, throwing it over the foot of the mattress before I climbed into bed and passed out.

CHAPTER
FIFTEEN

When I opened my eyes, it felt like only five minutes had passed, but based on the light streaming in through the blinds, it had to be mid-morning or even closing in on noon.

Goddess, I was exhausted.

I glanced over my shoulder but knew that I'd find the bed empty. The blankets weren't askew, so I knew Dax had come back to bed sometime after I slept. Or at least he'd taken a few moments to smooth them out.

I sat up in the bed and listened, wondering if Dax had left me alone in the house. He said that he wouldn't, not after the spell Sommerton managed to cast over me, but after last night, I was a little afraid he'd changed his mind.

Then, I heard the water come on in the bathroom and realized he was about to take a shower.

I leaned over and tapped my phone screen so that it lit up. It was nearly ten in the morning. I'd managed to sleep over six hours after the excitement last night. I wasn't sure if it was the adrenaline dump or the power burst that did it, but I was still so tired that I could have gone right back to sleep.

But I couldn't. Dax said yesterday there was a contingent of cat shifters coming to the resort today for a meeting with the local cat clan. Apparently, they could be difficult to deal with and he didn't want to leave Poppy to deal with them.

I tossed the blankets to the side and headed into the bathroom. As soon as I opened the door, Dax turned to face me. The shower walls were glass but lightly misted from the rising steam. I could still see him clearly.

At the sight of the water running in rivulets over his naked body, my hesitance and residual irritation with him became something else. Something hot and insistent.

Without taking my eyes from his, I shoved the sweatpants I wore down my legs and stepped out of them. As I took another step, I tugged my tank top over my head and dropped it on the floor as well.

When I stopped in front of the shower stall, I hooked my thumbs into the waistband of my panties and skimmed them down my legs, leaving them on the bathmat.

Then, I opened the shower door, letting out a plume of damp steam.

Dax hadn't torn his eyes from me since I opened the bathroom door, but he wasn't watching me with heat in his eyes. He seemed just as hesitant as I'd felt moments ago.

He backed up when I stepped into the shower and shut the door behind me, closing us inside. He kept moving until his back hit the tile and my body was against his.

"Ally," he murmured. His hands came to my hips to hold me still.

I pressed my hands to his chest, sliding them up until I reached his neck. He didn't resist when I pulled his head down toward mine, but he did try to speak.

"Ally," he repeated. "I'm not sure we should—"

I used my lips to tell him to shut up, but without actual words. I kissed him, slipping my tongue into his mouth. He froze for a split second until I lowered one of my hands from his neck to the space between us. His cock was already half-hard when I wrapped my fingers around him and stroked.

Dax groaned against my mouth as I let my fingers trail down his length to cup his balls and squeeze.

His hands moved to my ass, lifting me off my feet. I yelped against his lips and released his cock to grab his shoulders with both hands. My legs wrapped around his hips so I could lock my ankles behind him. He spun around so that my back was against the tile. The smooth surface was still chilled. I gasped, my back arching, and he took the opportunity to lift me higher, bringing my breasts even with his mouth.

My head fell back when he ran his tongue over my nipple before sucking it deep into his mouth. With each pull, sounds escaped from my lips. My hands went from his shoulders to the back of his head, holding him close.

When his teeth closed over the tip of my breast, I cried out, arching even harder against his lips. The pleasure held a razor's edge, bordering on pain.

He released my nipple before moving to the next, his mouth becoming rougher. I writhed in his arms until he used his weight to pin me against the wall of the shower.

"Dax!"

My voice echoed in the bathroom and seemed to snap something within him. He carried me to the bench that ran along the back corner of the shower and sat down. Once he sat down, he lifted me off his lap, set me on my feet, and turned me to face away before bringing me back down to sit on his thighs.

His ankles came between mine and shoved my feet apart. Only his hands on my hips kept me from jumping off his lap. His hands moved to my inner thighs and down to my knees, shoving them wider apart until I was completely exposed, and my only choice was to lean back against his chest.

His knees trapped mine, forcing me to keep my legs spread. I could feel the hard length of his cock against my ass, and I writhed against it, but his hands clamped down on my hips again, holding me still.

"Don't. Move," he commanded.

There was something in his tone, an edge I hadn't heard before. Instinctively, I stopped wiggling and sat stock still, perched precariously on his thighs.

His hands smoothed up my sides, his fingers barely brushing the outside of my breasts until he reached my shoulders. Then, his palms glided down my arms to my wrists and he grasped them, lifting them over my head and around his neck.

"Stay just like this," he whispered, his lips touching my ear as he spoke. His voice had taken that deep, gravelly tone that made me shiver.

I linked my fingers behind his neck and held on for dear life because he didn't hesitate again. His hands went straight to my breasts, cupping them and kneading them before he grasped both my nipples and gave them a light tug.

"Ah!" I cried out, my back arching as the pleasure took on more than a hint of pain.

My nipples tingled and burned, but somehow it still felt good.

One of his hands released my breast, flattening on my belly as it moved down my torso. His other kept torturing my nipple, alternating between rubbing it with his thumb and giving it another tug that bordered on too much.

His middle finger slipped over my clit before it pressed in, slipping deep inside me. My legs tried to close as the sensations he wrought from my body threatened to overwhelm me, but his knees kept me from bringing my thighs together.

"I told you not to move," he murmured before his teeth closed over my earlobe.

Then, he gave my clit a light smack.

I jerked on his lap, unable to do anything but absorb the impact on the most sensitive part of my body. It hurt, but the pain immediately transformed into something much more. He smacked me again and I released a short scream.

His hand released my breast and covered my mouth. "Shhhh."

When my whimpers faded, he asked, "Do you want me to stop?"

I shook my head wildly. I was desperate. I needed more of whatever he was doing to me. It was exhilarating and unexpected and I wanted every second of it.

Another light slap to my clit. My hips jerked as he then ran two fingers over my clit in a rough circle before reaching down to slide them inside me. I was already wet and ready, which made him smirk against my neck. I felt his lips curve on my skin.

"You're ready for me, aren't you?" he asked.

His hand was still over my mouth, so I nodded.

Dax shifted on the bench, his hands releasing my mouth and pussy to move me. When his cock nudged the entrance of my pussy, I moaned, rocking against him. With his knees still forcing mine apart, I couldn't do anything but roll my hips to try and slip him inside me.

Nothing I did would make him move faster. He lowered me down, slowly entering me from behind.

"Please, please, please." I kept repeating the word, too lost in what he was doing to my body to stop.

"Are you begging me to stop?" he asked, his hands gripping my hips to stop my descent.

"No! Don't stop!"

His answering laugh was low and dark, but he let my body move again. He didn't stop this time, letting my weight bear down on his cock until he was deep inside me.

My heartbeat was frantic in my chest. Dax moved his hands again, one moving down my hip to my inner thigh. The other trailed up to my breast. His touch was so light now that it nearly tickled.

I jerked beneath the caress, unable to hold still.

When I did, the hand on my thigh moved to smack my clit again. With his cock stretching me wide, the sensation the impact evoked was even more intense.

"Dax!"

I couldn't stop myself from writhing on his dick, and each time I did, he gave me another slap. The orgasm that exploded inside me was as unexpected as it was overwhelming.

My body went rigid, and my fingers dug into the back of his neck.

But Dax wasn't done torturing me just yet. His index finger rolled over my clit, pressing deep, and the spasms that wracked my body increased. I drew in the breath to scream again, but his hand clapped down over my mouth before the sound escaped me.

The sound was muffled by his palm but still echoed in the bathroom. I shuddered against him until the pleasure actually became pain. I whimpered against his hand, and he stopped torturing my clit immediately, his fingers moving to dig into my hips.

Gripping me tightly, he lifted me a few inches before slamming me back down on his cock. My head lolled back on his shoulder as he hammered into me, wringing the last of my orgasm from me.

A few moments later, he thrust inside me one last time before he groaned into my throat, the sound vibrating from his chest against my back. I felt the prick of fangs against my skin, which brought another gasp from my lips. Just as the pinch began to edge toward an actual bite, he growled and jerked his head away from my neck.

One of his fangs scratched me and I flinched at the swift pain.

"Fuck," he whispered behind me, but he sounded as though he was in agony rather than riding out his own pleasure.

I couldn't move, my body completely boneless. Dax's hands flexed on my waist, and he was panting behind me. I wasn't sure if I was shaking or he was, but neither of us moved for a long moment.

"Fuck," he repeated. This time he sounded displeased.

"What is it?" I asked, trying to find the energy to move.

"Your neck is bleeding."

I glanced down and saw a tiny stream of blood trickling down my chest. It wasn't much, just a little.

"Oops," I murmured.

"Oops?" he repeated.

"Did you get me with your teeth?" I asked.

His body went rigid beneath me. "Yes. I'm sorry."

I shrugged one shoulder and realized I was still gripping the back of his neck. "It's okay. I'm pretty sure the back of your neck would be scratched into a bloody mess right now if you weren't a gargoyle."

I released him and lowered my arms, hissing as pins and needles rushed through my muscles.

"What's wrong? Are you hurt?" he asked.

I wished I could see his face, but the way we were sitting made it impossible for me to turn around.

"I'm okay. Just some pins and needles in my arms."

"Gods, Ally," he murmured, lifting me to my feet.

My legs nearly gave out and I would have crashed to the bottom of the shower if he hadn't grabbed me.

"You are hurt," he insisted.

"No, I'm not hurt," I shot back. "I just came so hard that I can't feel my legs, okay? Will you please calm down?"

Dax was silent but got to his feet behind me, still gripping my hips.

I glanced over my shoulder at his face, but, once again, he wore his impassive mask. The one that kept anyone from knowing what he was thinking.

"I shouldn't have been so rough with you," he finally rumbled.

"I don't recall telling you that you were hurting me or telling you to stop," I retorted.

My legs were steadier, so I stepped forward into the shower spray. I turned my back to the water, tilting my head back to wet my hair. I studied him as I grabbed my shampoo off the built-in shelf.

"I made you bleed," he finally said.

"My neck is fine. I've cut myself worse shaving my legs."

I lathered up my hair and started scrubbing my scalp. I wasn't sure how long we'd been in the shower, and I didn't want to run out of hot water.

His eyes trailed down my body, stopping at my waist. "You're going to have bruises on your hips."

I glanced down and saw four round bruises spread out just inside my hipbones. I twisted but couldn't see the back, but I assumed I had a matching thumb-sized bruise on my ass as well.

"Cool, my first sex bruises. Maybe I need to put that on my list."

"Dammit, Ally, this isn't a joke!" Dax burst out.

I grabbed my conditioner bottle, and my eyes narrowed. "No, it's not. Why are you beating yourself up for something we did together, something I really enjoyed?"

It was Dax's turn to study me in silence. I smoothed conditioner through my hair. I didn't let it sit as I usually did but rinsed it out almost immediately. I really didn't want to take an ice-cold shower. Nor did I really want to continue this conversation while I was naked.

Dax didn't say anything else as I washed my face and my body. He did shift out of the way when I stepped out from beneath the spray and started squeezing the water out of my hair. I met his gaze with a level stare of my own.

"I am perfectly capable of telling you when I don't want something, Dax," I said. "I demonstrated that last night when we argued. If you were hurting me earlier or if I didn't like it, I would have no problem telling you."

"Ally, you're inexperienced and I treated you like—"

I threw my head back and laughed, which made him shut up.

When I stopped, I leaned forward and patted him on the chest. "You've met Minerva. Don't you realize that she was extremely frank when she discussed sex with me. She was also the first to tell me to invest in some decent sex toys. She said that I wouldn't be able to tell someone else what I enjoyed if I didn't know that for myself. She also said that I had no business having sex with someone if I didn't feel like I could tell them no or talk about what I liked. So, while I may not have had sex before you, I have experimented on my own." I leaned forward slightly and whispered, "I've even watched porn, some of it a lot more intense than what we just did. While I may not have had sex with anyone but you, I am by no means a prude or uncertain about what I like."

By the time I was done speaking, Dax was looking down at me with an astonished expression.

"Now, I'm going to get dressed because we have to get to the resort soon, right?"

He nodded, his eyes never leaving my face.

I exited the shower, reaching for a towel from the rack next to the stall. As I bent to wrap it around my hair, Dax swore.

I straightened and turned my head to see that he'd stepped under the shower spray. Judging by the stiff way he was holding his body, the hot water had run out.

Biting back a laugh, I grabbed another towel, wrapped it around my torso, and left him to his cold shower.

TWO HOURS LATER, we were standing in front of the main lodge of the resort, watching as Poppy stepped forward to greet the alpha of the visiting cat shifter clan.

The man stared at her as though she were diseased, but he did give her outstretched hand a brief shake.

Dax tensed behind me but didn't move. Poppy insisted that she could handle the arrival of the cat clan, so Dax had agreed to stand back unless something catastrophic happened.

I was too far away to hear what they were saying to each other, but Dax must have been able to because he shifted slightly behind me, as though he were about to step forward.

Poppy must have sensed the movement because she glanced over her shoulder at him and gave her head a single, slight shake.

Dax took a deep breath but settled back into his stance behind me.

As I watched Poppy deal with the cat shifters, my chest began to feel tight. It was a feeling I recognized. One I would never forget.

"Oh, shit," I whispered.

Dax leaned down. "What is it?"

The tightness increased and I felt the swelling inside me, the same pressure I'd felt last night.

Before I could answer Dax's question, the alpha who was speaking to Poppy stiffened. His head turned until he was looking straight at me.

Power crackled along my skin, invisible, but there was a scent of ozone in the air. Even with my human senses, I could smell it.

I knew Dax sensed it too when he whispered, "Shit."

The alpha skirted around Poppy, heading straight for where I stood with Dax. The pressure inside me suddenly increased and I doubled over, wrapping my hands around my stomach, groaning.

"What is the meaning of this?" the alpha hissed.

I felt Dax move then, but I couldn't lift my head to see what was happening.

The cramp in my abdomen eased for a moment and I managed to straighten. When I did, I saw that Dax was standing between me and three cat shifters—the alpha, a female who must have been his mate, and another large male who must have been the clan enforcer.

"Back away," Dax rumbled. His body grew larger, his muscles swelling beneath his shirt, and his skin turning dark grey.

"You dare bring a witch to this meeting?" the alpha asked, not backing down an inch.

I saw horns appear above Dax's head and ducked just in time to avoid his wings when they burst out of the back of his shirt. He was shifting into his full gargoyle form in front of me. To protect me.

My heart started hammering and the power on my skin gave an audible snap as it intensified.

The alpha made a strange roaring sound. "You have insulted us with this. What spell is she casting? Did Harold send her?"

Harold was the alpha of the cat clan in Devil Springs. While he could be sneaky and even downright mean, he was always straight-forward. If he had a problem with this alpha, he would have attacked him on his own, not hired a witch to do it.

I couldn't say that though because another pain wracked my body. I couldn't contain my cry. As I grabbed the waistband of Dax's pants, my eyes met the alpha female's gaze. Whatever she saw in my face must have frightened her because she paled. Her hand went to the alpha's shoulder, and she tugged him back a step.

I had to say something, to let them know that I meant them no harm, but they needed to run. The pressure was building, and I knew it was only a matter of time before another shockwave of power escaped me and shot through the group of shifters in front of me. I didn't want to hurt anyone.

As I clutched his belt, Dax reached behind his head and a sword hilt appeared in his hand like magic. He drew the weapon from the back of his shirt in one smooth motion and crouched slightly, flaring his wings wide. I saw then that the enforcer had been sidling around, trying to sneak up on his flank.

I leaned around him, looking at both the alphas. "I-I'm sorry. I don't want to hurt you." I groaned as another pain gripped me in its massive fist. "I can't control it. I'm trying, but—"

My knees almost gave out, but I managed to keep my feet. I kept trying to fight it, to keep the burst of energy back, but the crackling on my skin became a white light.

When the alpha female saw it, her eyes widened. "Back away!" she shouted. "Take cover!"

Using her grip on the alpha male's shirt, she yanked him back and started running for the trees.

Somehow, she knew what was about to happen.

Goddess, if I couldn't control the direction of this burst, I would end up killing someone. I saw Poppy standing in the middle of the drive, staring at where Dax crouched in front of me. I could kill my friend.

I couldn't hurt her.

Magic was all about intention. That's what Talant had said.

I fought through the agony, focusing on what I wanted. As the magic rushed through my veins, I threw my head back, my arms lifting toward the sky, and screamed.

The power shot out of me, an intense beam of white light, going straight up toward the sky. About a hundred feet above the trees, it seemed to hit a barrier. The same lacy dome I'd seen last night flashed against the bright blue of the sky.

The power continued to rush out of me, stronger than it had before.

Finally, the flow stopped abruptly, like a faucet being shut off.

My legs gave out and I crashed to the ground, ass first. My body flopped over until I was lying face up on the dirt, staring at the sky. The dome of the ward pulsed with white light, brighter than it had before. It was almost blinding against the cloudless, blue sky.

It was so pretty.

Dax's face appeared over me. "Ally, what are you talking about?"

I realized I'd said my last thought out loud. I tried to tell him that, but everything was hazy.

The last of my energy seemed to slip away and I descended into the haze, letting the black fog roll right over me.

CHAPTER
SIXTEEN

The yelling brought me out of the haze. I was still lying on the ground. All I could see above me was a pair of jean-clad legs, black wings spread wide, and the sound of snarling and yipping.

"What is that noise?" I whispered.

My throat was dry, so my voice was barely audible, but Dax still heard me. He stepped over me and crouched down by my side, his attention split between me and whatever was happening nearby.

"Ally, thank the gods. Are you okay?"

I took a moment to take stock of my body. Other than my fuzzy head and weak muscles, I felt fine.

"I'm okay. What happened after I passed out?"

"Let's just say that the cat alpha decided that Poppy was a spy from the wolf pack, especially when Zeke Marshall showed up from the police department and mentioned that Garrett was on the way. It didn't matter that Zeke explained that Garrett is the police chief and would be expected to show up anyway. The cats know Garrett is the alpha of the wolf pack here and then, when they realized that Poppy was his sister, things went to absolute shit."

Dax sheathed the sword in his hand down the back of his shirt, reminding me that I needed to ask him how in the heck the magic for that worked, and reached down, lifting me in his arms.

When he straightened, we were face-to-face with the alpha's mate. Dax snarled at her, but she raised her hands, palm out.

"I'm not here to hurt her," she said.

"Back up," Dax barked.

"Please, I mean no harm."

I put my hand on Dax's shoulder. "Let her speak," I murmured.

He shot me a glare, turning so that most of his body was between me and the female. "Fine, what do you want?"

She kept her hands raised and took a small step forward, her eyes on me. "You're a Conduit, aren't you?"

"I've never heard of that before," I said.

"You channel the power of the gods."

I shook my head. "No, I don't channel their power."

It wasn't a lie, but I wasn't about to tell her all of the things that Talant had shared with me. I didn't know her.

"I've met one of your kind before," she said.

"I'm not a Conduit," I insisted. "I've never even heard that term before."

"That may not be what you call yourself, but it's how I know you."

"Who is this Conduit you met before?" I asked. Why was this shifter so insistent?

Her eyes darted around, as though she were making sure that no one else was near us. "My mother."

I blinked. "I thought shifters couldn't hold magic power."

"My mother wasn't a shifter."

I realized then that she was half human. It was rare for a half human shifter to achieve alpha status. Most packs and clans would reject an alpha with a human parent.

She inched closer, which brought another snarl from Dax. Her gaze flicked to him. "I swear, she is safe with me. I know what this sort of power can do to a witch. My mate can be reactive, but he knew and loved my mother like his own. Once I explain it to him fully, he will understand and calm down."

"The damage will already have been done," Dax replied.

She flinched. She knew he was right.

"The police officer your mate is fighting with right now is Harold's son."

All the color leeched from the female's face.

"The wolf shifter he insulted is the alpha's sister."

She took a step back.

"And that police officer views Poppy as family. So, I suggest you go get your mate calmed down now before he destroys this situation beyond all hope of repair."

The female turned and sprinted toward the tree line. Now that I wasn't distracted by a cat shifter, I saw two males in partially shifted forms, battling. Poppy hadn't shifted as they had, but she was facing off with the enforcer of the cat clan, with nothing but claws and fangs to reveal that she wasn't fully human.

She moved fluidly, avoiding his lightning-fast strikes and kicks.

"You need to go help her," I said to Dax.

"She's doing fine," he replied.

I winced when she barely evaded another swipe from the enforcer's claws. He was partially shifted like the alpha and Zeke and nearly a foot taller than her now.

His other hand caught her bicep, leaving four bloody slashes on her arm, and I nudged Dax with my elbow.

"Go help her. I'll be fine."

He shook his head. "My first concern is your safety."

I started to argue with him some more, but Poppy closed in on the enforcer, catching the next strike he threw her way with a hard block. Then, her own claws came up and jabbed him in the throat.

It was a quick, brutal move, one that made me cringe.

The cat enforcer went down, clutching his throat. I knew that he would survive the wound, but it would be painful as it healed.

Poppy threw a violent kick at his head, and he fell face-first onto the grass in a boneless heap, obviously unconscious.

"See? I told you she was doing fine," Dax murmured.

I hadn't realized that Poppy was such a good fighter, but I should have. Her brother was alpha, and she could have been, but she didn't want the position. She joked that shifters couldn't take any drug strong enough for the kinds of headaches running a pack could cause.

As soon as the enforcer crashed down, Poppy whirled toward where Zeke had been fighting the cat alpha. But it was no use.

At some point, Zeke had pinned the alpha onto the grass by the throat. The male had clawed him up but hadn't been strong enough to beat him. The alpha struggled weakly in Zeke's grip. I realized that Zeke was choking him.

The alpha's mate was crouched next to him, her mouth moving rapidly. I couldn't hear what she was saying, so I asked Dax, "What's she saying? Can you hear?"

"She's talking to both of them, saying this is all just a big misunderstanding. She's telling her mate he needs to calm down and asking Zeke to give them a moment to talk."

Judging by Zeke's body language, that wasn't going to happen. He looked like he wanted to rip the male's head off.

Finally, the cat alpha went limp and stayed that way. I could see that his eyes were open, but he was no longer fighting. It was only then that Zeke released him and got to his feet.

The sound of sirens caught my attention, and I looked up. Garrett Kent's SUV tore up the drive and slid to a stop next to Zeke Marshall's patrol car.

As soon as he climbed out, he glanced over at Dax and gave him a nod. Without a word, he turned back to the group of shifters and approached them.

"Let's go," Dax said.

Before I could respond, he leapt into the air, holding me tightly in his arms, and headed toward the cabin.

"Dax, what the heck?" I yelped.

"Garrett will meet us at the cabin later to get our statements. Right now, I'm taking you where I can keep you safe. I didn't want to risk distracting them while they were fighting or carrying you while you were unconscious, otherwise we would already be there."

I didn't argue because there was nothing I could say. Honestly, I didn't want to stay there and watch all of this unfold. I wanted to lie down on the couch and cover my face with an ice pack. Now that I wasn't distracted, I realized my head throbbed with each beat of my heart.

Dax landed in the yard and carried me into the cabin, locking the door behind us.

"What about your car?" I asked, my voice faint.

"Poppy will drive it and follow Kent over."

Dax seemed to know that I was in pain because he was incredibly gentle when he set me on the sofa.

I looked up at him when he straightened and said, "We have to stop meeting like this."

His expression said he didn't find my joke funny in the least.

I didn't have the energy to give him a hard time. I just laid my head back against the armrest of the sofa and closed my eyes.

"What do you need?" he asked.

"Ice pack," I whispered. "My head hurts."

I heard his footsteps retreat as he walked to the kitchen and opened the freezer. A few moments later, an ice pack wrapped in a towel was laid over my eyes.

"Lift your head up," he murmured.

I did as he directed and sighed as he slid another pack beneath my neck.

"That already feels better," I said.

"Do you need Minerva?" he asked.

"No, I'll be okay. She left me some tea the other day. It's in the cabinet in a purple box. Can you put a small spoonful in a cup of hot water for me? It will help."

I tried to relax, letting the chill from the ice packs ease the ache in my head. I was almost asleep when the floral scent of tea penetrated the fog of exhaustion surrounding me.

Dax's voice was close when he said, "Ally, I need you to sit up and drink this."

I reached up and removed the ice pack from my eyes. Dax sat on the coffee table, a steaming mug in his hand. The liquid inside it was pink.

I sat up slowly and reached out for the cup. He didn't release it when I took the handle, making sure to support it as I brought it to my mouth. I took a couple of sips, letting the warmth wash over me.

"Just a little more," Dax insisted when I tried to lower the cup.

I kept my eyes closed and took two more sips. "There. Give me a few minutes and I'll drink some more."

Dax took the cup from my hands, and I heard it click when he sat it on the coffee table.

Within a minute, the ache in my head began to fade. I leaned back against the couch and let my head rest on the cushion behind me.

"You ready for more?" Dax asked.

"Not yet. It's starting to kick in, but I need a few minutes."

After another minute, the pain was much more manageable, and my thoughts no longer seemed to be moving at the speed of molasses.

I raised my head and leaned forward to grab the cup, but Dax was already there, taking it in his hand and guiding it into mine. Once again, he supported the cup as I lifted it to my lips. I drank about half the cooling brew this time before I lowered the mug.

"I can hold it on my own now," I assured him.

"Maybe, but I don't want to explain to Minerva how you got burned on my watch."

I let Dax keep his hold on the cup as I finished off the last of the tea.

"There, I'm done," I said.

He took the cup and set it aside. "Why don't you rest until Garrett gets here?"

"Sounds like a plan, Stan," I replied.

He didn't even crack a smile, just swept the blanket over me when I laid down.

As I closed my eyes, I said, "I'm getting tired of ending up exhausted and on this couch every day."

If Dax replied, I didn't hear it.

TWO HOURS LATER, I was awake and watching as Dax walked the police chief out of the cabin. I'd just finished giving him my statement of what little I could remember. When I asked him what would happen with the cat shifters, he told me not to worry about it, which didn't ease my mind at all.

I felt responsible for this entire mess. After all, it was my inability to control my magic that had caused the issue in the first place.

After Dax shut the front door behind Garrett, he kept his back to me and stared down at his feet, his palms resting on the door frame.

When he didn't move, I called out, "Dax, are you okay?"

He didn't answer me. He only sighed and lifted his head. When he faced me, his face was once again an impassive mask.

"I can't do this," he said. "I shouldn't have done this at all."

"What are you talking about?" I asked. My headache was gone, but my brain still felt fuzzy. I knew a good night's sleep would help, but the trip up the stairs seemed too difficult right now.

"I shouldn't have gotten involved with you. It was a mistake."

I blinked at him as my brain tried to process what he was saying. When I finally understood, I got to my feet. "You mean you shouldn't have brought me to your cabin? Or that you shouldn't have kissed me? Or that you shouldn't have fucked me?"

With each question, my voice rose. A dark flush spread over Dax's cheeks, but I ignored it. I was too focused on the pain tearing through me. It was worse than when my magic pulsed. Worse than the headache I'd experienced earlier.

It was as bad as what I felt when my parents died.

I knew this pain. It was grief and loss and a sadness that might ease over time but never fade.

"Ally, you know we can never be together. Not like you want."

I laughed. A high-pitched sound of hysteria that pierced even my ears.

"How would you know what I want, Dax?" I asked. "Have you asked?"

His impassive mask was back. Goddess, it hurt so badly to have him looking at me like that again. Like he felt nothing.

"We've made no promises to each other," I continued. "We're friends. We've only had sex a few times. I didn't expect you to declare your undying love for me or propose marriage. We haven't even discussed being exclusive to each other."

"Exclusive to each other?" he repeated.

"Meaning whether we'll see or sleep with other people, Dax."

His face changed and I could read this expression. He was pissed as hell.

"What?" The question was low and dangerous.

His body seemed to grow, and his eyes turned into pure silver. His hands fisted as he lowered his head to look at me from under his brows.

It was a terrifying stance, one that I'd never seen him take before.

Instinctively, I took a step back. Then, another.

The movement seemed to break through whatever Dax was thinking because his face changed again. He looked horrified.

He spun on his heel and stalked back toward the front door. He leaned his head against the wood and took a deep breath. After a few moments, he faced me again, his face completely blank.

"You should go to bed, Ally."

I didn't argue with him. Whatever had just happened in Dax's head, I wasn't sure I could deal with it right now. I was tired and weak, my heart hurting and my emotions a wreck. There was no way I could have a calm, reasonable discussion with him right now.

I needed to lick my wounds and calm down.

I turned my back to him and trudged up the stairs to the loft. I went through the motions, getting ready for bed on autopilot. I stripped my clothes off and let them fall on the floor on my side of the bed, slipped on a tank top and shorts, and crawled into the bed. I didn't worry about washing my face or brushing my teeth. I didn't have the energy to deal with it.

When my head hit the pillow, that was when the tears came. Goddess, this hurt.

The cabin was completely silent. I couldn't even hear Dax moving around. I forced my breathing to remain even as tears trickled down my face to soak the pillowcase. I didn't understand why, but something inside me didn't want him to know how badly he'd wounded me with his words.

Because he was right. I did want a relationship with him. And after the way he'd been acting the past few days, the seed of hope had bloomed inside me. I thought that maybe I was getting through to him. That he could let himself love me.

But it seemed that I was wrong.

I cried for a long time, but the events of the day finally took their toll on me, and my eyes drifted closed. I didn't think I would be able to sleep, but I was going to try. Anything to escape this feeling. To forget the words that Dax had thrown at me.

I wasn't sure how I could face him again, but I knew I wouldn't have a choice.

Maybe tomorrow I would know what to do.

CHAPTER
SEVENTEEN

I wasn't sure when the dream started, only that I knew I was dreamwalking when I became aware.

The sky was filled with dark clouds and thunder rolled, echoing off the mountains that surrounded me. Wind tore through my hair as lightning arced across the sky, a web of violet electricity.

Even as the wind howled, there were huge grey figures flying past on black wings. They carried swords, spears, and bows and arrows. In the distance, there was a castle set on the side of the mountain.

My mouth fell open as I stared at the aerial battle above me. They were all gargoyles. Thousands of them. It was a vicious battle, full of blood and screams. Their blades were as black as their wings and the tips of their arrows gleamed like obsidian. Whatever metal or stone their weapons were made of, I'd never seen it before.

Suddenly, the world shifted, and I found myself on the roof of the castle. The battle raged around me, closer than before. There were gargoyles all around me. Some wore red and black. The others were clad in grey and white. They fought fiercely.

I screamed when I saw one of the gargoyles swing his sword in a sharp arc, slicing off the head of his opponent.

My stomach lurched and tried to revolt at the sight of such bloodshed. It was only after I managed to suppress the urge to vomit that I realized how easily the gargoyles were injuring each other. I'd always thought they were nearly invincible in their full form.

It seemed I was wrong.

The world spun again, and I found myself running down a hallway. I was moving faster than I ever had before. It was then I understood that this wasn't my dream. I was within someone else's dream.

A gargoyle's dream.

As I raced down the dark hallway, my heart pounded as fast as my feet. I held a sword in one hand and a broken spear in the other. The wounds on my chest and side burned like fire, but I couldn't stop. They were counting on me to protect them, and I'd been caught unawares.

I knew there was unrest in the kingdom, but I never expected the war that raged around me.

A scream pierced the air, feminine and full of rage. I forced my feet to move faster, even though my head was growing light with blood loss.

I came around a corner and crashed into another warrior, this one wearing grey and white. Without hesitation, I stabbed the broken spear into his throat, twisted it, and yanked it free.

He gurgled as he fell to the floor, clutching his throat. It was a mortal wound, so I didn't take the time to finish him off. I had to get to them.

I killed two more warriors clad in grey before I burst through the double doors that led to the queen's chambers.

As I entered, my eyes took in the scene before me in a flash.

The prince lay on the floor in a puddle of blood too large to belong to a child so small. His skin was no longer grey but the pure marble white of death.

I saw the warriors surrounding my queen and howled in rage.

183

Moving faster than I ever had before, I attacked, wanting nothing more than to kill them all.

What kind of warrior killed a defenseless child? There was no honor in what they had done and so I would not give them the honor of a clean death.

I met their attack head on, using my sword and spear to tear them apart. As I slashed and stabbed, my back met the queen's. We fought side-by-side, but there were too many. They swarmed us.

When the first blade pierced my spine, I screamed. I tried to turn, to fight off my attacker, but another spear skewered my abdomen in the front.

My legs stopped working, folding beneath me.

Another blade sliced through my shoulder, piercing all the way through my body. My sword arm immediately became useless, and the weapon dropped from my grip.

I screamed again, not because of the pain, but at the agony of what was unfolding before me.

My queen fought valiantly, a sword in each hand, but they outnumbered her as they did me. Right before my eyes, they cut her down, their spears piercing her body and pinning her flat to the floor.

I fought with everything I had, my blood splattering on the floor, but I couldn't get free of the weapons spiking through me.

All I could do was watch as the largest gargoyle separated from the group, a heavy black crown on his head. The Usurper knew he couldn't win in an honorable battle, so he intended to take the throne by whatever means necessary. The crown he wore was nothing more than a false declaration.

I managed to knock one of my attackers off his feet, but another took his place before I could lunge forward, his spear stabbing me through the thigh.

I screamed again as the Usurper's sword lifted and fell, my queen's head rolling across the floor after he cleaved it from her body.

I would make them pay in blood. I would tear them apart for what they had done.

The words flowed from my mouth, vows before the gods themselves, bringing the Usurper's attention to me.

He smiled, a terrible, ugly smile of triumph, and sauntered in my direction.

"Daxys Tremalsys, how did I know you would find your way here?"

I tried to lunge forward again, and this time I dragged the three warriors pinning me to the ground with me. The Usurper stopped his approach, watching as his minions wrestled me back under control.

"You chose the wrong side, Dax," he continued once he was assured I wouldn't free myself.

Even now, he was a coward. I laughed in his face, spitting blood at his feet to demonstrate my loathing.

"You will never hold the throne, Paraxys. A coward like you will fall beneath the sword of another, probably while your back is turned." I chuckled at the thought. "It is a more merciful end than you deserve."

"Still your tongue, Daxys, or I'll remove it from your head before I kill you."

My left hand still clutched the spear. I was weak from blood loss, but I was willing to sacrifice my life if it meant that I could plunge the weapon into his black heart.

"Go ahead. Cut out my tongue but know that you will always be a coward."

I prepared myself to move when he took another step forward. My muscles trembled and I fought not to tense my body, not to do anything that would betray my intention.

Before he got close enough, the skylight above the throne shattered and every window in the throne room erupted. Gargoyles clad in red and gold filled the room, cutting down every enemy they encountered.

The queen's brother had arrived.

But it was too late. Far too late.

The males pinning me to the ground tore their weapons free of my body, turning to fight their new opponents.

I didn't hesitate. From my knees, I leapt forward, the spear slipping beneath the breastplate the Usurper wore. Yet another indication of his cowardice. Unlike the rest of the warriors, he wore armor, demonstrating his weakness. A true gargoyle warrior needed no armor. His stone skin and skills with a weapon would be enough to protect him.

As the spear pierced his gut, he cried out, trying to lift his sword to strike at me. I grunted and gripped the spear even tighter, driving it higher into his chest, past his ribs. I felt the tip tear through his flesh until it finally reached his heart. I felt the muscle give as the blade pierced it, popping like an overripe fruit.

He shriekd as I twisted the spear inside him, his arms falling to his side, useless. His weight took me to my knees when it collapsed, but I didn't let go. I stared into his eyes, snarling.

"The gods will damn you in the next life, Paraxys," I said. "Enjoy the hell you made for yourself."

He gasped, his last breath rattling in his chest, and exhaled. As the last of his lifeblood leaked out of his chest, his skin paled, the grey becoming white.

When I could no longer hold my body up, I released the weapon and fell to my side. The Usurper remained on his knees, his body nothing but stone now.

As my heart slowed, I knew that I was dying. And I was at peace with it because I had avenged their death as my last act. Even so, I didn't deserve to live. Not while they turned to white stone.

I SCREAMED before I even opened my eyes.

Strong hands gripped me, lifting me off the mattress. I tried to fight them off, clutching at my side, my shoulder, and my leg. The phantom pain of those stab wounds was fading, but I remembered it still.

"Ally!"

Dax's harsh voice broke through my panicked thoughts.

I opened my eyes and looked up at him. I could feel the tears flowing down my face, but there was nothing I could do to stop them.

It was him. I'd been in his memories in my dreams.

And now I knew why he could never love me the way I wanted him to. Why he couldn't let himself feel anything for me except friendship.

He didn't think he was worthy of life, much less happiness and love.

This was an enemy I couldn't fight because the enemy was also the man I loved.

"Ally, what happened?"

"I'm sorry," I gasped, grabbing at his arms, my hands locking onto his wrists. "I'm so sorry."

"You have nothing to apologize for," he said.

"I saw it," I continued. "I saw it all. The battle. The prince lying in his own blood, his flesh the color of marble. The queen falling to Paraxys' sword. All of it. I'm so sorry, Dax."

His body went rigid at my words, his hands grasping my shoulders so hard that I flinched.

He released me as though he was burned. "What did you say?"

I sobbed, wrapping my own arms around my waist, rocking back and forth on the mattress. "I understand now. And I'm so very sorry."

With a groan, Dax wrapped his arms around me, pulling me into his chest. "Shhh. Ally, calm yourself."

I shook my head, the tears still falling as the ragged sobs tore through my chest. "I understand now. I do."

"Shhh."

He stroked my hair, rocking me as he tried to quiet me.

The storm of tears continued on and on until I thought I would never be able to stop crying.

Finally, I had nothing left. My body lay limp against his, my breath coming in little, weak gasps, and my heart was broken beyond repair.

Dax laid down, taking me with him, so that my head was cradled on his shoulder, and he had both arms around me.

"Rest, Allison," he said. "Just rest."

My body gave me no choice but to obey him.

CHAPTER
EIGHTEEN

The next morning, I woke in the bed alone. Again.

I supposed I should get used to it because that would be my future now. Going to bed and waking up alone.

I didn't bother with my clothes, only pulling on the sweatshirt that I'd left on the floor the night before.

When I crept downstairs, I found Dax standing in the kitchen, the blinds above the sink open so that he could look outside. He had a cup of coffee in his hand, but it was no longer steaming.

His head turned toward me when I stopped at the bar. His expression was shuttered, and his body was tense.

I didn't wait for him to speak, for him to try and smooth over the awkwardness. I jumped straight in.

I was right yesterday when I decided to give myself some time. I did know what to do this morning.

But that didn't make it hurt any less.

"I understand now, Dax," I began.

His hand lowered the cup to counter, moving slowly, but he didn't speak.

"You're right. I do want more than friendship from you." I rubbed my chest with one hand, trying to soothe the ache in my heart. "But I also know that you won't give me that. Maybe you can't."

I took a deep breath, but he remained silent, so I continued.

"I can't force you to open your heart to me and I deserve more than whatever scraps of affection or attention you can give me. You do, too, but I can't control your choices. Only my own."

One more deep breath and I finished it.

"So, you're right. This can't continue. It will only hurt both of us in the long run, you because you won't be able to let go of your guilt and me because I will be settling for less than I deserve."

He remained perfectly still when I walked toward him. I rose up on my toes and pressed my lips to the underside of his jaw. It was all I could reach of him because he didn't bend down for me as he usually did.

"Still, I don't regret my time with you here or what we did together. No matter what you believe, I don't think it was a mistake."

I dropped back down to my feet.

"I'm going to shower and then I want you to take me to Minerva's. I think I know what I need to do to wake Talant."

That was a lie, but I knew I couldn't stay here with him any longer. I had to move on...starting today.

Dax was still silent when I walked away, but I forced myself to keep going. It was better to end this now, clean and simple.

My head was surprisingly clear as I showered and dressed. I would probably be a mess once I was in the safety of Minerva's house, but, right now, I felt like my decision was the right one.

I'd just finished getting ready when it hit. The twisting inside me made me double over. I bit back a gasp, clutching my belly. Dear goddess, the pain was worse today than yesterday. The pressure eased off and I pulled myself up, using the counter to support my weight. When I straightened, I nearly stumbled back.

Sommerton's image gazed back at me from the mirror above the sink, a smug smile on his face.

"It's almost time," he said. "You can feel it, can't you?"

The magic inside me bubbled at his words, rising higher as though it was responding to his statement.

"It's time for you to come to me, Ally," he continued.

He leaned closer, his face coming further into the light. His eyes were pure black, shot through with violet light streaks. The black veins surrounding his eyes had branched out to encompass his cheeks, jawline, and down his neck to disappear behind his shirt. His body seemed leaner than before, almost gaunt.

"And to give you a little incentive, I have a special guest here to witness your manifestation."

Sommerton stepped to the side, disappearing from the mirror as though he were stepping out of the frame of a camera. Behind him, her hands tied above her head to a metal hook jutting from a rock wall, was my aunt.

Her dark red hair was tangled and matted. A bruise marred her cheekbone just below her eye, the lid already turning such a dark purple it was almost black. Her eye was so swollen that she couldn't open it.

Sommerton appeared again, this time next to her, kneeling on one knee. He clutched a knife in his hand, the tip of the blade pressing against her throat, denting her skin.

My heart stuttered when a thin stream of blood trickled from beneath the point of the blade.

"Come to me, Ally, or suffer the consequences."

"Is this your way of convincing me that you'll give me whatever I want if I just wake your brother?" I whispered.

The triumphant smile he wore faded. "You still don't understand, I see." His hand dropped away from Minerva's neck as he got to his feet. Her one good eye focused on me and she shook her head violently, but I ignored her silent directive.

I wasn't going to let anyone take the last living member of my family from me, not even if he was a god.

"I'm helping you make the right decision," Sommerton said,

bringing my attention back to him. "You'll understand once Talant is among us."

I leaned forward, my voice still a whisper as I said, "I want to help Talant. And I would help him willingly, but now you've pissed me off. So, when I wake him up, I promise I will do everything within my power to make you pay for this."

My aggressive response must have taken him off guard because he flinched at my words.

"Come to me, Ally. Let's finish this." The smirk returned to his lips. "And then I'll look forward to seeing how you intend to make me pay."

At that moment, I was so angry that I would have been willing to sacrifice almost anything to have enough power to punish him for what he'd done to my aunt.

"I don't know how," I admitted.

"Think of your aunt. How much you love her. How much you want to help her. Magic is all about intention. Make your intention to be by her side and you will come here."

For a moment, he sounded just like Talant. I could hear their similarities in his words.

I closed my eyes, took a deep breath, and centered myself. I focused on Minerva, reaching out to her with my mind. I thought of how much I loved her and how much I needed her. How I needed to help her right now.

I felt a tugging sensation and then the air rushed around me as I fell through the floor, just as I had when I dreamwalked before.

This time, I couldn't slow my descent. I landed on my hands and knees on a slab of rock, the breath knocked out of me at the impact.

The cave was dim, but even in the low light, I could see that it was Talant's cave. The one I visited in my dreams. Only there wasn't an enormous cushion and pillows in the center as there had been in my dreams. Instead, it was a thick slab of stone, like an altar. Or the top of a sarcophagus.

I struggled to catch my breath, but the pain in my chest returned.

This time I didn't fight it. I listened to my instincts and thought about my intention.

If the entity possessing Sommerton wanted me to wake Talant, I was going to make sure that I used enough power to be certain that it happened.

My arms couldn't hold my weight anymore. I fell to my elbows as the pressure inside me grew. For the first time, I reached for it, grasped it with my thoughts.

Immediately, the agony eased. I could breathe again. I embraced the magic, bringing it deeper into my psyche. The power built further, growing more than it ever had before.

My upper body flew back, and my arms opened wide as I looked up at the ceiling. I could hear Sommerton speaking but couldn't understand what he was saying over the roar inside my head.

Wake.

The thought echoed in my mind, drifting through the magic filling me up.

I focused every fiber of my being on Talant, insisting that he wake up, that he rise from his prison.

"Wake," I said, reaching out for him.

There. He was stirring beneath the rock I knelt on. His magic twined with mine, winding through the cracks in the rock.

"Wake," I demanded, louder.

The slab beneath me trembled. The rock snapped and cracked as it shifted.

"Wake!" I screamed, shoving every bit of the power spilling through me down into the slab, willing Talant to rise from the depths of the stone.

A huge crack appeared beneath me, running from the front of the slab to the back. The white light of my magic glowed as it flowed from my body and deeper into the mountain. It felt like my body was cracking along with the stone. I convulsed on the slab of rock, my back arching and my neck stretching. Now that I'd pulled on the magic filling me, it was flowing, no, exploding through me. I had no control over the force within me. I could only ride the tsunami that was about to devastate me.

My magic crashed around the spell surrounding Talant's form. It was the same reddish-gold as his eyes and his magic, but it vanished at the first touch of mine.

My body rose above the rock, floating in mid-air as the slab crumbled and disintegrated beneath me. I moved back until I hovered over the solid part of the floor. My feet touched the ground as Talant's power spiraled out of the hole forming in the floor, his magic the color of blood and gold as it overtook the white light of mine.

The wind howled through the cave, blowing my hair back, as the floor continued to split. I felt him rising, faster and faster, until his body flew through the hole. There was a loud roar of rock and magic, and the cave went completely dark.

I rocked back on my heels, my balance wavering now that I didn't have the insane amount of power running through my veins.

My magic was still there, humming beneath my skin, but it was gentle and calm. A warm glow that filled me rather than a maelstrom that threatened to swallow me whole.

"Ally."

My name echoed in the cave, the whispered word resonating all around me.

I blinked, trying to focus my eyes in the darkness after all the bright lights that had filled the cave moments before.

Then, I saw him, standing only a few feet from me. Naked as a damn jaybird again.

I turned my back to him. "Gah! Put some pants on."

"Where am I supposed to find pants?" he asked, amusement clear in his voice.

"Conjure some up. You're a god, after all."

Talant laughed. "Done."

I turned to face him again, finding him much closer to me. The cave was also brighter. I realized that he must have conjured up some candles and lamps as well.

"I can't believe you're here," I said.

I reached out and hugged him, so glad to finally see him in person.

Thunderous footsteps echoed in the cave and Talant was yanked from my arms. He went flying across the space, somehow managing to land on his feet. I stumbled back, tripping over my bare feet, yelping when my heel landed on a sharp stone.

Dax was there, in full gargoyle form. He towered over me even more than usual, at least seven and a half feet tall. Maybe even eight. His skin was grey and stretched over muscles that swelled and tensed beneath. His wings flared behind him, spiked and curved, the membrane over them black as pitch but they gleamed like leather. Black horns spiraled over his head and his eyes glowed like molten silver. His mouth formed a snarl, showing his fangs.

Violet magic slammed into his back, rocking him forward. Dax whirled and roared at Sommerton.

"Enough!" Talant's voice filled the cave, making the walls shake.

Dax crouched slightly in front of me, his wings sweeping back to surround me. "You dare touch my mate," he growled.

My body stiffened at his words. Mate? What in the world was he talking about? Just last night he said that he couldn't give me what I wanted, and he hadn't said one word in argument this morning when I told him that I wasn't going to take whatever scraps he offered me.

"I see no mating mark on her neck," Talant replied.

I couldn't see him, but his tone was calm, almost taunting.

Dax snarled again, his body tensing even more.

"But Ally is my Anointed, not my paramour."

I rolled my eyes behind Dax's back at Talant's choice of words. Paramour? Good grief, he was laying it on thick.

I ducked beneath Dax's wing and stepped in front of him. "Tal, stop egging him on."

A grin spread across Talant's face. "But it's so easy."

"I don't care. Knock it the hell off!"

He shrugged. "Fine."

Dax grabbed my waist, pulling me back into his body. I didn't shove his hands away, but I did hold myself perfectly still and rigid.

Talant turned toward Sommerton, holding out his hand. "Brother."

Sommerton stared at him for a moment with his creepy black and violet eyes before he took gripped Talant's forearm. "Brother."

"While I understand why you wished me to wake, I can't say I approve of your methods."

Sommerton's eyes narrowed. "I don't recall you complaining about how I did things before."

"Ally is my Anointed and her aunt is special to her. What you have wrought means you will likely not be welcomed here when you're free."

"We have no need of this place," Sommerton said, releasing Talant's arm.

"You have no need of this place, but I must train my Anointed. It is my responsibility to prepare her for what she will face when it comes to her power."

Sommerton scowled. "Then, bring her with you. The world is a big place now, brother. We can go back to the old ways. They will serve us again. We have only to take what we want as we once did."

Talant shook his head. "I don't want my old life. I want a new life. I want to honor her the way I should have then."

Her? Who were they talking about? Me?

Sommerton looked as though he'd been slapped. "You lie. She imprisoned us both!"

Talant shook his head. "No, she didn't. I chose to sleep. It was for the best."

Sommerton stepped back, a sneer on his face, and a portal of black smoke and purple lightning forming behind him. "You will change your mind once you've had a taste of what this world offers,

Talant. But, first, you must free me. I am weakening here as they feed from my power. I do not know how much longer I have before I fade."

Talant nodded. "I will come for you. Then, we will talk."

Sommerton stepped back through the portal, his form disappearing in the black smoke.

CHAPTER
NINETEEN

As soon as he was gone, I moved away from Dax, heading straight for my aunt but Talant beat me there. He knelt next to Minerva, his fingers curving around her chin where it rested on her chest.

I skidded to a halt next to them, crouching down. Minerva seemed to be unconscious. I reached out and took her hand in mine, rubbing her forearm gently.

"MinMin, you need to wake up."

Her head shifted, turning side to side. The bruise on her cheek was even uglier than it had appeared in the mirror. Tears welled in my eyes when I saw the small slice on her throat, the blood dried where it had flowed down her neck and over her collarbone.

As my tears fell, I wished I could heal all these injuries on her. I hated to see her hurt and in pain.

All at once, my hands began to glow with white light. The light encompassed Minerva's hand and ran up her arm. The shimmering magic moved beneath her skin, spreading up her chest to her throat. The small cut on her neck vanished as though it had never been.

I could feel my magic moving under her skin, into her muscles and bones. There were small fractures in her ribs. They healed with a thought. The bruise on her face shrank and the swelling faded until both were gone as though they had never been.

When my magic sensed that she was fully healed, the flow from my hands into her body trickled to a stop.

Once the white light faded, Minerva inhaled deeply, a low moan coming from her throat, and her eyes opened. As soon as she saw me, she sat up, her hands grasping at my arms.

"Ally, dear goddess, are you okay? What are you doing here? I told you to stay away!"

I patted her biceps. "I'm okay, Aunt Minnie. I'm safe. Sommerton is gone and Talant is awake."

At my words, she turned and saw Talant kneeling beside her. They locked eyes for a long moment, and I felt something shift in the air, a sort of electricity that seemed to crackle between them before it vanished completely.

"I missed everything, didn't I?" she asked, turning back toward me.

I nodded. "But that might be for the best because it was pure chaos for a while."

Her hands came up to cup my cheeks. "You've come into your power. I can see it inside you, shining like a star."

Tears filled my eyes as I nodded. I'd given up hope a decade ago, convinced I would always just be human. I thought I'd come to terms with it, but it seemed I was wrong. Feeling this power shimmering inside me, it was indescribable, and it felt...right.

"Sweet girl, you are exactly who you were meant to be, even before you manifested."

I nodded, sniffling.

"Now, I think I need to go home," Minerva said. "My injuries may be healed, but my body still wants to rest."

"I'll take you," I said, getting to my feet. I wasn't ready to be parted from her just yet. Not with the terror still swirling in my mind at the thought of how close I might have come to losing her.

Dax's arm wound around my waist, something Minerva noted

with a small smile. "Ally, I love you, but I don't want to be fussed over. I just want to lie down and sleep for twelve hours straight. I'll be fine on my own."

Minerva sat up, ready to get to her feet. I reached down to help her, but Talant was already there, his hands beneath her elbows.

"MinMin," I started to say, but I was interrupted.

A low moan came from the corner, and we all turned together, peering into the darkness. Talant waved a hand and more candles appeared against that wall, flaring to life with flame.

A woman huddled in the corner, her bare legs dirty and bruised. Her blonde hair was matted with dirt and goddess knew what else. She groaned, turning her head toward us and I gasped.

It was Leona. Her hands were bound with silver shackles and attached to her waist with a chain.

Minerva approached her, crouching down just out of arm's reach. "Leona, can you hear me?"

The shifter cracked her eyes open and stared at her. "Minerva?" she asked.

"Yes."

"Has the blood god awoken?" she croaked.

"Yes," Minerva answered. "He's here."

Leona's head craned as she looked around until her eyes pinned to Talant. "I have a request."

I blinked at Leona. With everything that had happened and the fact that she was freaking chained, all she cared about was speaking to Talant?

Talant walked over to her. "I'm not in the habit of granting requests from those who offer no compensation."

Minerva's head whipped around, and she glared at him, her eyes gleaming with blue fire.

"But on this occasion, I'll consider it," Talant said, crossing his arms over his bare chest.

Leona moved, shoving herself up until she was standing. She

swayed on her feet and the shackles on her wrists jangled. Talant glanced down at them. The chain around her waist fell and the shackles followed immediately after.

"Ask your favor," he said, studying her as though he knew he wouldn't like what she wanted.

"As the god of blood, you can control blood bonds, yes?" Leona asked, lifting a hand, pressing it to the rock wall beside her to keep her body steady.

"I can," Talant agreed.

"I want to remove my mate bond," she stated, lifting her chin to meet his eyes. "My fated mate is weak and holds me back. I want it removed."

Talant cocked his head, his gaze sharpening. "The bond of a fated mate is a blessing. One meant to bring shifters in balance. His strengths should complement yours. That was the intention of the bond. Are you sure you don't wish to keep it?"

Leona shook her head. "I don't want it. I want to be in charge of my own fate. My own mate."

It was on the tip of my tongue to point out that she wouldn't be able to have another male in her life because he would leave her for a fated mate or always mourn the loss of his mate if she was no longer of this earth.

Minerva seemed to sense my thoughts and shook her head.

It was difficult, but I remained silent.

"Very well. I will remove the bond, but it is not a favor for you," Talant finally said, lowering his arms from where they were crossed over his chest. "I'm doing this for your mate. He deserves far more than you and I will ensure that he receives it."

Leona sighed, an impatient sound, and nodded. "Fine."

I understood then why Talant wasn't telling her to fuck off, as I assumed he would. He felt sorry for her mate, not her.

He lifted his hands in front of him, gathering a ball of blood-red magic between his palms. There was no gold threaded within it. He murmured a few words beneath his breath in a language I didn't understand and released the magic.

The ball split in two as it flew from his hands. One beelined straight for Leona and the other zipped through the cave and out the same opening that Dax had appeared through.

The red glow sank into Leona's chest and dissipated beneath her skin.

"It's done," Talant said.

"My thanks." With that reply, Leona strode toward the same exit the magic had taken and disappeared into the darkness. She didn't look back.

I shook my head. I didn't understand her at all. Was that all she had wanted? To have her mate bond broken? She'd kidnapped Sela and tried to use her to free the blood god for nothing more than her desire to get rid of her fated mate?

Talant turned toward me. "Well, that was interesting," he said. "Is everyone in this town like her?"

Somehow, I found myself smiling, but I shook my head. "No. Most of us are friendlier and not as bitchy."

His lips twitched into a brief smile as well. "Well, I look forward to you showing me around."

Before I could answer, Dax's arm went around my waist again, pulling me into him. I scowled down at it. But now wasn't time to bring it up. Once this was over and I knew my aunt was going to be okay, he and I were going to have words. It wasn't right for him to tell me one day that he didn't want me and then the next to behave like a possessive Neanderthal.

My aunt saved the day because she jumped right in. "You will stay with us at my home," she said.

I knew it was because she wanted to keep an eye on him and keep him from creating problems with his mere presence.

He looked back at her, a twinkle in his eye. "I'm delighted to accept your gracious invitation."

It was Minerva's turn to give him a skeptical look.

An awkward silence fell, but I was saved from having to address the big gargoyle in the room by the appearance of Garrett Kent, the police chief of Devil Springs, and Daniel Ayers, the mayor.

They burst into the cavern, skidding to a stop when they saw it was only the four of us inside.

"Where's Sommerton?" Garrett barked.

"Gone," Minerva answered.

"Who's that?" Daniel asked, pointing at Talant.

"The blood god," she answered before anyone else could speak.

My aunt swayed on her feet, her face suddenly paler than usual. Talant reached out and scooped her up in his arms.

She scowled up at him. "I'm fine. You don't need to carry me."

"I'm a god, I do what I want," Talant drawled.

Minerva started to struggle a bit, but even I could see that it was a weak resistance.

Talant looked at me. "It's time to head home. Your aunt needs rest."

I nodded and tried to step forward, but Dax's arm around my waist stopped me. I looked over my shoulder at him, a frown on my face.

"Dax, I need to go home."

"No," he growled.

Talant's expression grew distant and cold. Suddenly, he looked every bit like the god he was as he seemed to grow taller before my very eyes. "Release her, gargoyle."

Dax shook his head. "No. She comes with me." When I gaped up at him in astonished anger, he continued. "For now. I will bring her to her home tomorrow."

Before I could say anything else or refute his words, Minerva sighed, her head drooping to rest on Talant's shoulder. "It's fine," she murmured. "He won't hurt her."

Her eyelids were drooping as well.

"He already has hurt her," Talant growled, ruby fire burning in his eyes.

"Ally," my aunt said, ignoring him.

I looked from Talant to her.

"Go with him for now," she said. "Talk it out. I'll see you tomorrow."

I swallowed and shook my head. "I...can't."

My whisper was tortured, and her expression softened. "Trust me, sweet girl."

Tears threatened to overwhelm me, but Talant distracted me before the first could fall.

He walked closer to us, stopping just in front of me, and glared at Dax with angry eyes. "If she wants to come home tonight, you bring her, stone man. Or I will find you and I will take her wherever she wants to go."

Dax snarled at him, a wordless sound of anger. "Your magic is useless against me."

Talant's mouth curved, but it was sharp, more a baring of teeth than a smile. "Remember, Daxys, gargoyles aren't immune to all magic. I've been around much longer than you and I know exactly how to turn you to dust."

Dax's arm tightened around me, pulling me back until my shoulders crashed into his abdomen.

"If she wants to come home after we talk, I will bring her," Dax agreed.

Talant studied him and the ruby fire in his eyes banked. "Very well." He looked at me, his eyes the color of aged gold. "I will see you soon, little witch."

I nodded, still frozen at the idea of being forced to go anywhere with Dax after the things that had happened last night and this morning.

"So, we missed everything?" Garrett asked, interrupting the interlude.

"Yep," Minerva said. "But it's probably for the best." She paused. "Wait, didn't you see Leona on your way in."

Garrett and Daniel exchanged a glance and then they both shook their heads.

"She was here?" Daniel asked.

Minerva nodded. "You should send someone to check on her mate—" She paused at the sound Talant made deep in his chest. "Her former mate. Talant broke their mate bond and I'm worried what it might have done to him."

"He should have no ill effects," Talant murmured.

"Still, just in case," my aunt argued.

Talant's eyes came to mine, and he sighed as though my aunt was already exhausting him. I merely shrugged. I'd warned him what Minerva was like and he still wanted to meet her. I wasn't going to say *I told you so*, but I wasn't going to step in to save him either.

"I'll take care of it," Garrett said. "I need to see if she went home, anyway. She has some explaining to do. And crimes to answer for." His voice was little more than a snarl.

"I can go," Daniel insisted.

They began to argue in whispers. I couldn't understand what they were saying, but Dax's arm grew even tighter around me.

"I need to go home and sleep," Minerva murmured, interrupting the hushed conversation drifting between Daniel and Garrett. She lifted a hand to me. "See you tomorrow, sweet girl. Not too early, though. I'm not kidding about needing the twelve hours of sleep," she said.

Talant didn't wait for my response, he turned, a portal of red and gold magic shimmering into sight behind him. He glanced down at my aunt and said, "Think of home."

Then, he stepped through the portal, and they vanished from sight.

"Dax, we should—" Garrett began, coming toward us.

Dax took a step back, dragging my body with him. "Stay back," he growled.

Garrett froze, his eyes flicking between Dax and me. Slowly, he raised his hands and took three steps back. "I'm not a threat, brother. I'm mated, remember?"

Dax growled again, a wordless vibration. "Don't care. Get out of my way."

It was Daniel's turn to try to reason with him. "Dax—"

"Tomorrow," Dax rumbled, his voice so deep that the rocks around us seemed to vibrate.

He didn't wait for their response. He scooped me up, clutching me to his chest, and took to the air, swooping past them into a long, rough stone hallway. The sun hurt my eyes when we burst out of the cave, and I gaped at how high up we were. I didn't even know there was a cave here.

The mountains in Texas weren't as tall or rugged as the Rockies or green like the Appalachians. They were more like big hills, but they were still beautiful.

Dax soared through the air, rising higher as he wove through the mountains. I shivered at the chill in the wind this far above the ground.

He cradled me closer, as though he wanted to share his body heat with me.

We flew in complete silence for about ten minutes, before Dax began to descent, spiraling down near the peak of another mountain.

I didn't see the ledge leading into the cave until we were right above it and Dax was dropping down to land.

His wings flapped once, curving to catch the air as he dropped down onto the rock outcropping. He didn't stop moving, immediately transitioning from flight to walking without a pause.

It was only when we were in the shadows beneath the overhang that I saw the stone wall with a heavy steel door set in it. Dax shifted my weight so he could reach behind a rock on the other side of the ledge. He pulled out a skeleton key after fishing around for a few minutes.

I didn't say anything at all as he went to the door, unlocked it, and shoved it open. I squinted as he crouched and carried me inside the dark space.

I remained still in his arms until he shut the door behind us. It wasn't until I heard the key re-enter the lock and the bolt slide home with a clang that I realized he was locking me inside.

With him.

CHAPTER

TWENTY

"Stay here," Dax murmured when he sat me on my feet. The room was completely dark, not even a stray sunbeam peeking through the door.

I heard nothing but the air around me felt empty, so I knew he'd walked away from me.

I waited for a long moment, my breaths sounding loud in the pitch-black silence. The magic hummed in my blood, reminding me that I was no longer human but a witch. A very powerful one.

I bent my arm at the elbow, lifting my palm up even with my waist. Then, I focused on bringing light to the cavernous space.

Quicker than ever before, a ball of white magic formed over my open palm. It swelled until it was the size of a huge paper lantern, but it was three times as bright. I tossed it into the air, imagining it floating five or six feet above my head.

My magic responded effortlessly rather than with the sluggishness I'd felt before. It seemed now that I had manifested, I had no trouble shaping my power with my intentions. Which reminded me that I couldn't wait to try some of the spells that I'd memorized when I was younger, and my aunt was still teaching me about magic because she thought I was a witch.

While she and Talant both insisted that intention was the most important part of magic, I knew that spells could sharpen that intention to a fine razor point, guiding the magic to work in a chain reaction to achieve a desired result.

As the light spread throughout the room, I saw that there was a bed against the stone wall to my right, the mattress even bigger than the one at his cabin. Also, unlike his bed at the cabin, it was piled with pillows of all shapes and sizes and covered with a fluffy duvet and what looked like an insanely soft faux fur blanket.

My gaze moved from the bed to the back wall. There were two passages exiting the back of this cave, but it was what was against the back walls that caught my attention. There were huge shelves made of wood and stone that soared eight or nine feet into the air and stretched along the entirety of the wall.

On those shelves were books, knickknacks, photographs, paintings, and sculptures. A huge, low sofa faced a firepit in the center of the cave, flanked by two rustic wooden tables that appeared to be handmade.

Another wooden table stood to the left with one chair shoved beneath it, also appearing to be handmade.

A primitive kitchen was against the far-left wall, a short cabinet that held a tiny sink and drainboard for dishes. There were three shelves above the cabinet, and they held a basket of spices, a set of four plates, bowls, and cups, and a jar filled with silverware and cooking utensils. The middle shelf held several pots and pans and the one above that held a kettle, a teapot, and a Dutch oven.

As I surveyed the space, I realized that this was where Dax actually lived, where he was actually himself. I heard a loud clang followed by a low hum. My eyes widened when I looked and saw bare light bulbs strung along the walls above where Dax's head would be in full gargoyle form. There was a lamp on the nightstand next to the bed that also blinked on.

I glanced up at the ball of magic still hovering in the air and released it with a thought. By the time Dax made his way back into the space, the white ball of light had completely dissipated.

Dax was no longer in full gargoyle form. His body had shrunk back to his normal human dimensions and his wings were gone. His skin was still grey, and his horns still spiraled above his head, but he wasn't quite as intimidating as he'd been earlier.

I watched in silence as he dropped the leather strap that held the key to the door over his head. Then, he walked to the fire pit, laid out a few longs, and started a small fire. He didn't look at me or speak to me.

I prowled past the bed to the back wall of shelves and started looking through the books and other detritus. To my surprise, most of the books were fiction, everything from classic literature to the latest thrillers and even a few romance novels.

But what truly caught my attention was the photographs. They were scattered throughout the shelves, all at eye level with Dax or below. There were none on the upper most shelves.

My heart began to pound in my chest as I paced back and forth, studying each one.

I was in every single photo. Some were of Minerva and me together, either embracing or doing something. Others were of me alone, usually when I wasn't even looking at the camera. There were even a few of me as a child or a teenager. He even had one of my baby pictures!

Confused, I turned around to find Dax standing right behind me, his hands clasped behind his back. He didn't look implacable right now, just solemn, and maybe a little sad.

"Dax, why do you have so many pictures of Minerva and me?" I asked.

His dark blue eyes stayed glued to mine. "Because, somehow, the two of you became my family."

My heart was no longer pounding, it was racing, so fast that I wasn't sure I could stay upright. I stumbled over to the small kitchen table and collapsed into the chair.

Against my will, tears formed in my eyes. "You don't hurt your family the way you hurt me last night." I sniffled but blinked the water away from my eyes. "And then, when you were facing down Talant and his brother today, you called me your mate. I'm pretty sure I have whiplash from how quickly you changed your attitude." I waved a hand toward the front of the cave. "And you've locked me in here with you!"

"I will regret the way I spoke to you last night for the rest of my life," Dax murmured. "And I will never forgive myself for not talking to you this morning." He glanced at the door. "As for locking you in here, it has more to do with making sure we're not interrupted rather than keeping you here."

He crouched down in front of me, his face nearly level with mine even though he was basically on his knees.

"Ally, no one is good enough for you. Least of all me. But the idea —" His voice cracked, like a stone breaking in two. When he continued, his words held a tremor. "I may not be worthy of you, but I know I would work harder than any other male to make sure that you were happy for the rest of your life. That you know without a doubt that you are the center of my world, and the sun doesn't rise in the morning if you aren't there when I wake up. No one deserves you but you deserve to have someone who will do anything for you. And I think that's me."

Damn, the tears were back. His words chipped away a bit of my resolve to remain distant. I hardened myself. I couldn't let myself be easily swayed just because he was saying all the things I wished he'd said yesterday.

"I don't know if I can trust that, Dax," I said.

He looked tortured at my word. He didn't reach out, but his hands twitched as though he wanted to. "It's not an excuse, but you have to understand that I have lost anyone and everyone I've ever loved. Everyone I was meant to protect was murdered. There are still nights, centuries later, where I relive those days over and over again in my dreams." He leaned closer. "My biggest fear is adding your face to those dreams. And to that loss."

My breath caught in my chest. There were tears shimmering in his eyes. This man, this gargoyle, who always seemed to be in perfect control of his emotions, was crying at the mere thought of losing me. My heart wanted to soften again, but I didn't allow it. I couldn't give in just because he gave me a sweetly worded apology. He had to understand that, yes, he was correct—I deserved better than that. And also, that I wasn't going to sit back and let him do it over and over again just because he said he was sorry.

"Shat happens when you get scared again, Dax?" I asked. "You say I deserve someone who will do anything for me but what happens when you realize that nothing in life is guaranteed, and it gets the better of you?"

My words were soft and gentle, but he winced as though I'd slapped him across the face.

It was my turn to lean forward, our faces only a few inches apart. "While I do deserve better than the way you treated me, I think I should be the one to decide if someone is worthy of me or not," I said. "That's not your decision unless I ask you to select my future husband. Am I clear?"

Dax blinked at my stern question but nodded. His hand reached out to take mine, lifting it from where it rested on my lap.

"I am truly sorry, Ally. More than I can ever explain with words." He took a deep breath and released it. Then, he continued, "I think I fell in love with you the first time I saw you after you graduated college. But I was convinced that it was wrong. That your aunt wouldn't approve. That I would be taking advantage of your youthful feelings for me."

I squeezed his hand, shocked that he was able to admit all of that out loud. It was another chip in the wall I'd been trying to build around my heart since last night.

"What I felt for you when I was a teenager and in my early twenties, it was love, but it wasn't what I feel now. Before this week, I never saw your flaws, Dax. To me, you were perfect."

His expression began to shutter.

I cupped his cheek with my other hand. "But now I see that it's not true. You're not perfect. You're just perfect for me. You say I deserve someone who will do anything for me, and I've always thought the same thing about you."

He leaned forward until our foreheads touched and his eyes closed. His horns were surprisingly smooth where they rested against my head, and I could feel the slight roughness of his grey skin.

Goddess, maybe it made me weak, but I wanted to give him another chance. But, just as he was scared that he would lose me, I was afraid that he was going to push me away again.

We were going to have to lay it all out with each other. It was the only way I could move past this.

"I want you to give me an honest answer to a question," I said.

He leaned back, his eyes opening to gaze into mine. For once, I could read every emotion, every thought, on his face. "I will tell you anything."

Another brick knocked out of the wall I'd desperately built last night.

"What do you see in your future?" He looked confused, so I reworded the question. "If you could have any future between us, what would it look like?"

He swallowed hard. "What I want?"

I nodded.

"I want to wake up next to you every morning and have breakfast together. I want to share the highs and lows of life with you. The good days and the bad days. I want to have dinner with you in the evening and go to bed beside you every night. Whether we travel the world or never leave Devil Springs, I want to be by your side."

It was my turn to swallow hard. Dear goddess, his vision of our future was mine. The wall around my heart began to crumble, shaken by what I could see in his eyes and hear in his voice. He was sincere.

His mouth was a breath from mine when he continued speaking, "And, someday, if you wanted, I want to build a family with you."

My mouth went dry. "Are you talking about...children?" I asked.

"Yes," he whispered. "Do you think that is something you would want?"

I released a shaky breath. I wanted to pinch myself. He was saying all the things I sometimes dreamed he would say to me. There was no shield I could build that would hold up against the sight of him on his knees before me, asking me if I would want children with him.

He released my hands, shifting closer to cup my face. "Ally, I can't promise I won't hurt you because there will be times that I upset you or that we argue, but I will never do it intentionally. I will never lie to you. And I will never make you feel as though I don't love you."

My thoughts were racing even faster than my heartbeat. I lifted my hands to clasp his wrists.

"Now, Ally, tell me what you want."

"Everything you do," I whispered.

He frowned at me. "No, I want to know what you want for our future, too. Not for you just to agree to everything I said."

I shook my head, a tear trickling down my cheek. "You don't understand. I'm not saying this because it's what you want, and I want to please you. Everything you talked about is what I've always dreamed of. I want a simple life. I learned far too young that the things we take for granted can be snatched away in the blink of an eye. Those are the memories I want to build. To cherish."

He kissed me then, his lips brushing mine like a whisper.

"Can you forgive me?" he asked.

"I can," I said.

"Can you give me time to prove to you that you can trust me not to push you away again?"

"I can," I repeated.

His hands moved from my face to my sides and down to my hips. Dax got to his feet, bringing me with him. I squeaked and wrapped my legs around his waist.

"What are you doing?" I asked, my voice breathless.

He answered my question with another question. "How do you feel about make-up sex?"

I couldn't completely bite back the smile that wanted to surface. "I don't know. I've never had it."

"Me either," he said.

I slipped my hands from his shoulders to the back of his neck, running my fingers through his hair.

I didn't know what to do with this Dax, the one who wasn't actively hiding what he was thinking and feeling from me.

"Want to try it and then decide if it's a good idea?" he asked.

I couldn't hold back my laugh this time. "Absolutely."

He walked across the cave to the bed and leaned forward, putting one hand and one knee on the bed before he lowered me to the blankets.

He wasn't wearing a shirt, so my hands wandered over his shoulders and chest, stroking his skin. He was still grey, and his skin held the faint roughness of stone.

Dax's hands went to the bottom hem of my shirt, his fingers sliding under it to skim over my belly. Then, he tugged it up and off me in a swift motion.

His hands returned to my body, moving to cup my breasts through my bra. His thumbs brushed over my nipples before he tugged the thin cotton aside. He leaned down and I gasped when his mouth enveloped my nipple and he sucked, soft at first and then harder and deeper.

My back arched as heat spread through my body, leaving tingles in its wake.

Dax released my breast and focused on the button and zip of my pants. A few seconds later, my pants and panties were on the floor next to the bed. He slid his hands behind me to the clasp of my bra and stripped it from me as well, leaving me naked on the plush fur blanket that was spread over his bed.

Then, he worshipped every inch of me.

His mouth started at my throat, his tongue and the tips of his fangs skimming over my skin and bringing goosebumps up on my arms. My nipples hardened as his lips cruised down my chest to my breasts. He tugged each of my nipples in his mouth, leaving them wet and aching before he moved down to nip the flesh of my stomach.

He moved down, his palms slipping down my thighs. In a swift motion, he shoved my knees up and apart, spreading me wide.

I gasped at the suddenness of the motion.

He ignored me, his eyes glued to my pussy. Then, he leaned down and ran his tongue over me in one long, slow lick. I gasped again, my entire body jerking. His tongue wasn't smooth any longer but ridged. Each one seemed to tug at my clit as his tongue dragged over it.

"Dax!"

I grabbed his horns and shoved his head up a bit. He stopped, his swirling silver eyes locked on me.

"Your tongue," I panted. "It's different."

He smirked at me. "It's not the only thing that's different about me in this form."

I blinked at him, confused, until his hand went to the waistband of his jeans. Then, the penny dropped and my mouth fell open.

"What?" I asked, unable to take my gaze away from where he was flicking open the button of his jeans and unzipping them. He climbed off the bed and shoved his pants off, kicking his boots off at the same time.

When he moved, I rolled over and crawled toward the edge of the mattress. His cock jutted out in front of him, darker grey than his skin. I saw then what he was talking about. There were ridges around the base of his dick, thick and rounded on top. They extended nearly halfway up, spaced closer together at the bottom and further apart as they rose.

I reached out, grasping his hard length. His cock jumped at my touch. I stroked him, feeling the firmness of each ridge as my hand moved down to the base of his dick.

I squeezed at the base, and he hissed as he exhaled. I crept closer and flicked the tip of his cock with my tongue.

His body jerked and his hands fisted at his sides.

"Ally, now is not the time to check off another item on your list."

I lifted my gaze to his face, and I sucked the tip of his erection into my mouth. His cock was as smooth as his horns. I drew him deeper, my hand stroking his base as I did, and Dax's entire body tensed.

"By the gods, Ally," he said, his voice full of gravel and deeper than usual.

Before I could continue my exploration, Dax pulled his hips away before he shoved me onto my back.

"I wasn't done," I complained.

"Later," he said, lowering his head between my thighs.

His hands pinned my legs down to the mattress and he attacked my pussy with his mouth. He sucked my clit hard, wringing a cry from my lips, before lashing it with his tongue.

I cried out, my back arching, at the intensity of the sensation. The ridges on his tongue added an edge to the pleasure.

As he focused on my clit, driving me toward orgasm with single-minded intensity, he released one of my legs to push one finger deep inside of me. Then, another. He crooked his fingers, rubbing a spot deep inside me. The pressure inside me intensified, winding my body tighter.

"Dax," I gasped, my hands flying to his horns, gripping them tightly.

He growled against my pussy and his mouth became ravaging. I lifted my hips as I tugged his horns, and he added a third finger inside my body.

He sucked my clit harder, flicking it with his tongue rapidly, and I imploded. The orgasm was a wave of pleasure spiked with pain as it wracked my body, every muscle shuddering as I spasmed.

But he didn't stop. His tongue and his lips kept torturing my clit until I was trying to shove his head away. The orgasm never waned, only built higher until one climax became two.

I screamed as I thrashed on the bed, unable to escape. Just when the pleasure was about to become too painful, he released me, rising up over me and wiping his mouth with the back of his hand.

I was panting as I collapsed against the blanket, a fine sheen of sweat on my entire body. The air in the cave was cool, bringing up goosebumps all over me as it touched my damp skin.

Dax levered his body over me, his mouth crashing against mine. I locked my legs around his hips as he kissed me, rough and urgent. I reached between us, wrapping my fingers around his cock and angling my hips. I shivered when the tip of his dick slipped over my clit, sending another shockwave through me.

Dax didn't make me wait. He tilted his hips, his hand over mine, and slipped inside me in one long, deep thrust.

I tore my mouth away from his as the breath left my body. I shuddered beneath him, my hands clutching his waist.

"Dax," I gasped.

He wasn't smirking anymore. His face was fierce as he withdrew from me and pushed inside me again. I could feel every single ridge and they were destroying me.

Neither of us spoke as his hips moved, keeping a slow, steady pace. He kissed me again, his tongue mirroring the motions of his cock inside me.

He groaned when my nails dragged down his back to his hips before I gripped his ass hard, trying to urge him to move faster.

The tension was building inside me again and I moaned when he changed the angle of his thrusts, dragging those ridges over my sensitive clit with each movement.

Dax tore his mouth from mine, his quicksilver eyes swirling and glowing. "Will you wear my mark?" he asked.

When I stared at him in a daze, he stopped, making me cry out in denial. "Dax! Don't stop!"

His hands grabbed my hips when I tried to move, holding me down. "Ally, will you wear my mating bite?"

It wasn't until then that I understood what he was asking me, and I nodded. "Yes."

He withdrew further from me, and I made a noise of pure frustration.

"Are you sure?" he asked. "I don't have to—"

"Dax, I said yes. Now, fuck me and bite me," I demanded, reaching up to grasp his horns and yank his face toward mine.

He was smiling when he kissed me. At least until his hips slammed into mine, his cock rubbing that spot inside me that drove me wild. He thrust into me, hard and fast, hammering that spot until I was writhing beneath him.

"Goddess, Dax," I panted. "I'm going to—"

The orgasm tore through me like a wildfire, scorching my nerve endings. Dax nudged my head to the side, and he sank his fangs into my neck.

I screamed as the pleasure increased twofold. My hands left his horns to curl around the back of his neck, cradling his face against my throat.

He groaned into my neck, his thrusts losing their steady rhythm. He slammed into me one last time, his hands pinning me to the bed as his big body shuddered over mine.

We stayed locked together, riding the wave of pleasure together until it receded and left us breathless and wrecked on the bed.

I opened my eyes, blinking at the bright white light above me. I realized that my right hand was glowing with magic. As I stared at it, the light faded.

Dax ran his tongue over the bite mark on my throat. It throbbed for a moment, and I felt bone-deep satisfaction. But it wasn't my emotion. It belonged to Dax. Beneath that satisfaction was something far better—the warm embers of his love.

He lifted his head, looking down at me, and his silver eyes were glowing with the same white light of my magic. And, on his neck, my handprint glowed. I ran a fingertip over it and felt his surprise.

"What is that?" he asked, staring down at me.

"I marked you," I murmured. "It's my handprint."

A smile spread across his face. "You marked me?"

"I didn't mean to," I said. "But I'm not sorry."

His smile widened. "I'm not either." He stared down at me, his hand coming to my face. "I can feel you. In my heart," he said.

I let my hand slip down his chest until it rested over his heart. "I can feel you, too. Does that mean we're mated?"

"It does," he answered.

He wore his happiness on his face, his eyes losing the white glow of my magic and returning to the beautiful swirling silver I loved.

"You look happy," I whispered.

"I'm happier than I have ever been," he murmured back, moving down to press his lips to mine in a soft kiss.

"I can feel it." I sighed as contentment washed over me, this time, the emotion was my own.

Dax kissed the bite mark on my neck, making me shiver again. "Thank you," he murmured.

"For what?" I asked, smiling a little.

He lifted his head, staring down at me. "For not giving up on me."

I couldn't stop the tears that welled in my eyes and trickled down my temples to my hair. "I won't give up on you as long as you don't give up on me."

"Good, because I never want to be apart from you again."

After he kissed me again, he asked, "Are you hungry?"

My tears had dried up and I smiled up at him, my right hand going to the handprint on his neck and pulling him down. I laughed a little when he shivered against me, his softening cock suddenly getting harder.

"Not for food," I answered, nipping his bottom lip.

"But—"

"Later," I said. "Kiss me."

As he promised, he gave me what I wanted.

CHAPTER
TWENTY-ONE

As soon as I walked into Aunt Minerva's living room the next afternoon, Dax's fingers laced with mine, her eyes zeroed in on the mating mark on my neck and a huge smile spread across her face.

She jumped to her feet, clapping her hands. Little gold sparkles flew up into the air with each clap, her magic leaking due to her excitement.

"You're mated!" she squealed.

She crossed the room and yanked me into her arms, hugging me so tightly that the breath left my lungs.

Dax released my hand so I could hug her back. Just as quickly as she grabbed me, Minerva released me and lunged toward Dax, wrapping her arms around his waist.

"I'm so happy!" she said.

More golden sparkles flew through the air, dancing around the living room like magical fireflies.

"I can tell," Dax drawled.

She released him and smiled. "Your grumpy face won't work on me anymore," she said.

He sighed, his eyes sliding over to me as though he was put out.

"I see that you finally claimed her."

We all looked toward the doorway to find Talant leaning against the entry, his arms crossed over his chest. His bare chest.

"Why aren't you wearing a shirt?" I asked. "You aren't a caveman anymore."

He smirked at me and then at Minerva when she sighed. "As I told your aunt, I will wear clothes when I'm in public. As long as I'm somewhere private, I will be comfortable."

Talant straightened, his arms dropping to his side, and came forward. He held his hand out to Dax, who stared down at it with a blank expression. It was the first time I'd seen that look on his face since we entered his private cave yesterday.

"Congratulations on your mating," Talant said.

When Dax still didn't take his hand, he chuckled and lowered it. "I'm not going to challenge you for your mate, Daxys. She is a friend and my Anointed. That is all."

When Dax still stared at him in silence, I moved closer to him and nudged him with an elbow. He glanced over at me.

"Be nice," I hissed softly.

It was Dax's turn to sigh. Then, he held out his hand to Talant, who took it immediately.

"Thank you for protecting her," Talant said. "She has told me so much about you. All of it good."

Dax grunted as he released Talant's hand but said nothing else.

I rolled my eyes and came forward, giving Talant a quick hug. Dax growled behind me, but I nudged him with my elbow again when I stepped away from the blood god.

"Chill out," I whispered. "He's more like a big brother than anything else. An annoying big brother at that."

Talant chuckled again and moved to stand next to my aunt. My eyes narrowed when I realized my aunt stiffened slightly at his nearness. She didn't look uncomfortable, exactly, but there was a tension between them that made my magic stir.

"Are you ready to explain what an Anointed is?" Minerva asked.

I stared at Talant. "You haven't told her?"

He shook his head, once again smirking, and I knew from that alone that he was trying to drive her nuts. It was funny. In a little over twenty-four hours, he'd figured out exactly how to get under her skin.

"Then, let's sit down so you can tell us all now that we're together," she said, her tone saying that she was done waiting.

Minerva sat in her usual chair, flashing a glare at Talant when he perched a hip on the arm and rested his hand on the back, basically looming over her. He merely winked at her.

Goddess, was he *flirting* with her?

"Please, enlighten us," Minerva invited him.

Dax and I took a seat on the couch. He put his arm across the back of the sofa and wound a lock of my hair around his finger. I leaned into him, noting the way my aunt's eyes lingered on his hand in my hair. She smiled slightly when she saw it.

I was still getting used to the fact that Dax wanted to touch me all the time. He held my hand, or sat close enough that our thighs touched, or he kept an arm around me. At night, he clutched my body against his like a human-sized teddy bear.

After how he kept me at arms' length for so long, it was taking some adjustment. I loved it, but it was definitely not what I was used to from him.

"An Anointed is a witch with the potential to become a god," Talant began. "But they have to make sacrifices to achieve it. Some choose to sacrifice those around them, not with blood sacrifice, but they sacrifice the love, respect, and good relationships they have with those closest to them in order to increase their power."

Minerva made a sound of distress but didn't interrupt.

Talant laid a gentle hand on her shoulder as he continued. "Some sacrifice of themselves. Their time, their magic. They give of themselves so much that the magic rewards them. Though most Anointed aren't of this ilk, there have been a few who have earned their godhood through their good deeds." He smiled at Minerva

224

and then at me. "I have a feeling your niece is this type of Anointed."

"What if I don't want godhood?" I asked.

Dax's hand stilled in my hair. In fact, his entire body went still. I wasn't even sure he was breathing.

"Then, you won't have it," Talant answered.

"You should consider it, Ally," Dax said, shocking me.

My head twisted around as I gaped at him. "Seriously?"

He took my hand in his free one, the hand in my hair moving to my shoulder. "Ally, gargoyles live a very, very long time. We are practically immortal. Your magic and my mating mark will give you some longevity, but nothing like my lifespan."

I opened my mouth to disagree, but I closed it again, still speechless from surprise.

"You have time to decide," Talant interrupted. "It doesn't have to be today, tomorrow, or even a year from now."

I laid my hand over Dax's. "We can talk about it later."

Dax looked like he wanted to argue, but he finally nodded. Huh. It seemed mating had calmed his need to control everything somewhat.

I turned back to Talant and asked, "What is a Conduit?"

He froze at my question, his body tensing. I could tell because all the muscles in his torso stood out in stark relief.

"Where did you hear that word?" he asked.

"There was a cat shifter here. She believed that's what I was. She saw me when I had to release a pulse of power before my manifestation."

Minerva shifted and looked up at him. He met her gaze, but his expression was shuttered.

"Answer her question, Talant," she said.

"It's a complicated answer."

"We have all damn day," she retorted.

He released a breath. It seemed that my aunt was learning how to get under his skin as well. "While an Anointed has the potential to become a god, a Conduit is the channel of a god's magic. They carry the heart of a god or goddess's power."

"What does that mean?" I asked.

He shook his head, rubbing his forehead with the tips of his fingers. His long dark hair fell over his shoulders and chest.

"He means that a Conduit is a god or goddess reborn," Minerva murmured. "Energy never dies and neither does magic. When a god or goddess dies, their energy has to go somewhere. It usually chooses the witch whose power resonates with their magic the most."

Talant stared down at her, a shocked expression on his face.

"I'm right, aren't I?' she asked.

He nodded. "How did you know?"

"Yeah, Minerva, how did you know that?" I asked.

My aunt shrugged. "Sometimes my intuition tells me what I need to know."

I squinted at her but didn't openly disagree with her.

"I thought gods couldn't die," I said, looking at Talant.

A fleeting expression of sorrow crossed his face. "While their magic can never die, sometimes their bodies will. Especially if they choose to give up their godhood. It's not easy to kill a god, but it has been done. Most who die do so because they feel they have lived too long, and it is time to move on."

That was definitely something I needed to know. If I ascended to godhood, I would have to live forever.

"After that lovely morose chat, I think it's time to discuss something else. Let's have some tea and snacks," my aunt said, getting to her feet.

She walked out of the living room and toward the kitchen. I watched how Talant watched her.

Then, I looked up at Dax. "I'm going to help her. And have a chat. No fighting with Tal."

He stared down at me, his expression clearly saying no promises.

I kissed his cheek, whispering in his ear. "I mean it, Dax. Be nice."

"Nice?" he rumbled.

"Polite then."

His only answer was a grunt.

I got up and followed Minerva's path into the kitchen. The kettle was on the stove to boil and there was a teapot and four teacups set out on a tray, but she wasn't there.

I found her standing in the sunroom off the back of the kitchen, surrounded by her potted herbs and flowers. She even had a dwarf lemon tree in one corner of the room.

Her back was to me, and her eyes seemed to be on the riot of green and color in her backyard. It was the middle of March, and her spring flowers were just beginning to bloom.

"MinMin?" I asked, coming to stand beside her.

She inhaled and looked over her shoulder at me. "You startled me."

"What's going on with you?" I asked.

She shrugged one shoulder. "Nothing really. I'm not sure if it was getting conked on the head by Sommerton or the healing you did on me, but I've been feeling a little off since yesterday."

"Do you need to see the healer?"

Minerva shook her head, her arms still hugging her waist. "No, I think I'm fine. I just feel...strange. Like something is supposed to be happening but I don't know what it is."

"You still haven't had a premonition?"

"Not a single one in days," she admitted with a sigh. "It's frightening me a little because I know that means I'm facing something potentially life-altering and this is fate's way of making sure I don't intervene."

I put an arm around her and rested my temple on her shoulder, much as I did when I was a child. It was just now that I was a little taller than her.

"Nothing can happen to you," I murmured. "I wouldn't be able to stand it."

Her palm rested on the side of my face, and she kissed the top of my head. "Sweet girl, life-altering doesn't necessarily mean potentially dangerous. Just something that will change the trajectory of my future that must happen. I won't be able to stop it."

I couldn't understand how she was so calm about all of this. Especially since she couldn't know which she would be facing—death or her life changing completely.

The tea kettle on the stove began to whistle. Minerva gave my head another kiss and released me, walking back into the kitchen.

"I'm surprised you and Dax made it here today. I thought you would be holed up, having insane amounts of sex."

My face heated and I knew I was blushing. "Aunt Minnie, stop it!"

I didn't mention to her that Dax and I had already decided to pack up my duffel and fly back to his cave for a few days. It was rustic, but it was also completely private, something we both wanted.

She chuckled and went about putting cookies and chocolate truffles on a plate with the tea service as she waited for the tea to steep.

"Well, I'll give you a couple of days before I call," she murmured.

I walked over to her and leaned my hip against the counter, crossing my arms over my chest.

"What are you going to do with Talant?" I asked.

She shrugged a shoulder. "Try to keep him out of trouble and make sure he truly understands the modern world before I send him on his way."

"That's it?"

Minerva shot me a piercing look, her golden eyes shimmering with an emotion I couldn't place. "What does that mean?"

"It's just that...you two watch each other, but I can't tell if it's like two fighters circling each other before they attack or the way an enemies-to-lovers romance starts out."

Her mouth dropped open and she gaped at me. "There will be no enemies-to-lovers romance. He's not my enemy and I'm not going there."

I cocked my head to one side. "Why not?"

"Because he's arrogant, high-handed, and pushy!"

"Aren't high-handed and pushy the same thing?"

"Allison Grant, stop picking apart my words and actually listen to what I'm saying. That won't happen."

"What won't happen?"

We both whirled toward the door as Talant and Dax came into the kitchen.

"Nothing," Minerva answered, brushing off his question by picking up the tray.

Dax hurried forward to take it from her and she smiled brightly at him. "Thank you, Dax."

Then, she swept past Talant without even glancing at him and headed back to the living room.

I sighed and followed her. This afternoon was going to be interesting.

AN HOUR LATER, Dax was flying us back to the resort when he veered off in a different direction.

"Where are we going?" I asked.

He glanced down at me, his eyes dark blue. "I have a surprise for you."

I smiled up at him. "Okay."

When I didn't ask anything else, he chuckled. "You're not going to pester me with questions?" he asked.

"Nope. I'm hoping it's a good surprise and I don't want to ruin it."

"It is. I promise."

A few minutes later, he circled a clearing in the woods. We were probably a ten-minute drive from town and the closest house was the mayor's, but it was still at least a mile, maybe a mile and a half away.

When Dax landed in the middle of the clearing, he set me on my feet, keeping his hands on my waist and holding me close.

It was beautiful, full of wildflowers that were just beginning to bloom and tall, bright green grass.

"What is this place?" I asked, looking around.

It was beautiful and secluded and there was a small pond in one corner of the clearing, a single oak tree soaring over it and providing shade to one part of the shore.

"If you don't have an objection, this will be where we build our home," Dax answered.

My head whipped around so I could stare up at him. "Our home?"

"I bought this property a couple of decades ago, but I didn't do anything with it because it was easier to live in the cabin at the resort."

"Won't we continue to live there?"

He used his hold on my hips to turn me toward him. "For a while, maybe, but I don't think I want to go back to managing the resort."

That statement shocked me. "What? Why?"

He squeezed my waist. "I've been there for a while, and I enjoyed it. Now, I want something different for my life."

I rested my hands on his chest. "What's that?"

"I want to enjoy living it with you. I might decide to do something else after a while, but, right now, I just want to be with you. I have more money than I could spend in three lifetimes, and I don't need a lot of things. Except time with my mate."

Goddess, I loved the sound of that.

"And, when our children come along, I want to be there as much as I can to watch them grow, to teach them. To love them."

I faceplanted against his chest and sniffled. One of his hands moved from my waist to the back of my head, cradling me against his heart.

"I'm hoping this means you like the idea," he murmured.

I tilted my head back and made a face at him. "You know it does, you can feel it through our bond," I retorted.

He smiled down at me. "I can."

"Then, stop teasing me."

He kissed my forehead. "But I'm finding that I enjoy teasing you."

I sighed, pressing a kiss to his heart. "I would love to build a home here with you. Though I want some time with just the two of us before we start working on filling it with baby gargoyles."

"Gargoyles? Plural?"

I moved back so I could see his face. "I hated being an only child growing up. I always wanted brothers and sisters. I'd like two or three children. I might even consider four if I don't feel completely overwhelmed." I saw the look on his face. "I'd be fine with just one if you don't want that many—"

He shut me up with a kiss, his mouth taking mine firmly. That was when I felt it. Pure joy. Through the bond, his emotions told me that he would be happy with however many children I was willing to have. And that he would love them all as much as he loved me.

When his mouth released mine, he hugged me close so that my cheek rested against his heart.

"I'll call Martinez tomorrow," he said.

I shook my head. "Next week."

"Why next week?"

I hugged him tighter. "Because we're going to go back to your cave and spending the next few days in bed. We can begin preparing for our life together next week."

He laughed, sweeping me up in his arms. "If that's what my mate wants, then that's what she'll have."

Once he had me securely in his grip, he launched us into the sky. And I could feel his love for me through every beat of his heart and every breath in his lungs.

And I knew he could feel my love for him the same way.

EPILOGUE

Minerva

I couldn't sleep.

Since I'd woken up on the floor of the cave after Ally healed me, something just wasn't right. I felt restless and uneasy, as though I was missing a vital part of my body or memory.

I turned over in my bed again, trying to find a comfortable position. To find the peace that I usually felt every night.

But it wasn't possible.

Finally, I sighed and tossed back my blankets, climbing out of bed.

I would make myself a cup of herbal tea. My own personal blend that I took when the voices in my head got too loud and the world seemed too bright. It always helped me relax and eased my anxiety.

I slipped a light cotton robe over my satin nightgown and left my room, my footsteps nearly silent on the stairs.

I walked through my silent house, listening to the silence of the spring night. Devil Springs wasn't always quiet at night, especially during the week of a full moon, but tonight, it was perfectly calm and still.

Almost unnaturally so.

When I entered the kitchen, my steps stuttered.

He was there, stretched out in one of the chairs at my kitchen table, a glass of milk and a plate holding a huge slice of chocolate cake in front of him.

"You're up late," I murmured, getting over my surprise as quickly as I could.

I didn't want him to know when he caught me off guard. Or that he affected me at all.

It wasn't because he was a god. And not just any god, but one of blood magic. The magic that I had a strong affinity for.

No, it was because there was something familiar about him. As though I'd known him my entire life. And maybe for lifetimes before that.

But it was clear that I couldn't ask him about that. Any time I tried to ask him questions or learn more about him or his past, he would shut me down or change the subject. It was never in a nasty way.

No, Talant would flirt or smirk or say something unbelievably arrogant to distract me and then pretend I'd never asked him anything at all.

His evasiveness combined with my lack of visions was making me edgy. And I didn't like to feel edgy.

It had taken me two decades to feel in control of my magic, to not feel as though the premonitions and the intuitive magic were driving me insane.

It had also taken me that long to recognize that my abilities with blood magic were nothing to be ashamed of. And that the stigma attached to it by the coven in Devil Springs was unfounded.

I had finally settled into my power and into myself. I had created my place here and I was happy with it and with myself.

But Talant's presence was stirring all of that up again, making me question myself. Making me anxious and knocking me off balance.

I set about making myself a cup of tea, taking the smoked glass jar that held my special blend out of the cabinet next to the stove.

"I wanted something sweet," Talant replied, his velvety voice filling the kitchen even though he spoke softly.

The way he said it made me think the sweet thing he wanted had nothing to do with cake.

I ignored the shiver that wanted to crawl down my spine and put the kettle on to boil.

I also ignored the fact that I'd been making him cakes, cookies, pies, and other assorted treats since he'd awoken in that cave and come home with me. The first night, when I'd been too tired to do anything, he'd gone through the kitchen and put together a plate of fruit and cheese for me to eat in bed. He'd also brought a plate with a few cookies on it, asking me what they were.

Once I explained, I'd offered to let him try one. When he did, his eyes had lit up and he'd smiled as though he'd discovered something marvelous.

He asked me where I got them, and I told him I'd made them. The way he looked at me in that moment...it had made my knees weak.

So, as soon as I had regained my strength, I'd started making him treats. Even on the days I was ready to cast a spell that would trap him back under that damn mountain because he was driving me absolutely insane.

"Why are you still awake?" he asked.

For once, his question didn't have a sarcastic edge. He sounded as though he cared.

"I'm not sure," I answered, pouring hot water over the tea ball resting in my cup.

"Did you have a bad dream?"

I shook my head. "No. I haven't been able to fall asleep yet."

He fell silent. When I finished making my tea and turned around, I found him watching me closely, the plate that had held his cake empty. He must have inhaled it.

I didn't want to, but I walked over to the table and took the chair on the opposite end, facing him.

I grabbed the honey from the center of the table and drizzled some into my cup.

He waited until I'd taken my first sip of tea before he said, "We need to talk about my brother."

I lowered my cup, the flavor of lemon and herbs on my tongue. "What about him?"

"About how we'll free him."

I put the mug down on the table with a snap, the tea sloshing over the side and spilling across the scarred wood. "We're not freeing him. He threatened to kill me, and he could have killed my niece with his asinine plan to have her wake you."

A muscle in Talant's jaw ticked as he stared at me. His eyes had brightened, their gold color was now tinged with a hint of ruby light.

"I gave him my vow that I would come for him soon and it's been two weeks. You needed that time to recuperate from your ordeal, but now, we must act."

"I won't help you," I argued.

He sighed. "I'm afraid you don't have a choice."

"And why is that?" I asked, my question biting.

"Because you're the Conduit of the goddess who imprisoned him and only your power is capable of setting him free."

ABOUT THE AUTHOR

Born and raised in Texas, C.C. Wood writes saucy paranormal and contemporary romances featuring strong, sassy women and the men that love them. If you ever meet C.C. in person, keep in mind that many of her characters are inspired by people she knows, so anything you say or do is likely to end up in a book one day.

A self-professed hermit, C.C. loves to stay home, where she reads, writes, cooks, and watches TV. She can usually be found drinking coffee or a cocktail as she spends time with her hubby and daughter.

ALSO BY C.C. WOOD

Novellas:

Girl Next Door Series:

Friends with Benefits

Frenemies

Drive Me Crazy

Girl Next Door-The Complete Series

Kiss Series:

A Kiss for Christmas

Kiss Me

Westfall Brothers Series:

Texas with a Twist

Paranormal Romance

in the Blood & Bone Universe:

The Witch's Gift

The Wolf's Winter Bride

-

Novels:

Seasons of Sorrow

All or Nothing

Romantic Comedy Series:

Crave Series:

I Crave You

Wild for You

Only for You

NSFW Series:

In Love With Lucy

Earning Yancy

Tempting Tanya

Chasing Chelsea

Paranormal Romance:

Bitten Series:

Bite Me

Once Bitten, Twice Shy

Bewitched, Bothered, and Bitten

One Little Bite

Love Bites

Bite the Bullet

Blood & Bone Series (Bitten spin-off)

Blood & Bone

Souls Unchained

Forevermore (Contains Destined by Blood)

Ensnared in Shadow

-

Paranormal Romcom:

Mystical Matchmakers:

Rock and Troll

Made in United States
North Haven, CT
17 May 2024

52556661R00135